# MY MISTAKEN IDENTITY

By

## L L Eadie

Revised Edition

Copyright © 2020 L L Eadie

Originally Published in 2013

Under title "Mistaken Identity"

ISBN: 978-1-7347371-4-1

Library Congress Control No:

Dolly Dimple Ink

508 NW Scenic Lake Dr

Lake City, FL 32055

Email: LLEadieAuthor@gmail.com

## Dedication

This book is dedicated to the two people in my life that always had the faith in me, even when I experienced apprehension about my own ability - my mother, Barbara Briscoe and my husband, Robert Eadie.

## Books Published

Yearning for the Unattainable - 2019

Alligator Warrior: Halpatter Tustenuggee - 2020

Pedro Menendez: The Adelantado of Florida - 2020

## Get in Touch with the Author

Author Email: LLEadieauthor@gmail.com

Author Facebook Page: https://www.facebook.com/L-L-Eadie-141069182765272/

Twitter Page: https://twitter.com/lindaeadie

Author Website:
https://lindaeadie.wixsite.com/booksbylleadie

YouTube Channel:
https://www.youtube.com/channel/UCOqwdnT40rPwg7HSE6GmKlg

# Chapter One

## *My Mistaken Identity*

A re you there?

I can't find you.

I thought I saw you once,

But...

I was mistaken.

It wasn't you.

She only looked like you.

~~~~~~~~~~~~~~~~~~~~~~~~~~~~~~~~~~~

I slid across the white leather upholstery of our limousine as if were slick ice. The backs of my legs felt chilled. I tugged at my skirt. It wasn't really a skirt. It was more like a pair of baggy shorts. Whatever it was, it fought back and refused to cover my exposed thighs.

"Why do I have to wear this ridiculous outfit?" I pulled at the sash on the blouse untying it. I closed my eyes, leaned my head back and rubbed my throat.

"Did you say something, Miss Tuesday?" asked Philip, our driver as he stood like a soldier holding the door open. I'm only surprised mother didn't make him salute us in his white gloves. "Is there something I can get for you?" He knelt down and peeked in at me. I could see my reflection in his mirrored sunglasses. I appeared small and fragile. Is that how I looked to everyone? "Perhaps," Philip said, "I can freshen up your water? Or, are you hungry? Rosa prepared some finger sandwiches and..."

"No thank you," I said. I snagged a black throw lying across the L-shaped couch that wrapped around the car's interior. I tossed the blanket across my lap. "Philip…"

"Yes, ma'am?" He removed his black hat. His hair fell across his brow and he ran his hand through it before placing the chauffer's cap back on his perspiring head.

When did Philip's hair turn grey?

"You don't have to call me ma'am, Philip."

"Yes, Miss Tuesday." He smiled. His teeth were stained. Did Philip smoke? "Is there something else?"

"Please, turn off the air conditioning."

"Right away, Miss Tuesday," Philip said as he started to shut the door.

"Don't!" I reached out. "Please, Philip, leave it open, it's freezing in here."

"Of course, Miss Tuesday. It's only in the seventies today I'm so sorry. I should have set the temperature for…"

"Forget about it," I said as I shook my head. "It's okay." Philip disappeared but now my mother was in my panorama view. She tugged at her skirt too, but not for the same reason. She was covering her signs of aging – cellulite. Her sexual market value was deflating and she knew it. Tomorrow the masseuse would pay.

Mom held the V.I.P. s of Glissando Records in her sticky web – snagging their undivided attention. I shivered, pulled the blanket up around my shoulders and tucked my knees to my chest. I began to rock.

My life planners were shaking and nodding their heads outside the studio doors. The same doors I had entered and exited from for the past ten years. I pinched my bottom lip. Some people bite their nails and others pick their nose. My nasty habit, as my mother called it, was to squeeze my lip. I pulled harder on it as I watched Mom smooth away my faults, which lately were stacking up quite nicely. Uncle Monty, her battery-operated boyfriend, stood next to her agreeing as usual.

I didn't care anymore, especially about performing those parental approved songs and dance routines. It was as if they were all still convinced I was the bucked-tooth six-year-old instead of being the bleached-tooth sixteen year old.

When will this bubblegum Jazmyn and Justyce fairy tale world ever end? Stormy, my co-star, had shaken the label. What a bitch. Why couldn't I?

I uncurled myself and reached for the door handle and slammed my cheesy life from my mind. I could taste blood. I released my lip. Only my purse was sitting next to me. There was nothing new about that. I dug around inside it, pushing stuff from one side to the other.

"Where is my damn lip gloss?"

I flipped the bag over and dumped everything onto the seat next to me. I clawed through the loot. There it was. Another note. Folded just like the others into the shape of a triangle. I peeled the tucked corner open and unfolded it.

To Tuesday,

You SUCK!

From Zelda

I crumbled it up and tossed it across the limo as Uncle Monty opened the door.

"Are you feeling better?" Uncle Monty asked as he slipped in next to me.

"If you're asking me if I still have a headache?" I said, "The answer is yes." I sucked on my bottom lip as I kept my eyes on the crinkled note lying next to the fluorescent lit bar. My mother's half-drunk martini had beads of perspiration running down the bulb and the stem. Philip must have turned on the heat. I dropped the blanket.

Uncle Monty wrapped his arm around my shoulders. I stretched out on the sofa and leaned into him. Good ole Uncle Monty what would I do? Or, Momma do? Without him?

"Well," Uncle Monty said, "the medicine should kick in pretty soon."

I nodded and closed my eyes. I could smell his familiar musky cologne. I felt safe here in his arms. Safe from Momma.

"If it's okay with you, Tuesday honey…" Uncle Monty ran his fingers through my hair and then rubbed my back. Up and down. Up and down. "We're going to straighten everything out over dinner with…"

I looked up. "I don't have to go, do I?"

Uncle Monty shook his head. "Of course not, Philip will take you home and tell Rosa to put you straight to bed."

"I think I'd like to take a bath first."

"Whatever you'd like, Tuesday honey." Uncle Monty kissed the top of my head then exited the stretched Mercedes. "I'll come up and check on you when we get home."

I smiled. "Okay, thanks, Uncle Monty."

I crawled across the carpeted floor and grabbed the crinkled note from Zelda. No reason for anyone besides me to read it. It was almost as if I protected every one that appeared unexplained. Looking back maybe I should have trashed them. Or, refused to have read them.

Before I was aware of it the limousine had pulled through the gates of my hell and offered me up as bait. Rosa greeted me with a warm wash rag for my face and hands, a peppermint for my mouth and scurried me up the stairs to my private suite, which included a kitchenette, sitting room, bed and bathroom. What more could a girl want? She filled my tub, my thoughts with her sweet humming. and my wishes.

# My Mistaken Identity

I wonder how much of the English language Rosa really knows. And, what country did she come from anyway?

"Thanks, Rosa," I said as I stepped into the oversized bathtub with the black streaks swirling through the white marble like a threatening cloud. I sank into the warm cleansing water. Rosa lit the candles and dimmed the lights as she dropped my silk robe on the chair and left me alone. I reached next to me for the hand carved letter box and retrieved the other notes from Zelda. This had become my nightly ritual. My bedtime story. It fueled my misery and went perfect with a long soaking bath. Particularly after another bumbled performance at the studio. That's what my mother had called it.

I held the letters high above the vanilla scented bubbles and away from the flickering candles. I opened the bottom note first. I always started with that one – the inaugural one. I began to read once I was settled – legs stretched out, back matching the slope of the tub and my head resting against the suctioned satin pillow.

Zelda had nice handwriting. I liked the way she wrote her name with a giant Z. It reminded me of Zorro – the fictional dashing masked outlaw dressed in black with a flowing cape; that defended the helpless from brutal rulers. Zorro was a hero. He humiliated his screwed-up enemies. No one could catch him. And no one knew his true identity.

"To Tuesday,"

Zelda began every letter like this. Never – Dear Tuesday. Of course, by now I didn't expect it any other way. It wouldn't have seemed right. It wouldn't have been – From, Zelda.

"Did you know a for-real smile is not crooked, lasts more that a nano-second and totally affects your eyes and cheeks? Maybe you don't want to know. Or you don't give a shit. Just thought I'd share that bit of trivia with you since you barely grinned the last time I spied you on TV. Not that I search out your show. Get real."

She was right. I didn't care.

"To Tuesday,

Just wondering why you wore that lame outfit to the even lamer teeny-bopper award's show? Who dresses you anyway? Your mommy?"

Zelda was right again.

"Next time wear layers of colorful vintage jewelry and high-top sneakers with your Cinderella fantasy. Now, that would be way cool."

I squeezed my eyes shut and pictured myself teetering across the stage in the backless heels wearing the strapless plum-perfect gown. The dress exposed the bulk of my breasts, squeezed my waist and forbid me from wearing underwear. Funny how sometimes mom thought it was perfectly okay to dress like a slut, but most of the time I was a virgin.

I read on. "Are you really going to record that bubblegum song you sang? Well, your fifth-grade groupies seemed to like it. But when are you going to start singing songs that are like the way it <u>really</u> is?"

I had no idea how it really was. My life was not my own. It belonged to those who had invested in me – my mother, Uncle Monty, Glissando Records, and my fans. Everyone had a preconceived image of my identity.

I opened the next one.

"To Tuesday,

Is there some reason why I never see pictures of you in the tabloids just hanging out? Don't you ever feel like partying to the wee hours of the morning? Letting loose? Is it because you don't have any friends? Or because your mommy won't let you?"

I wondered how she knew so much about me.

"I know why! It's because you really do think you're thirteen years old, don't you? Just like the goody-goody Jazmyn character you play on TV. No one likes her either. Grow up!"

Jazmyn. Would I ever be thought of as anyone else except her? Pure stereotyped.

# My Mistaken Identity

"Tell me are you socially alienated? Let me know when you're ready to break away and become a free-range chick."

I wish.

"What an airbrushed life you live!

From, Zelda"

"You'd be surprised, Zelda," I said as I unfolded the fourth note. "It's not as perfect as it appears."

"To Tuesday,

I think we could be friends. In fact, I know we should. You would totally like me. Because…I'm not anything like you."

Looking at my life through Zelda's eyes always made me realize how much of myself I had given away. I wanted to relate, to be the real deal, to be myself. But who was that? How do you get to know yourself? Is there some kind of a check-off list or a how-to book to read? Maybe there's a class to take titled – 'To Know Thyself'. The only thing I knew for sure about myself was that I had perfected the ability to pretend to be who everyone in my life wanted me to be.

"To Tuesday,

Is there anything real about you? Or are you all fake? Is your hair really yours? Or do you wear extensions?"

I ran my acrylic nails through my waist length hair floating around me like seaweed. There wasn't anything wrong with my own hair. So what if it was a little thin and never seemed to grow past my bra strap. Was my mother right about me needing to have everything Stormy Gallagher had bought, or even grew naturally?

I'm going to have to start thinking for myself. It's about time! My time! But what if I make the wrong decision?

Zelda's letters, however, weren't always just about her disapproval of my star-studded life. In fact, she related to me. Well, sort of. In the last letter she told me how she had never met her father. I can relate to that. Uncle Monty fills in quite nicely, but he's not my father. And, neither is he really my uncle. Zelda also said she lived in an apartment. That is kind of similar to me too since I have my own suite within my house.

I sat up and laid the letters on the tub's massive ledge. I didn't really need to read them. I knew what they said. In fact, I could recite them in my head – which was still doing that drum-pounding thingy. Headaches were also starting to be something else I could count on.

I stretched out once again and breathed in the sweet smell of vanilla, held it in my lungs and exhaled into the bubbles tickling my chin. The candle flames trembled next to me. I cleared my throat. It wasn't really sore. I had lied about that. Or, was that my excuse last time? No, last time it was my ankle I claimed I had twisted. I shut my eyes and told myself to relax. To just forget about it. There was always next week to work out the vocals and dance routine. I'll get it together. I just need some time. I wish they'd leave me alone.

I wish…shit...I don't know what I want.

I honestly don't think I ever did. I never had a choice to start with.

I cleared my throat again. It did tingle a little bit. And last week my ankle did kind of throb. But that was only after I unwound the boa-constricting bandage.

But, Glissando Records was not pleased with me again. I wondered, was this it? Was my career really over? Good. I think. I tugged on my bottom lip.

"You are so ungrateful!" The pointed toe of a designer stiletto kicked my jeans across the bathroom tile as the intruder entered. She slammed the door shut with its sole.

Why didn't I hear her coming? I should have been on guard. I knew better than to think she wouldn't show up. Of course she would. She also had no other choice.

# My Mistaken Identity

"Momma!" I scooted up from my slouched position. "Please don't."

"Don't what? This?" She snatched my blouse off the floor, balled it up and threw it in my direction. It landed only a foot away. Not good enough. She reached for one of my patent leather sandals and slam-dunked it into the toilet. Now, that was a new move.

Second shoe. Second splash.

On a scale of one to ten, I appraised my mother's most recent revival of craziness – a three. Of course, she had only just begun. However, this totally psycho performance, starring my mother, wasn't how our life had always been. I vaguely remember the earlier one that was so much simpler; where money was a necessity and not an accessory. I swear I never asked to be famous. It was my destiny according to my mother.

"Look at all of this!" My mother stood rigid and stared with darting eyes into my rock-star closet.

This was not the average girl's wardrobe. It was not humanly possible to have worn every designer label hanging in there, even if I had changed six times per day for an entire year. Most still wore their price tags.

Next, as was my mother's moment-of-madness habit, her eyes blinked a couple of times along with her clucking tongue. "None of this," she said, "absolutely none of it would have been possible if it wasn't for me!"

"Of course, Momma, I know that." I reached for my robe without climbing out of the warm water. It lay draped across the zebra striped chair beyond my reach. My fingertips grazed the black silk belt only causing it to slip from my grip to the floor. It seemed to have taken up sides with my mother.

"You have always had it so good." Her scolding index finger inched closer to my retracting body. Her nicotine breath snuffed out three of the seven dripping white candles standing at attention in a silver candelabrum. "You think you're so damn special! Don't you, Tuesday? You've never had to lift your hand! You have no idea what real sacrifices are all about. You're a sixteen-year-old spoiled brat!"

"You're right," I said trying to convince her. But I knew it was of no use. I closed my eyes and shook my head, "You've done everything for me. I'm so lucky, Momma, to have you." And, I was. She was all I had. She was my family.

I dared to peek when I heard her pencil height heels strike the tile. Her anger drew her into my closet and the one-shoulder number that I wore to the 'A Time for Heroes' bash in L.A. exited. It slid to a stop next to the door. A second later my empire silk sundress hooked up with it. "You don't deserve any of this! Do you hear me, Tuesday? Answer me when I'm speaking to you! Damn it!"

I inhaled the sweet scent of the bath again. But this time it was different. No more calm only confusion. I exhaled my answer, "Yes, ma'am."

"Yes, ma'am? That's all you have to say?"

There was nothing I could have said that would have changed my so-called life. I had secretly craved the end of The Jazmyn and Justyce Show. Five years on cable. Finally over. God forbid a spin-off. Enough.

I ducked into the bubbles as a shoe whizzed above my head, parting my hair and splashing behind me in the oval shaped tub. I fished it out. A velvet wedge. Ruined. I let it drop to the floor – DOA.

"Momma, please," I begged. "Stop." My heartbeat thundered behind my eyes beckoning my lids to close. "I'll nail it next time." I clasped my hands as if in prayer. "I'll churn out an awesome song that will be a hit." I shook my head and further attempted to boost my mother's endorphin level. "A diamond record, Momma! It'll sell millions of copies!"

My mother appeared. Sort of. Her appearance always changed when she became possessed by the inner demon. Her face became scary contorted and mimicked Edvard Munch's painting - The Scream. Her nightmarish eyes popped along with the veins on her temples and forehead that were pulsing madness.

"I promise, Momma, I'll smash it next time." My arms draped over the side of the tub in defeat while my mouth pleaded for forgiveness. "I'm really, really sorry."

"Sorry isn't good enough," she said, as her next victim – a cashmere sweater - was twisted, tugged and stretched frantically into a dress. "Your latest effort at a hit is crap! Do you hear me, Tuesday? Crap!"

My mother disappeared, but not her in-my-face report. "And your former costar – that lil' bitch Stormy Gallagher's single will be in the top ten in no time!"

Shoes number four, five and six headed in my direction, tailed by a purse. I batted them as if they were volley balls, over the net, and onto the floor.

"Your CD sales are down. You'll never have a tour of your own at this rate!"

Zelda's letters that had mistakenly tumbled into the tub now floated around me as I sank back into the evaporating bubbles. Only my throbbing forehead and runny nose were visible. My eyes were slammed shut where fresh tears were forming.

"There will be no more Jazmyn and Justyce tours! That's over! Now you have to make it happen without Stormy. And you're doing a shitty job at it!"

My mother paced from the closet door; three feet to a stack, and back. "What makes you think you'll even get another chance? This industry doesn't give second chances. Most people never get a first shot." She laughed as she kicked one of the vulnerable piles. It was a mocking laugh that stabbed my heart.

I am your Sugar Plum, Momma – your Sugar Plum fairy.

"Have you forgotten about that opt-out clause in your record contract? There are a thousand and one more Tuesday-Greenwood-wannabes out there." She reached for one of the Chinese ginger jars positioned on the shelf. "Damn it, do you hear me, Tuesday?" The porcelain dragon one shattered as it attempted to bounce off the unforgiving tile.

"I hear you, Momma."

"I don't think you really do. Don't you see they're just waiting," my mother said, "for you to slack up, my darling, so they can take your place?"

Another jar. Second crash.

"And, ruin everything I made for YOU!"

Final jar. Final crash.

But she wasn't finished. Oh, no, Momma needed a bigger finale. She found it in my favorite memory from the past. An earlier childhood made up of dolls and playing pretend. No more time for dolls. However, plenty of times for pretend.

"Not Sissy! Please, Momma, NO!

My baby doll's legs popped from their sockets as her torso dressed in a gingham pinafore dropped. Her bonnet flew off as her head cracked open like a raw egg when it met the floor. My mother held each of Sissy's plastic legs by their ankles as if they were her trophies. She tossed them over her head and darted back into the closet for more ammunition. My vision blurred as Sissy's glossy blue eyes with the thick black lashes blinked a couple of times at me, and then closed.

After so long you would think I would be numb to my mother's manic episodes. But, I wasn't. Perhaps, because each one took me closer to the edge – the edge of a cliff. Or, was it a bridge in my last fantasy? The mind can be a really, really dangerous place to hang all alone. You start to believe there is a way. An easy way. A quick way. To end it.

# My Mistaken Identity

"CONSTANCE!" Uncle Monty shouted at my mother from outside the door. "If you don't come out, I'm coming in to get you! I mean it, Constance! Come out! Right now!"

Please help me, Uncle Monty. And, if you can, please put Momma back together again. I miss her.

I focused on the eight-foot mahogany door and willed it to open as another armful of my belongings belched forth from the closet, along with my mother's shameless verbal assaults. She was on a gargantuan roll now as she detonated my wardrobe.

Score adjustment – a nine.

"I'm coming in, Tuesday." Uncle Monty informed me. He was, and had always been my save-me-from-the-mommy-monster special need's unit. Especially, when that Mommy stopped taking her necessary bipolar disorder meltdown meds.

Please say this is not hereditary.

I scooted up and snagged the washcloth dripping from the faucet to hide the obvious. My uncle attempted to swing the door wide, but his progress was halted by the foraging raid of clothes, purses, shoes, and shards of porcelain blanketing the floor. His balding head appeared before the toes of his four hundred-dollar handmade tasseled moccasins.

I wonder what would happen if he didn't show up one time?

Rosa, our live-in help, followed Uncle Monty. He headed for his darting target while Rosa began dipping and filling her arms with my scattered belongings with each step she took.

I shook my head. "Not now, Rosa. Please."

Rosa nodded and smiled an all-knowing sigh. She'd been here and done this all before. She set the heap down and scooped up Sissy's torso and amputated limbs. Rosa shook her head and mumbled something about loca in Spanish while Sissy's broken face smiled at me over Rosa's left shoulder as she left.

Bye bye, Sissy.

Uncle Monty dragged my weeping mother from the closet. "Let go of me, you asshole! Damn it, Monty! Let me go!" Her padded-wall image was hard to take in. I shivered, as if a black widow spider was scaling my bare back. I pinched my lip till blood dribbled into my mouth.

"You son-of-a-bitch!" My mother grabbed hold of a framed painting, unhinging it from its fastener. She held on just long enough for the nail to rip through the serene scene, before releasing the torn canvas to the cluttered floor.

"She'll be all right, Tuesday." Uncle Monty wrestled my mother into his way-familiar sympathetic arms and out the door. It slammed shut. And then, the sordid little scene was over. For now.

However, my mother's scary, unbalanced sickness echoed down the marble hallways of the eight bedroom, ten bath, gourmet and commercial kitchens, wine cellar, theatre room, recording studio, clay tennis court, six car garage with guest residence, designer swimming pool, and alarm system – sprawling 20,000 plus square foot gated early 1900's Spanish architecture ocean front home in Florida.

An asylum.

For her.

For me.

# Chapter Two

## *Just a Farce*

We're different,

You and me.

But alike.

We're best friends,

Aren't we?

Or...

Was it all,

Everything,

Totally,

About Us...

Just a farce?

~~~~~~~~~~~~~~~~~~~~~~~~~~

I scooped up Zelda's soaked letters. The black ink had smeared the words across the page into the likeness of the black and white marble. I rung them out like a washcloth and tossed them across the bathroom. They seemed unimportant now.

My head sank back into the pillow suctioned to the tub. My lip felt swollen while my ears still rang from my mother's manic episode and tears burnt my eyes. Or, maybe it was my mascara. The water had chilled and I scooted forward to refill it. I set the left faucet to scald and the lighting to dusk. The steam began to fog me in. I only wished I could forget. I tried to think of something else to block it all out. But every time I opened my eyes I saw the reminders – my scattered glitzy clothes, the torn oil painting, the shattered dragon, and Sissy's bonnet.

As a little girl when I was upset my mother would help me feel better by telling me one of her famous fairy tales. However, the one that came to mind was the story of the evil fairy. The fairy that went bonkers after being forgotten, left behind, neglected, and betrayed by all the others. Her unbalanced revenge frightened the fairy kingdom for years. It was said she would sneak into the fairies' hiding places and destroy their most precious possession – their wings!

"Shhh," whispered another intruder as her index finger raised to her puckered lips. It moved like a second hand on a clock ticking off the last thirty seconds to twelve. A disheveled looking girl was coming into my bathroom from the private balcony. Half of her face grinned. The other half I couldn't see. It was hidden behind choppy hair that covered one eye. This intruder was different in another way too. She was someone I didn't see much of at home – a stranger.

"Oh my God!"

She shushed me again. "Don't scream, please." She shook her head but not hard enough to jolt her chin-length hair that was as dark as the night she walked out of. "It is you, isn't it? Tuesday Greenwood!"

"Who are you?" My startled limbs sprang into panic mode and hugged my bare torso as she took several more timid steps inside. "GET OUT OF HERE!"

"It's okay, Tuesday!" She waved her hands in a please-don't-freak-out motion. "Don't yell for help! I promise it's okay."

I shook the nano-nap from my eyes and snagged the washcloth from the side of the tub to shield my chest. The bubbles had long ago evaporated. "Do I know you?" She did look sort of familiar. "Have I met you before?"

"No," she shook her head, "you've never met me." Then nodded, "But, yeah, you do know me. I'm Zelda!"

Of course, it was her. Zelda looked just like I had pictured her – fashionably second-hand. Her eyes, set behind dark horn-rimmed glasses, darted manically around the room picking objects out of the gloom.

Is she here to rob me?

Or, is she going to...oh my God! Hurt me?

"Zelda?" I asked. My body began to quiver.

This so isn't happening. I'm dreaming. Of course I am. I'll close my eyes and when I open them again...

"Yes! It's me!" She laughed. "This is so cool being in your bathroom! And with you soaking in it!" She spun around taking it all in. "My entire apartment could fit inside this room alone!"

She reached for the sink's faucets turning them on and off. "Are these swan heads real gold?"

"I don't know how you found your way in here, but you need to leave! NOW!"

"Damn, Tuesday, I just got here," Zelda said and snarkled. "Hey, are you okay? You're shaking."

"I'm fine." I clasped my hands together to control their fear.

"I guess you're still upset. I don't blame you. Wow! I thought your mother was going to lay into you. Were you scared? I'd probably have pissed on myself." Zelda kneeled down to pick up a piece of the broken vase. "Too bad," she said turning the shard over and over in her palm. "What do you really owe her anyway? You're the freakin' ATM around here. I seriously don't know how you deal with her psycho side." Zelda watched the broken porcelain break into another jagged piece as she dropped it. "I guess I mistakenly got a glimpse of the other side of up, huh?"

How did she find me?

Did she climb the fence?

Wasn't the alarm on?

How did she get in here?

"If I was you, Tuesday, which I'm way glad I'm not, I'd invest in a dead bolt for your nice dollhouse."

I'll say, like a couple of hundred thousand dollars nice. Momma had it remodeled for me. The former owner used this area with its adjoining office and kitchenette for his girlfriend. I wonder if he was married. Does anyone really get married anymore? Or, stay that way?

I could hear Zelda's snarky giggle. The rubber on the bottoms of her canvas slip-ons squeaked as she headed for my walk-in shower. She upped the lighting and began counting the shower heads pointing them all out. "I bet an entire soccer team could clean-up in here!" she yelled.

My shoulders shrank and my voice shrilled as I spoke, "What do you want?"

Zelda left the shower behind and raced for my closet. She disappeared. The chandelier lit up. "You've got to be kidding me!" She reappeared, swung on one of the marble columns and laughed. "I could so get used to this!"

She took several more steps in my direction, scooting the mounds of my clothes out of her way. "Forgive me for invading your privacy, Tuesday." Another step closer. "I guess I kind of surprised you, huh?"

Watching Zelda was like watching a tiny jumping spider skitter across your floor in every direction, afraid all the while that he would launch onto you.

"Didn't you get my last note?" she asked.

"The one that said I sucked?"

"No." Zelda shook her head. "The one after that. Shit, I really should explain. You really must be freaking-out!"

I nodded. "Yes, I am. And, no, I didn't get that one."

"Sorry, Tuesday, I told you I'd be visiting my mother – Rosa and...."

"Rosa? Your mother is our Rosa?"

Zelda nodded her head and laughed in that quirky way of hers. It was almost as if she was making fun of me because I didn't know. What else wasn't I aware of?

"Since when?" I asked.

"Since she pooped me out!" Zelda said and laughed.

"Rosa never said anything about you. I don't believe you! You're lying!"

Zelda shrugged her shoulders. "I don't give a shit if you believe me or not, Tuesday!" She walked towards me. "Actually, I've only been here a few times. I come once a month and stay in that apartment above the garage. Maybe you've never been up there before but it's really cool. I have my own fridge, TV and bed. I am forbidden, though, as the help's bastard, to hang with you. Ain't that something?" She laughed.

"So," I said, "if you're telling me the truth where do you live the rest of the time. You told me in one of your letters that you lived in a small apartment. Who do you live with? Rosa lives here. With us."

"Like I didn't know that?" Zelda peeked into the water at me and chuckled. I sunk a little bit deeper and held onto my lip. "I have an aunt. She fills in quite nicely, but she's not my mother."

I nodded. Where had I heard that before?

"Jeez, Tuesday, how else do you think I was able to deliver those notes to you?"

Maybe she's telling the truth. How weird that I never knew Rosa had a daughter, but what do I actually really know about her anyway? Have I ever even asked her about herself?

"You said you live with an aunt, so, where's your father?"

Zelda's face turned into an enormous smirk. I pinched my bottom lip. "Monty's… my daddy."

"What? No way! You're lying!"

"Think about it, Tuesday, Monty moved in with your mom and you when you were six years old. Right?"

I nodded while twisting my lip to the right. Then. Left.

"Isn't it a fact that Rosa came with him? She was his housekeeper first. Remember?"

I didn't answer. Why didn't anyone ever tell me this?

"Does my mother know?"

"Of course!" Zelda said. "But, it was her idea that you had absolutely, positively no fucking contact with me! Can you believe that?" She smirked and snarkled again.

My bottom lip nodded. "Do you call him daddy?"

She shook her head. "No way! In fact, my mother had to make him take a prove-it test." Her laugh was sarcastic. "DNA – the molecular basis of heredity. Works every time," she said with another chuckle. "But DNA isn't an automatic bonding adhesive, you know? I'd rather not. At least not with him. Rosa hasn't pushed him though to give her anything, you know, money. She just asks that I get to come here. So ya see, Tuesday, I hang out here for my monthly visitation rights. Thank God, for just a week at a time. Not my idea, I promise."

"How long have you known this? How long has he? My mom?"

"Count your notes." Zelda laughed.

# My Mistaken Identity

I stared at the crumbled ball dripping black ink onto the tiled floor.

"Yeah, Monty's a real winner. What a jerk. He creeps me out. He's always trying to touch me, hold my hand and squeeze me. Can you believe that? And he actually kissed me! Shit! His old man breath is totally fatal." Zelda's face scrunched up into a gagging reflex move. "Are you sure you're okay, Tuesday? You don't look so hot."

"I'm fine," I lied.

"I mean, you're really pretty. Even if you are all wet." She chuckled. "You're actually even more movie-star gorgeous in person."

"Uh…thanks." I scooted up a little taller and wiped my eyes with the washcloth. There were two dark smudges left behind.

"You really don't know how amazing you are, do you?"

I shrugged. "I don't know. Sometimes yes. Sometimes no."

"Ironic isn't it?"

"What?" I bit one of the terry cloth threads of the white wash rag stretching it several inches.

"How the girl whose seen and done it all in commercials, sitcoms, movies, and the music industry doesn't even realize how awesome she is." Zelda shook her head and then focused on me. "Look at yourself! You have the perfect face – stunning big blue eyes, tiny turned-up bud of a nose, full smackin' lips…and your teeth! Oh my God, they don't even look real! Are they?"

"Of course they are!"

Maybe she's right. I am pretty.

But, I wish I were thinner, taller…

"Remember, Tuesday, nobody's perfect. It's those imperfections that make us unique. Flawless is fake."

I smiled. "Thanks, I'll try to remember that."

"Wow! You really have some nice clothes. Very chic, of course." Zelda said as she turned and dragged her foot through a pile on the floor. "Maybe, I could borrow something sometime. Or maybe be your wardrobe assistant." She snickered while picking up a black lacey dress. "Hey, we wear the same size! Cool!" She held it up to the shoulders of her T-shirt. "What do ya think?"

No! I don't think so!

Zelda tossed the dress into the sink and stood at the doors leading outside onto my rooftop meditation garden. I could hear the gurgling of the three-tiered Italian fountain. Uncle Monty had bought it for me on our vacation last summer to the Amalfi Coast of Italy. I had fallen in love with it along with the mountainous coastline. Momma had raised hell about the cost of shipping it back, but he had insisted. Good ole Uncle Monty. Damn him!

"What a cushy-ass life." Another snicker as Zelda rose to her toes and pirouetted. Her sneakers screeched. She shut the doors. "But just look at little ole welfare-soup- kitchen-free hand-outs' me now!" She laughed. "I'm hanging with you – Tuesday Greenwood, the reigning pop princess, with her very own lines of Jazmyn mini-me dolls, perfume, jeans, shoes, shampoo, jewelry, greeting cards, and whatever other must-have merchandise her tinsel-teeth groupies gobble up."

Zelda held up a plastic decanter shaped like a guitar from the marble countertop. "Add bubble bath to that list." She grinned.

Is she making fun of me?

Zelda spun around again, laughed and raised her arms in a what-are-you-thinking pose. Her hands beat out each syllable. "But honestly, Tuesday, do you really, really enjoy all that stupid shit?"

No.

Yes.

Do I really?

# My Mistaken Identity

I think I do.

"You're not just an object for others' enjoyment, you know, Tuesday?" She was inches away from me now. "Why do you let them get away with exploiting you?"

I stared. I didn't know what to say.

"Let me ask you a simple question," Zelda said. "What's your favorite color?"

"Yellow, because it reminds me of sunshine and smiles."

"Wrong."

"How do you know?" I said.

"That was one of your trained responses, wasn't it?"

"Well…maybe," I said. "What's your favorite…?"

Zelda shook her head. "Not fair. I asked first."

I didn't answer. It was sad. I really had no idea what color I liked best.

"Okay, I'll give you another chance to answer a basic question. What's your…"

"No more questions," I said. "You made your point."

Zelda's I-told-you-so expression changed. And so did her question. "Hey, you got any smokes?"

I shook my head before I answered, "No."

"Of course not, what was I thinking? What a brain cramp. That the Queen of the Tween Scene – Tuesday Greenwood – would actually smoke!"

She returned my gaze with stoic eyes. I shivered. The water felt cold again. But Zelda's eyes, which were shielded behind her glasses, suddenly pooled with tears.

"Sorry," Zelda whispered. "That was just brilliant." She sat down on the side of the tub and shook her head while looking up toward the soaring ceiling at the Strass crystal chandelier. A second later those vulnerable eyes gushed on me. "I'm sorry," she repeated, "that was not fair, or very nice. I so suck at first impressions."

I shrugged. My head throbbed.

"I shouldn't have crashed in on you. I guess I just wanted to meet you. I've never met anyone famous before. Maybe I should have just asked you for an autographed glossy and been satisfied."

Zelda imitated my I-don't-give-a-shit shrug and chuckled. "So, it's up to you, Tuesday Greenwood, if you rat me."

I shook my head. "Don't worry, I won't." I look back now and think I probably should have said something. But I didn't. I was lonely.

"I better take off anyway." Zelda smiled. "Rosa might come looking for me, but of course she has to hold dinner in case M&M want anything more. And, then clean up the kitchen, tuck their fat asses into bed, and who knows, maybe wipe them as well." Her shoes squeaked on the slick floor once again as she spun on her toes, avoiding the chaos, to head toward the closed door. "I'll vacate…that is…if you want me to."

"No, don't go," I said. "Stay."

Zelda turned back around. "Are you sure you don't want me to ripcord? I'm kind of a freak compared to you. I might screw up your nurturing, wholesome kiddies' channel image. I'm possibly a life-altering experience. And an extremely bad one at that." She rolled her eyes and stood. "Cause, I don't measure up. You know, Tuesday, to your high standards. I mean, just look at me!"

And, I did. She was right. Zelda was far from resembling me, or anyone I knew for that matter. Her bottle-dyed black hair was totally whacked-off by a bad pair of shears, her XS tee was strangling her, and her jeans, well, let's just say I'd never heard of them before. Shabby. Yes, that was it. Zelda was totally not put together. The fashion cops would be all over it. Totally arrest and convict.

"I'm a nobody compared to you, Tuesday."

Yeah but, it might be nice to be no one special for a change.

"You better be really sure."

I stared through her at the floor and remembered the mommy-monster scene.

"Yeah, I'm sure."

"You, Tuesday Greenwood," she said and snarkled, "must be hard up for company."

Jeez, maybe I'm the one, not momma, whose way insane.

It was my turn to laugh. "You have no idea."

Zelda reached out with her index finger and wiped a tear trying to escape me. She stuck the finger in her mouth and pulled it out with a smack. Then she smiled. So surreal. My mother used to do that very same thing.

Momma once told me a story about how the fairies would collect our tears, especially the tears of joy, and use them to clean their scraped knees and elbows after narrowly escaping the ugly troll. The salt she said would cure any boo-boo they had.

I was totally confused as Zelda and I checked each other out in silence. Just the crashing waves of the incoming tide in the near distance filled the space. Zelda frowned as she glanced out the opened balcony doors. The flood lights had poured in making eerie shadows across the damaged goods on the floor.

She looked up at me over the thick black frame of her glasses. "I could be some kind of psycho chick that's going to pull a pair of blunt scissors on you while you shower." Zelda snarkled. "Last chance – are you really sure?"

"Yes."

I think.

"But…"

"What?" Zelda's expression changed from wow-you've-got-to-be-kidding to I-knew-it-was-too-good-to-be-true

"It's just…just…that if my mom and Uncle Monty ever found out. I don't know what would happen. They would never understand so…"

"You're right," Zelda said, "M&M already despises me!"

That's so sad. However, I'm not surprised.

But I could never hate you, Zelda.

"I promise, Zelda, I will never tell them. Or, Rosa. It will be our secret."

# Chapter Three

## *Not a Friend-shit*

I need to subscribe,

To a friend.

Not one for six months,

But,

for a lifetime.

We all need a bestie,

Don't we?

A for-real friend.

A friendship.

Not a friend-shit.

~~~~~~~~~~~~~~~~~~~~~~~~~~~~~~~~~~~~

I checked my cell. Not a text or voice mail from a friend. Did I ever really have one? Some were just opportunists. I know that now. They wanted the whole celebrity lifestyle perks-thingy and they thought I was their way to get famous. Some got really stalker-ish and would want to hang with me everywhere.

I glanced at my cell again. There were only messages from Uncle Monty reminding me my voice coach would be here tomorrow, my dance teacher on Thursday, my acting instructor on Friday, and my...

Good ole Uncle Monty. What would momma and I do without him?

Or, Zelda? And, Rosa?

I stretched out on the lounge and closed my eyes. The sun felt good on my vitamin D starved body. The pool's waterfall and the distant wave action with its salty scent were lulling me to sleep.

"Senorita Tuesday, excuse me," Rosa said. "Here's your pepperoni pizza you asked me to order for you and an Orange Crush. Your favorito. In a chilled glass bottle with a straw just the way you like it."

My eyes clicked open along with my sudden ravenous junk food appetite. My new taste for the food of shame. I never would have thought of eating this stuff when I was working. Which it seemed was my entire life.

"Smells delicioso," I said, as she set it next to me on the poolside table. "Gracias, Rosa. You didn't tell Momma or Uncle Monty did you?"

"No, no, Senorita Tuesday." Rosa shook her head. Her thick ponytail swung side to side. "Anything else I can do for you?"

"No, that's all. Gracias, Rosa."

Maybe Zelda didn't dye her hair. Maybe she got it from Rosa.

"You need la amiga. Not good for a senorita to spend so mucho time alone."

Why don't you offer up your daughter?

"Don't worry, Rosa, I'll call an amigo," I said and smiled as I picked up my phone. "A delicioso one!" Rosa patted my cheek and shook her head. Her caring charcoal eyes smiled and then she left.

I checked my cell again. Just in case.

Why doesn't Stormy call me? She must think I'm still pissed at her. Oh well, she's just a bitch anyway. And I don't even want to think about Ashburn! What an asshole!

# My Mistaken Identity

I tossed my phone onto the matching lounge next to me. I snagged a piece of the forbidden pizza and took a bite. It smelled yummier than it tasted. I set it down and dove into the lagoon pool to wash away the junk food. There was no way I should have been eating this. I surfaced and swam to my monogrammed chaise. Climbed on board and drifted away.

I wonder if Zelda is still here.

"Young celebs are so vulnerable."

"Zelda!" I spun around on my float. Beyond were a cabana, an outdoor kitchen, workout spa, and a massage pavilion. And, the Atlantic Ocean.

"Shhh..." Her finger ticked off the seconds as it rose to her what-are-you-thinking mouth. She grinned. "You missed me, huh?"

More than you'll ever know.

I had spent the rest of that first surprise encounter with Zelda watching her pretend to be me – the teen queen. She dressed up in Jazmyn's clothes, caked on my make-up, jewelry and sang the words to my sappy songs karaoke style. Or, should I say Jazmyn and Justyce's repertoire. It was a total smack-down. But I have to admit I laughed at myself.

"Well, I did go to your room," I confessed. "But, you weren't there."

"Why? Because you thought I was going to rip you off? Did you take inventory?

Zelda pulled her Your Mommy's Worst Nightmare band tee over her head.

I have a two-piece like that.

Her breasts were tiny. Only tits.

"That never crossed my mind, Zelda!"

"So, did you go back on our little secret and rat me out?" she asked.

"No!" I shook my head and squinted behind my sunglasses, as I tried to focus in on Zelda planted on the sandstone pool deck. The sun in the constipated blue sky was blocking my view. It hadn't rained in a month. Total drought conditions.

"Okay, I guess we're not breaking up," she said and snickered. When Zelda snickered her nostrils would flare as she exerted a puff of air from them and her head would do a double shake. "By the way, Tuesday," she said while wiggling out of her generic jeans. "I hope you don't mind but I forgot to pack a suit. So I borrowed this one."

That is my bathing suit! Oh my God!

"Plus my week to hang with my newly-found daddy isn't up. But Monty's as annoying as chain emails." Zelda smeared coconut scented sunscreen on her color deficient bare body. "I can't wait for my visit to be up," she said and laughed.

I wish I knew who my father was.

"Hanging out with you should make it bearable." Zelda reached over and picked up a celebrity magazine from the pile on one of the teak deck chairs. "Teen-tainment," she said and snickered, as she pointed to my cover girl mug in a small square in the bottom right corner of the teeny-bopper collaged cover. Stormy was two pictures above me and four to my left. I swear she always got front and center coverage.

"What a tabloid-y life you live, Tuesday. So tell me, what's it like? Do you actually enjoy it?"

I shrugged. "It's all right. I mean it's my life. It's all part of it. You get used to it."

"Don't think I could handle it," Zelda said. "But, I have to admit it would be kind of cool to try. Having people fuss over me, dress me up, take my picture…I mean you have everything you want! And more! I have no idea what that life feels like. I'm lucky to get a pair of

Levis from a second-hand store." She pointed at me. "And to think, Tuesday Greenwood, you have your own worn 'n' torn rocker brand!"

"Be my guest," I said. "Take whatever you want. Including that two-piece."

"Really?" Zelda's eyes widened and her chin backed up into her chest.

"Yes. Really."

"Okay, I may just take you up on that offer," she said and laughed. "But come on, Tuesday, what's it like being rich and famous? I bet you're invited to some awesome parties with all the coolest people."

I shook my head. "Believe me, it's not what people imagine. It's a lot of work, long hours and not much recess."

"That sucks," Zelda said. "Hey, do you know Piper Milligan? She's one of my favorite actors? And have you ever met In Lieu of Flowers? They're one fierce band!"

"Yeah, I met Piper once at a charitable function."

For like a second. She so didn't want to hang with my baby-powdered ass.

"You're right," I continued, "she is awesome. But I've never met that group before."

"Really? Hey, they're playing tomorrow night at the Hurricane Evacuation Club down in South Beach," Zelda reached for a slice of pizza, picked the pepperonis off, tossed them behind her into the hibiscus bushes, and took a humongous bite. "You wanna go?"

"Can't."

"Why not?" Zelda wiped her mouth on my sheer white cover-up. "We could take your limo! You do have one, don't you?"

I nodded and then shook my head. "Just can't."

"You probably have some hot date, don't you?"

I wish.

"Tell me!" Zelda took a step closer to the pool. "Who is it? That hunk – Zane Hampton? No, no, I got it!" Pizza chunks plopped into the pool as she spoke. "It's that new guy from that scary movie – Bronx Simmons! Isn't it?"

"I don't have a date, Zelda," I said as I adjusted my halter. "Unless you want to call my voice coach one." I chuckled. "Not hardly."

"Too bad, maybe next time." Zelda headed back to the lounge and snatched another magazine – Rock, Scissors and Fly Paper – the pop culture icon reference. She held up the exclusive cover girl shot. "Look! Here's a picture of your co-star. What's her name – Justyce?"

She would have to bring that to my attention. The last photo shoot I had done landed on the cover of Lip Gloss with its eleven-year-old average subscribers.

"Actually, it's Stormy Gallagher."

"Yeah, her," Zelda said. "I heard her song on Hot Hits Radio. She's fair. I guess she's already moving on. Not only with her music, but out of your former G-rated world into a more R-setting. A reality show I hear." Zelda flipped through the pages. "Of course, she did play the bad bitch on your sitcom, right? And, you were the good bitch." She looked up at me over the thick horned rim of her dark glasses.

I nodded.

Yeah, you nailed me - always the mild child never the wild child.

"When are you moving on? I guess you have big plans now that your show was cancelled, huh?" Zelda folded the magazine back to a brief article about me on the What's Up page. "Are you really going ahead with that lame high school prom idea?"

"Well," I said, "we're looking at all our options." I pulled on my bottom lip.

# My Mistaken Identity

"Are you part of that?" Zelda asked as she dropped the magazine onto the table.

I released my lip. "What do you mean?"

"You know what I'm talking about." Zelda took another bite of pizza.

I lingered on the mosaic dolphin decorating the pool's bottom. I was unsure how to answer. "Momma and Uncle Monty...I mean...I...haven't decided yet what's next for me. We...I mean I haven't put the prom gig all together yet. You know, how I'll go about it. But singing at some random high school's prom is kind of cool though."

"Who said? M&M's?" Zelda smirked and then nodded. "I see how it is."

"What do you mean by that?"

"Nothing. I didn't say anything." Zelda licked the tomato sauce from the corners of her mouth. "Is there something you want to say?"

"No."

"I didn't think so." She crammed the final bite into her mouth.

"Okay," I said, "I can tell there's something behind that remark so go ahead and say what's on your mind."

"You might not like it." Zelda removed her glasses, setting them in the empty pizza slot.

"I'm a big girl that's been well seasoned and prepped for criticism. I've read everything that's ever been written about me.

And Stormy Gallagher.

"I don't need extra padding," I said, "or a pacifier. Do you really think you have something to say I haven't heard before?"

"Maybe not." Zelda licked her fingers. "But don't you want to have a say? Or don't you give a shit?"

"Of course, I care about my career!"

"Or, are you going to let your M&M's – Mommy and Monty always lead the way telling you what to do, say, wear, sing, or even when to piss? You're robotic! You sing. Then smile. You dance. Then smile. You act. Then smile. What are you smiling at? I mean think about it, Tuesday, do you pick anything out for yourself? Starting with your own furnishings for your bedroom suite. I bet it was constantly-in-charge-Constance that made all the choices for you. Do you really like it? It's so stuffy. It's so her! Not you."

I sat up taller. My voice got louder. And snarkier. "It was the interior designer's choices, thank you."

"Don't go and get all butt hurt on me," Zelda said.

"I'm not!" I exclaimed.

Zelda's voice lowered. "Sorry, Tuesday, I didn't mean to upset you. I have such a big stupid ass mouth. Do you forgive me?"

Why should I?

"Of course."

"I guess I'm just trying to help you figure it all out for yourself. But if you're cool with the prom thingy…" She shrugged. "Then go with it."

"Good, I'm glad I have your permission," I said and laughed.

Zelda picked up my Orange Crush and sucked till the straw hit air and made that annoying high-pitched sound. She poked it around on the bottom till she got the last drop. She looked up. "Tell me, Tuesday, where's your sperm donor?

Huh?

# My Mistaken Identity

"You know your daddy?"

I turned my distant gaze toward the east. Toward the ocean. A place on earth that still exists today with its many stingy secrets not spilled. I shrugged and said, "I don't really know. Momma won't tell."

"That sucks."

"I seriously don't know anything about him, Zelda. Like where he lives, what his name is, how old or tall he is, what color hair or eyes he has, what his favorite color, food or music is, or... if he knows...I even exist."

I was thankful I was wearing my sunglasses so she couldn't see, but I was crying and tugging on my lip as I turned and looked up, hoping the sun would dry my tears. "For all I know, he could be dead."

"That is just wrong! Make that crazy bitch, constantly-concealing-Constance fess-up. To know who you are, you have to know where you came from."

Yeah, you're right. My lip was free.

"Yes, but..."

"But what?" Zelda asked.

"Momma says he doesn't..."

"Listen, Tuesday, you said so yourself that you're a big girl now. It's your father! Not hers!"

Zelda's right. I'm way ruled and schooled by Momma and Uncle Monty.

"Maybe, I will."

"9-1-1!" Zelda cannon-balled into the pool – knocking me off my raft. I splashed her as she rose from the depths. She dunked me. I dunked her. Truce.

Zelda snagged my sunglasses off the top of my head. "I think I'll start with these since you're in such a charitable mood." She peeked out from under my former five-hundred-dollar pair. "Nice," Zelda said with a mocking laugh. A chlorine drool rolled down one of the lenses and landed on her cheek. She turned and swam over to the floating chaise. I followed.

"Check it out," Zelda said, as we clung to the raft and drifted around the pool. The latest copy of Teen Trivia lay spread in front of us opened to the 'Tuesday Greenwood Confessional Page'. "Did you for-real say you feel lovey-dovey in your dreams?"

"Are you serious?" I said and giggled. "You know now that Momma and Monty handle all my press."

"Of course. That figures. Teen myth busted!" Zelda tossed the magazine over her head into the water. "But, you were most definitely yakking-it-up in your sleep last night." Zelda cut her eyes at me. "Pure sweltering."

"No way!"

"Yes, way!" Zelda splashed my flushed face.

"Why were you in my room, Zelda?"

"Why were you in mine?"

"I…I was looking for you."

"Well," Zelda said, shaking her so-what-about-it head at me. "What if I was checking on you, too? Or, did you think I was ripping-off some of your shit?"

"No! Of course not!"

I hope I haven't screwed this up. I need her friendship.

Zelda stuck out her chin and smiled as if she had won something. Then, she punched me in the arm. "I was just testing the waters."

# My Mistaken Identity

My shoulders and voice sighed, "All right, fine, whatever." My head balanced on my right arm as I clung to the raft, while my eyes focused on my amusing new friend or whatever she was morphing into. "Okay, tell me now, what did I say in my sleep?"

Zelda released the float, rolled to her back and created a fountain spewing from her mouth before speaking. "Cancel what I said about it."

"No! So not fair! Come back!" I swam after her. "Tell me!"

"Who are you talking to, Tuesday?" Uncle Monty walked out onto the covered lanai twenty steps from the swimming pool. His head hit panic mode, jerking from left to right and back as his eyes searched out his suspicions.

Zelda stifled her laughter and ducked under the water. I reached for the raft and shoved it in her direction.

"Nobody," I said, shaking my head. I climbed up the steps and scurried in my uncle's direction to prevent any further progress on his part. "How's Momma?"

"Better," he said, as he handed me a plush oversized towel. Uncle Monty, as always, had called the doctor, filled my mother's prescription of mood stabilizers, put the mommy-monster to bed, and planted his extended-stay roots by her waffling side. And, always filled-in for Momma.

But, what about Zelda? And, Rosa?

"I just came out for a quick minute to check on you. Did you get my messages?" I nodded as he wrapped his arm around me. "Don't worry, Tuesday honey, your mother is resting. And, improving as we speak." He dried my back, arms and legs for me and then gave me a hug.

Thank God, for good ole Uncle Monty.

I think.

"She's been asking about you," he said.

"Really?"

He nodded.

"Is she still upset with me?"

"You know your mother, Tuesday, she could never stay mad at her Sugar Plum."

I strained a smile – the kind that is crooked, last only but a nano-second and refuses to light up your face. "Of course she couldn't," I said as he led me inside. I glanced over Uncle Monty's shoulder at the floating magazine and chaise. No sign of Zelda. Pure vanishing act.

# Chapter Four

## *Who Can I Trust?*

Such a sweet

Torment – trust,

I wondered.

As I wandered,

In my sleep.

~~~~~~~~~~~~~~~~~~~~~~~~~~~~~~

"You hoo, Tuesday!" My mother skipped to my side wearing a peek-a-boob nightie and gargantuan Colgate smile. "Surprise! I had Rosa prepare your favorite breakfast. Blueberry pancakes!"

Huh? That will totally blow my one thousand calories per day diet that you and my dietician have had me on since I could count that high.

We rarely ate together like a family. Momma preferred to go out to eat with Uncle Monty. Rosa stocked my suite's fridge for me: breakfast – bran cereal, half of a sliced banana and fat free milk, lunch – turkey breast salad, an apple and water, midday snack – carrot and celery sticks, dinner – frozen 300 calorie diet meal, and more water.

It had been eight days since my mother's latest psycho-scenester episode. Now, she was up. And, she had regained her charged-up capabilities for me. Her only genetic gift. Jeez.

"You look beautiful this morning, Momma," I said. And it wasn't a lie. She looked more like my older sister than my mother. And that fact alone pleased her more than I ever could.

"Thank you, Sugar Plum." My mother led me by the hand, like we were little girls, outside onto the covered lanai that overlooked our pool.

I could picture Zelda on the swimming pool steps just a few days before posed like a guardian-of-women – a mermaid. There was no way I would tell either of them about her. So, I kept Zelda's visit with me and future visitations a secret. She was gone now and, I missed her. I know, that's whacked. But I liked her. I didn't understand why I was drawn to her. We had absolutely nothing in common. Zelda was totally right about that. Absurd, but I trusted her already more than anyone else. Maybe it was because Zelda spoke the truth, even if it was hard to listen to.

I glanced over at my mother. It felt good to have her back. I smiled and lifted my face to the beyond. Beyond my isolation.

It was a normal wintry seventy-ish degrees morning in Hollywood. Hollywood, Florida that is. The Atlantic's turquoise soothing waves and its breeze were welcoming as the salty air stirred the palm trees, my tangled hair and my oh-so-sleepy head. The aqua pebble-sheen pool's bottom glittered and sparkled my eyes awake, along with my eleven o'clock sunrise. No way could you beat this view though.

"Good morning, Tuesday honey." Uncle Monty folded the Hollywood Gazette in half and set it down next to his china plate crowned with pancakes on the glass topped table. A tropical garden arrangement of fresh blooming orchids, birds of paradise and ginger decorated its center.

Things were back to normal. My mother's norm that is. Uncle Monty smiled a smile that screamed relief. I don't know what momma would do without him. Or, me. Sometimes I worried he'd get sick of it all and just take off during the middle of the night and I would wake and find him gone forever.

I told him that nightmare once and he promised if he ever left, he would take me with him. Of course, he was joking. It was his way. But Uncle Monty needed us too. Especially me. I was his only client. He gave everyone else up for my career. Just like momma had.

# My Mistaken Identity

But what was he giving up for Zelda?

"Have you read your horoscope lately, Tuesday?" My mother unfolded the Gazette.

Yeah, the last one I read suggested taking a bubble bath to keep my stress at bay. If only. Not happening.

I shook my head. "No, ma'am." My mother was a zodiac freak. She even had her own spiritual adviser, or as she preferred to call her – her life coach.

My mother read, "An opportunity will arise if you act right away and contact your connections. You will cinch a deal that will make others envious..." She glanced up and raised her voice, "You must protect your future plans and move forward with them, instead of sharing."

"Mmm-hmm," I said, nodding.

"That brings me to this, Tu-Tu." My mother sat down directly across from me. "Monty and I really think we should go ahead with the prom gig. It will give such a fresh spin for marketing your next solo charting single. It's totally unboxed."

No blueberry pancakes on constantly-calorie-counting-Constance's plate. Just fresh blueberries. And, ashes from a past cigarette. She lit another.

"This project will personify what you stand for, Tuesday, your positive and fun side as an artist. It will help promote you in a mega-unique way. What do you think?"

"Sure," I said, "I can't wait." I cut, swooshed and pushed my pancakes around on my plate. Not one bite had been chewed. I rarely ate breakfast. Lately, I rarely ate.

She took a sip of her Don Perignon mimosa. Her hazel eyes popped with life and her shoulder length blonde hair bounced with excitement as she exclaimed, "This will set you apart from the rest!"

Stormy Gallagher you meant to say, Momma.

She raised her crystal champagne flute in a toast with Uncle Monty, and then exalted as their glasses clinked in a celebratory salute, "It's Jazmyn versus Justyce!"

There, she said it. Will she ever get over the fact that Stormy, and not me, had won that acting award for her role as Justyce?

Of course, what really set my mother's latest chronic craziness off was when she heard Stormy was signed to do her own reality show on Rock-On-Videos. That sucked. But what's new? I was always chasing Stormy's image. And career.

Why can I never fulfill Momma's dreams?

No! My dreams!

"This will be fun, adventurous and possibly dreamy." She reached for my uncle's hand. There was an edge of impatience creeping into her voice. "Won't it, Monty dear?"

He smiled, nodded and squeezed hers. "It's your most awesome idea yet, Constance," Uncle Monty said massaging my mother's ego. He looked up at me and grinned. One of Uncle Monty's blue eyes, that mimicked the ocean, was smaller than the other. He said he landed on the right side of his face in a childhood accident – falling out of a tree. But his air-hair-comb-over was no accident. "I think you're going to like this, Tuesday."

Jeez. I so hope so.

"At least I don't have to come out that I'm an alcoholic, pregnant or been on the drug rehab merry-go-round," I said and smirked.

"Honestly, of course not!" my mother said. "Those are exactly the kinds of horrific outcomes that I have...I mean...Monty and I have protected you from. That's why we chose to stay in Florida and not move to L.A." She shook her head. "Thank goodness, the studios were in Orlando. Over my dead body would you ever admit to such blasphemous slanders!"

# My Mistaken Identity

My mother took a long draw of stress relieving nicotine into her lungs before providing me with secondhand smoke for brunch. She was wearing a new gold cuff bracelet. No doubt a hope-you-feel-better-soon gift from Uncle Monty. And, according to Zelda paid for with funds donated by yours truly.

I smirked.

"Are you laughing at me, Tuesday," my mother threatened in her narrowing-eyes-lowered-chin dark voice.

My uh-oh gaze hit my plate. "No, ma'am. I'm sorry." My mother was scary accurate. It was too soon to disagree with anything she said. A provoked relapse was way possible.

A second Z-moment surfaced into my conscience, "What are you afraid of, Tuesday? Clowns or Constance?"

Answer: The mommy-monster, Zelda.

"Apology accepted," my mother said. New face: round eyes, raised chin and light voice. "Now listen up, Tuesday, Monty and I agree that you really are too mature now to play the role of Jazmyn, anyway."

I'll say. How long can one pretend to be thirteen?

"And, Monty dear made sure your contract read per episode for syndication royalties. That's where the real money is."

That should make you happy, Momma.

My mother performed another lipstick-smudged suck on her Virginia Slim before continuing. "Besides, the filming shoots were getting in the way of your acting, dance, and voice lessons...your interviews... and...hopefully upcoming touring schedule, your own videos and recording sessions. So, just as well they cancelled the show this season."

Thank, God.

"We realize how much you've wanted to change your image, you know, reinvent yourself and break the Jazmyn and Justyce mold, since you're becoming…"

Say it, Momma – an adult.

"A junior in high school."

I am a junior, Momma.

"And we know how much you'd like to go to school instead of being tutored at home, especially for your senior year." She flicked a patient inch-long ash into her saucer. "But, of course, that's not possible."

Of course not, Momma.

"So, this high school prom gig is perfect. You'll have a date with one lucky young man from that school and sing a couple of your songs for them!" my mother squealed, shimmying her re-upholstered chest and head. Her tamed shoulder length blonde extensions kept tempo with her copycat Tuesday-looking bouncing melons. It was my sweet sixteen present – my boob job. And, her belated one. She had reminded me, "What's good for Tuesday is even better for Momma!" That was true with everything in my life. But maybe what she ought to have said was, "What's good for Stormy is even better for…

…me?

Or you, Momma?"

"But…but…what high school? And who would I go with?" I shook my head. "I wouldn't know anyone."

Uncle Monty answered the call of constantly-cancer-pursuing-Constance and lit her cigarette posed in her puckered pink lips. The ocean breeze blew the smoke in my direction along with Uncle Monty's attempt to fill-in the challenging-and-supposed rewarding blanks. "Have you ever heard of the movie – Bye Bye Birdie, Tuesday?"

# My Mistaken Identity

My quizzical face answered that say-what question. Besides playing the piano, Uncle Monty's other hidden passion was cable's old school AMC, Turner Classic Movies and TV Land stations. That explains it. How many times had I stayed up late with him, curled up on the couch eating popcorn drowned in butter, slurping root beer floats and watching reruns?

"Of course not," Uncle Monty said. "Come over here and let me tell you all about it."

Uncle Monty reached for my hand and I landed on his lap. "The movie came out in the early 1960's. A take-off of Elvis Presley being drafted into the army. It's about a rock 'n' roll singer, like Elvis, who travels to a small-town America as a PR stunt." Uncle Monty wiped the corners of his crusty mouth with his napkin and continued, "This rock 'n roll star stirs up this town to the point of hysteria before he enters the service. And, kisses his biggest fan." He kissed my cheek.

That's lame. And, way shallow.

I jumped up. "Please say I'm not going to some hick town and kiss some redneck, or have to really, really join the army!"

"No, of course not, Tu-Tu." My mother wrapped her arm around my waist and chuckled. "You'll go to the prom from the school that earns the most money for your favorite charity and peck the prom king on the cheek. See," my mother said, waving a horoscope clipping from a past newspaper. She held it up and read, "Getting involved in a charitable fundraising event will bring you in contact with exactly the types of people you need in your corner."

Jeez. Just great. Why can't I tell them no? Zelda was right. This is way stupid.

She glanced up from the stars-perfectly-aligned advice and proclaimed, "We'll announce the winning school on your website. And release a portion of your single at first as a digital download tease, and later it will appear on your best-selling album yet. It's sure to go double-platinum! It ain't over till Tuesday Greenwood sings!"

No doubt, your life coach's prediction, Momma.

My mother inhaled and exhaled some triumphant smoke before continuing, "Which charity did we choose, Monty dear?"

"Save the Whale Calves," he answered obediently.

My mouth was still fixed in the what-the-freakin'-heck position. I seriously had no idea what my favorite anything was, just as I had fessed-up to Zelda. It was way true.

I was never allowed to say what I liked. Or give an unrehearsed interview. Fill out any questionnaires. Select my own endorsement deals. Write my own social networking blog. Visit an internet chat room. Or even pick my own multi-licensed multi-bazillion dollar Jazmyn and Justyce merchandise with my cheesin' face along with Stormy's emblazoned on the packages.

My mother – my shrewd manager, and my agent – Uncle Monty, both my publicists and handlers, had always done it for me.

Or, is that to me?

# Chapter Five

## *Answers in the Night*

They come,

To you.

Tickling you,

Whispering, too,

While you sleep.

When your eyes,

A re slammed shut.

A nd your mind,

Is restless.

A nswers...

In the night.

~~~~~~~~~~~~~~~~~~~~~~~~~~~~~~~~~~~~~~

"So, do you play it, or what?" Zelda picked up my Taylor Guitar leaning in the corner of my spacious suite. "Wow! It's signed by Denton Rogers of Slippery Slope! To you! Way cool!"

I rolled over, swept my hair out of my groggy face and attempted to focus.

My bedside lamp was on. It was always lit. I admit – I am afraid of the dark. Way possessed with nyctophobia. My mother used to calm my fears by telling me stories about fairies that took endless flight around and around my bed to protect me from the evil fairy or ugly troll.

The glow of the bulb, she said were their wings flapping. And, as long as it was lit… "Zelda, is that you?"

"Shhh…" Her finger touched her lips. "Who else would it be the freakin' troll?" Zelda laughed as she strummed my guitar with her stubby black polished nails. Her face was barely visible behind her dark hair, which she wore mostly in her face. She peeked at me out of her hoodie.

Damn, it's good to see you again.

"So, do you?" she asked. "Or, is it just for show?"

Has it already been a month?

"Yeah," I said propping myself up on my elbows. "I play it."

"Why don't you then?" She laid my acoustic guitar down and stuck her hands into the hooded sweatshirt's pouch.

"What time is it?" I rubbed my eyes open.

"It's two. I just arrived." Zelda sat down on the edge of the bed next to me. "Did ya miss me?"

It's hard for me to believe, Zelda, but more than you'll ever know.

I scooted my legs over to make room and picked up my alarm clock. It was two all right. Two o'clock in the morning. "It's the middle of the night!" I dropped back into the billowing pillows.

"Got a match?" Zelda stabbed her mouth with a cigarette. "I swept it from constantly-cosmopolitan-sipping-Constance's pack on the bar. Do you think she'll mind?"

"No, Zelda, I don't have a light, and I doubt she'll even notice. But I way noticed that it's two o'…"

She smiled and said, "So, Tuesday Greenwood, have you written that platinum single yet? The one you're supposed to debut at some honky-tonk high school's prom?"

# My Mistaken Identity

She laid her head next to mine. The filthy bottoms of her Converse black high-top sneakers rested on my 800 thread count solid white silk duvet cover. I rolled my eyes and chuckled to myself.

If momma walked in right now, she'd probably lose it.

"No, Momma and Uncle Monty are working on it with some songwriter dude. He's supposed to be the best!"

Zelda rolled on her side to face me. "They don't know spit! Why aren't you working on it with that songwriter? You're the talent!"

I turned my head and looked at her. "Cause, I've never written a song before. That's why."

"Are you sure about that?" Zelda jumped up and skipped toward my dresser in a pair of sexually-assaulting tight black jeans. Her sneakers squeaked on the marble floor as she skidded to a stop. She opened the top drawer as if she had done it billion times before, dug underneath my collection of Euro-cool linen scarves and pulled out a bound notebook.

No way!

"What do you call these? Crap?" She stretched out her right arm and pointed the book at me with the wrist tattooed with a pair of wings.

Fairy wings?

I dug my nails into my palms before I leaped from the bed and rushed over to snatch it from her. "How did you know about that? It's none of your business, Zelda!"

She smiled, handed me my book and confessed, "I've read them all."

"Do you have some kind of search warrant, or do you just scope out all my stuff when I'm not here?"

"No, just some of your shit." She laughed and stretched out on her stomach on my oversized four poster bed and offered up a compliment, "I never knew you were so deep, Tu-Tu."

This is so not fair. I've never shared those with anybody.

Is nothing sacred in my life?

She turned and lay on her side, propped her elbow up and palmed her face. My mother's unlit Virginia Slim dangled from her bottom lip. "I enjoyed reading them. Are you surprised?"

"Zelda, nothing about you would surprise me." I walked toward the bed clutching my songbook to my chest like a life preserver. And, my bottom lip.

Damn. How did she know about these?

"Well, I was," Zelda said. "I didn't expect it."

"Why's that?" I asked. "Because the life and times of Tuesday Greenwood is made up of all yellow smiley faces? Am I not allowed to vent?"

"Please do! I don't blame you if you did. To grow up in solitary confinement in this fortress with Tuesday-arazzi crocodiles parked outside the no-trespassing gates waiting to gobble you up. And, constantly-cuckoo-Constance running, or, should I say ruining your so-called life!"

No she's not.

Or, is she?

Zelda reached over and set her menthol gasper on the nightstand. "And Monty dear, who's nothing but your mother's lap dog licking her wounds and nodding like a bobble-headed pooch in her BMW's rear window. I don't know how you tolerate him. I seriously can't stand to even hear him laugh. And what's up with his constant concern with bad breath? God, Tuesday, I'd be way whacked by now!"

You're right. I know you're right. I so need to stand up to them.

But do I really need to? They love me and would never do anything to hurt me.

# My Mistaken Identity

I lay next to Zelda. She grinned and then burped in my face. "For the sake of my air quality, could you not?" I said waving my hand in front of my face.

Zelda snarkled with yeah-I-did-and-I'll-do-it again wicked delight. I couldn't prevent it – I giggled, too. She was impossible. I had never met anyone like her. She was an original. Pure pain.

Why is she so irresistible though?

"Do me a favor and sing one of your favorites for me, Tu-Tu," Zelda said. "You really do have an awesome voice. It's very unique, you know?"

Is she lying?

No! She's right! It is!

Why then doesn't anyone else take notice? Stormy always sang the lead.

Oh well, what do I have to lose?

I nodded and opened the book between us, picked up my unplugged guitar and sang - It's My Turn - while strumming the melodic solo.

"You let me in,

And pushed me out.

I tried again,

You didn't care.

I did what you wanted.

You laughed,

Made fun,

Attacked me,

Inside and out,

Too many times

I lost count.

Did you count?


Now, I will do,

What I want.

And, I will laugh,

And, I will make fun,

And, I will attack,

Inside and out.


"Wow, Tuesday!" Zelda interrupted. "You had me at 'You let me in'. God, that's so edgy, but soothing." Zelda sat up. "It's daring! Relevant! And, damn serious!"

Is she being for-real?

She snatched my guitar from me and strummed an off-key chord. "I can just hear the fusion of your solid vocal chops wrapped in rebellious guitar-driven riffs now."

Oh my God! I think she really, really likes it!

She stood up and threw her arms above her head in an I-got-it moment. "A fierce band with horns! And, maybe a couple of guys for vocal back ups."

# My Mistaken Identity

I shrugged and blushed a bit.

"I think you should most definitely share your repertoire with that songwriter dude. Whoever he is." She smirked as she set my guitar next to the nightstand where her black Buddy Holly signature dark specks and her unsmoked menthol laid. "It would be the true you, Tuesday, for the first time." She clapped. "I got it! Your album should be called – The Third Day of the Week!"

"The third day of the week?"

"Yeah, I know it's way insane," Zelda said. "But totally more bitchin' than anything M&M's will come up with."

"Yeah, insane, I like it," I said. "The Third Day of the Week."

"Pure euphoric!" Zelda said with a voice that was close to crying and laughing at the same time. "It'll be the second coming of T.G. – The Evolution of Tuesday Greenwood!"

I tried not to reveal my total happiness, but my mouth couldn't prevent it. I smiled really, really big.

"Now all you have to do is scuff yourself up."

"Do what?" My grin disappeared with her crazy words.

"You know, Tu-Tu, how your image is so squeaky clean? You just need to tarnish it up a bit. Make it dirty, or at least dusty. We could actually start with this high-dollar-diva room of yours." Zelda groaned as she looked around my immaculate bedroom with a snarled lip and wrinkled nose – the custom-made blinds and curtains, the hand sewn tossed pillows, the overstuffed chaise, and the rest of the craftsmen-built furnishings. All in shades of ebony and ivory. "The decorator was most definitely influenced by constantly-coordinating Constance. I know this really cool secondhand store where we could refurnish this pampered-pad of yours."

"What's wrong with my room? I like it."

Her voice lowered. "Don't you want to make it yours? Just like your songs, Tuesday? You do have a voice. In more than one way. If you want to be an artist and not a pop star than you have to take chances. You do get it…don't you?"

I nodded and pinched my lip.

I think I do.

"That scarred-up reputation change along with your handwritten songs will catapult your career to mega-stardom!"

She really, really believes what she's saying.

Do I?

"Now, go share that totally brilliant nightingale songbird book of yours!"

Maybe she is right. This is amazing! I've never felt like this before!

But…

"I'll think about it." I thumbed through the hundred plus songs, stopping here and there to remember. It felt way weird having someone lust for my penned work. I still wasn't quite sure if she was being up front with me or not. It could be just pity.

"Absurd!" Zelda shook her head. "Do it, Tuesday! Don't be a conformist! They're stifling you! Everything you've recorded before is way shallow. Those songs didn't connect with anyone. Your songs, Tuesday, speak to people. They say the things we all care about."

You're right!

I think.

Zelda flopped onto the bed on her back. She pumped the air with her fists as she spoke. "There's no desperation, remorse, or suffering in your other stuff." Her eyes clamped down on mine. "No struggling for acceptance and identity. And, no sex appeal, for God's sake!"

It wasn't easy to imagine myself as a for-real rock singer. But it was fun trying to picture myself in one of those sleazy videos with those hunky-hard-body guy types draping themselves on me all seductive like. Maybe that could be me. Not just acting cool but being cool for-real.

However, I had no idea how to be cool. Should I wear sunglasses inside? And at night too? Adopt an accent or learn a foreign language? Maybe I should practice cussing out loud. Momma says being cool is how you hold yourself – your posture. Then I must be a leader. I'm pathetic.

"It's not that easy, Zelda, to change." I sat up and closed the pencil smudged book of lyrics and notes. "It really isn't."

"Why not?"

"Because, you see, my contract says they provide and decide what songs I record."

"That sucks!" Zelda said. "You should be more assertive, Tuesday. Just dump them and sign on with an indie label."

If only.

She sat up and drew her feet underneath her with her shoes still on. "That way you won't sell yourself out, your work won't be censored, and you can be faithful to your art. You risk not staying true to your muse otherwise. Make it your own, Tuesday. Possess it!"

I shook my head and said, "You just don't walk away, Zelda."

"Well then, at least let them poke it with a stick, Tuesday." Zelda's eyes pleaded more than her whiny voice. "Please."

She's right. I know she's right. I can do this.

I think.

But what if it doesn't work out? What if Momma and Uncle Monty don't agree?

"Aren't you tired of faking a perfect life?"

Huh?

"Do you dare to be real for once?

What are you talking about? I am real.

Aren't I?

"Are you a wimp or a winner, Tuesday?"

Winner!

Wimp.

"Being cool means you run things, Tu-Tu. Things don't run you!"

You're right.

But I seriously wouldn't know cool from a fool.

"It's a so-what-attitude."

So…what…does that mean?

A restless minute later, Zelda leaped to her feet snagging my hand and shrieked, "9-1-1! Five, four, three, two, one – Dance!"

This time it was ten seconds of spastic bouncing on my bed and waving pointy fingers in the air to invisible intoxicating music. We collapsed onto the disrupted Egyptian linens laughing.

"Come on," Zelda said breathlessly, "let's spoon."

I rolled to my left side as Zelda's body shaped itself to mine. Her chest rested against my back and she wrapped her arms around my waist.

# My Mistaken Identity

We had taken on this bonding formation on a couple of other mind-provoking conversational occasions. Mostly about my lifeless existence. My bed morphed into a confessional booth.

This cozy pose though reminded me of how it used to be when my mother and I snuggled – Momma's heart patting my back, and her warm breaths running through my hair keeping me safe. Just like a mommy fairy. Isn't that the way it's supposed to be? Of course, that was BM. Before Monty. I wonder if they spooned.

I also couldn't help but wonder – when does your life become your own? Do you demand it back? Or, do you just snatch it?

"My favorite song," Zelda spoke to my right ear, "was The Trip Inside My Head – What an Experience."

"Thanks, I like that one, too."

"Of course," Zelda said, "Parent-noia was brilliant. And No We Can't Be Friends. And My Soul is Being Raped, and Make Your Mother Sigh, and Pulsed Out…and…Slices of Me…and…and…"

"All right, fine, whatever," I said and laughed, "I'll ask! I'll ask!"

Maybe.

LL Eadie

Chapter Six

## *Step Up*

Sometimes,

You have to step up.

Many,

Steep,

Narrow,

Steps.

Before you can sightsee,

The sky...

That is,

Your future.

~~~~~~~~~~~~~~~~~~~~~~~~~~~~~~

"Don't worry, Tu-Tu," my mother said, "your song will sound current." She and Uncle Monty lay nude under skimpy white towels on twin massage tables. The bottoms of their calloused feet seemed to wiggle mockingly in my face. "It will captivate, be exciting, extraordinary. And youthful, of course."

Of course, the same ole playful lyrics. As Zelda would say, "Bor-ing."

My mother oohed and awed a bit before continuing. "Monty and I have come up with the most awesome title for your new solo album – Meet Tuesday Greenwood! It's a knock-off from the Beatles first album where half of their face was shaded. Isn't that the coolest?"

No, Momma, it isn't.

Mine.

A pair of masseuses kneaded their oil-upped skin to the piped-in melody of John Lennon's Imagine, compliments of our 340 hours of music storage. Lennon and The Beatles. Obviously one of her favorites.

Uncle Monty lifted his head out of the face rest to survey me standing emotionally naked by the opened pavilion door. There were no solid walls, only magenta colored flowers from a bougainvillea vine with its wicked thorns knotted through the white lattice work. It wrapped around the sides of the building allowing the sea breeze to sneak peek in. A restored vintage Spanish clay tiled roof shaded their bodies and the soft sandy floor.

A sea gull caught my attention as he cried out angrily at what was rightfully his to another gull on the beach.

I can do this. Go for it. Now!

Not sure I can.

"I spoke with Glissando Records," Uncle Monty said, "and they have agreed to your mother's simply awesome idea of debuting your next new single at a prom." His towel slipped over-sharing his nudity. There so should be a bun-ban in effect.

Note to self: Warning - refrain from entering spa pavilion when bare-ass adults are present.

"In fact," Uncle Monty continued, unaware of the eyesore damage he had caused, "they were so excited they suggested you should be involved with the prom committee, Tuesday honey. You know, help with the decisions on the decorations and making sure there's an adequate stage, sound system, lighting, etcetera. Of course, Glissando will provide whatever is needed to pull this gig off."

This is my chance.

I think.

## My Mistaken Identity

He laid his head back down and moaned as the masseuse targeted his lower back. He managed to muffle, "Glissando is already setting up a band, back-up singers, a choreographer, and, dancers as we speak. And, they are going to match the charitable funds raised by the winning high school."

Oh my God! I am so not going to punk-out this time. What was it Zelda said I was suffering from? Oh, yeah, - CTF – Chronic Tuesday Fatigue.

No more! Enough!

I shielded my songbook behind my back as I spoke and shook my head along with the CD I recorded in my studio, with the assistance of Zelda. My words though became budgeted. "No...No...No..." Then, I froze up like a computer. It was a cryptic message. M&M's puzzled say-what expressions bore into me, staring me down, and leaving eye tracks in the sand.

Bombarding Z-moment – "Constance has a weak game. Press her! No choke-ups allowed, Tu-Tu."

Okay, here it goes.

I hope.

"You see...I... um...have written some...um... songs with sort of uhh...between like a girl and grown-up woman lyrics," I said, as I stepped in one full length of my black flip-flops. I took a second brave step and attempted a smile.

Was it out of place? Should I frown? Cry?

Just say it already!

"What I really, really need," I continued, "is a fresh spin. I was thinking of ...uhh...a new name for my album – The Third Day of the Week. And, a new sound to ramp-up my image."

My hands hooked-up and pretended to wipe fine sand from between my fidgeting fingers. "Sorta, kinda, maybe like the pop-princess meets rocker-chick meets soul-diva," I said, as the salty breeze blew my hair and short skirt behind me. I hoped my words were not blown away, too. "But tinged with an…uhh…alternative vibe."

Yes, another giant leap forward. I'm almost there. I'm most definitely on a roll. For once.

"I'll need the usual instruments." I was becoming stronger, louder and more confident. "But add some jazz-kissed brass ones. You know like a sax, trombone, and a trumpet. It's an addictive mix of retro-tech meets old school funk." My voice filled with excitement. "With awesome beats you can dance to!" My hips got into the moment too. "And, maybe a couple of guy back-up singers! I think my new sound will win a crossover audience of all ages!"

I stared at the back of my mother's head shaking. My enthusiasm faded. And deflated. "That's it." I shrugged. "And, Momma, I made a demo for you to listen to. I think…I mean…hope…you're going to like it."

"Really?" Uncle Monty rolled to his side to view my possible inclement situation better. The masseuse thankfully guarded his fig-leaf of a towel this time. But a healthy patch of his silver-foxed chest hair was exposed; that grew in healthy fur swatches on his back as well.

"Why in the world would you do that?" my mother said, as she replicated my uncle's pose and took a sip of her designer water. A frown attempted to furrow her brow, however, it was Botox blocked.

Damn, I'm at the crossroads of T.G. and Jazmyn. Am I at risk?

WWZD – what would Zelda do? Go for it!

"I really don't want to sing the same ole songs anymore, Momma." I walked toward her with my hands clasped in prayer, as if I was walking toward an altar asking for a blessing. "I want to perform my own music and be appreciated for my true self. Don't you see, Momma? I'm older now. I'm sixteen. I'm on the edge of becoming a for-real adult."

Did I really just say that?

# My Mistaken Identity

Zelda would be so wowed!

However, my words were greeted less than enthusiastically.

"What is she talking about, Monty?" My mother rolled onto her back. "Did you know anything about this?"

"Of course not," Uncle Monty my mother's battery-operated boyfriend answered, as he turned his head to his left to speak to her.

My mother issued me her you-better-keep-your-mouth-shut look.

Is it fight or flight?

It's most definitely fight!

"I'm just saying Momma that I want to shed the queen-of-tween-scene image. A redefinition. I'm not seeking a total metamorphosis, more of a cross-pollination. A fusion of music genres."

My mother rose up onto her elbows as the masseuse took a required time out to fire-up her cigarette. She was lost in my translation as she repeated herself, "Monty, what in the hell is she talking about?"

Her second-hand smoke hitched a ride on a breeze and headed toward me. I waved my hand in front of my face.

Could you not?

Monty shrugged his loosened shoulders as he came up for air.

"Things change, Momma," I said. "You said so yourself. Give me some credit. Please. Isn't freedom of expression my right, too?"

"We already discussed the changes, Tuesday." My mother laid back down. Her masseuse, who pretended along with his partner, to ignore me being ushered down the rabbit hole, began at the bottoms of my mother's ticklish feet. Reluctantly, she smiled.

"See…" I said, as I held out my unknown-to-her talent. "I have written an entire book of lyrics, and I perform the melody with my guitar you bought me two Christmases ago. My guitar teacher, Mr. Tork, said my stick-to-it-iveness has really paid off. He said I have solid crossover potential for today's market."

I held out the book as if I were asking for it to be baptized. "Can I share them with the songwriter? And…and…you, Momma?"

"This is absurd and ridiculous! Bring that over here!" my mother said, stretching out her arm. Her fingers were spread and the pink acrylic claws were drawn.

Damn, I've done it. Now what?

I dragged my mid-youth-crisis feet in the sand as I walked in her direction. "Momma, I want to record my songs on an album. I know it will be way amazing. You'll be so proud."

Please, Momma, my time is now. I have to move forward with my life, even if that means leaving you behind.

Don't make me do that, Momma! I love you.

My mother snatched the songbook from my trembling hand and sat up, not caring that her 34 double D's were unleashed. "Imperfect, Reluctant, The Depression, So Marked, Too Sensitive," my mother read, as she flipped through the pages. "These are angry depressing songs, Tuesday! Do you really think your fans want to hear you belly ache?"

"But, Momma, you said so yourself that I was growing up and needed to update my image. I'm so tired of living this bubble-gum life. I'm older. Please hear me out."

"Not by changing your music genre to…to…some subgenre," my mother said still focused on my songbook. "Pop is what made you a commercial success. Why would you crossover and pull the pop plug? Dumb decisions stick, Tuesday. May I remind you, my Sugar Plum, there's little if any chance to rewind."

## My Mistaken Identity

I turned to my Astroturf uncle. "Please, Uncle Monty. I have a demo. Won't you listen to it?" He refused to pick up his face while his stress reducing massage continued.

Maybe Zelda was right about him.

"Are you talking about Stormy Gallagher here, Tuesday? I'm Not the Perfect Storm, Nor Do I Care to Be." She turned the page. "And what about I'm Tired of Being You, You Had Your Chance. What's that supposed to mean? Is that song about me?"

I started to lose it. I'd promised myself, and Zelda, that I wouldn't. But, I did cry. I was wounded deeply. Way burned. How could they turn me down without even listening to my song? My written words were raw, tender, vulnerable, and, truthful.

Or, as Zelda would say, "Pure exposure."

And yet, my mother had discarded them like her empty pharmaceutical bottles of chill pills. Nor did Uncle Monty divulge the slightest interest. Zelda was way right he was my mother's disciple-on-strings. My mother and Uncle Monty had always been my armor. Now it was rusting with age. My age.

I tossed my CD-demo into the sand, along with my tears. I only wish my voice had not trembled when I said, "I read my horoscope this morning, Momma. And guess what it said – Nothing should stand between me and what I want! Do you hear me, Momma?"

I snagged my baring-soul lyrics from her hands "And neither one of you can make me! I'm not going to that lame prom! Or sing your stupid song!"

# Chapter Seven

## *Who to Blame?*

I ask you,

Who should I blame?

The moonstruck?

The evil fairy?

The troll?

Or,

My mother?

Or,

Oh, my God!

Is it...

Me?

~~~~~~~~~~~~~~~~~~~~~~~~~~~~~~~~~~

My bare feet dug beneath the cooling night sand. I watched Uncle Monty the self-appointed momma-and-me-wrinkle-smoother study his freckling age spots, varicose veins, and fossilized yellowing nails on his sun-seasoned hands, as if he had never noticed any of these ick factors before.

He had found me on the beach, as he often did, following a domestic disagreement with my mother. In the past we might disagree over studying, practicing or what outfit I chose to wear. My mother called it back-sassing. But this was way different. I felt shaken but stoked at the same time. However, the mad-woman's soul-meter was running. Over-time.

Arrival of a Z-moment – "Constance is an obvious idiot."

True. And, a genius. A beautiful and talented one.

I had sat there alone on that exclusive beach until my butt suffered a migraine while turning off and on my tears of frustration about the what-ifs in my life:

What if I had never taken tap, ballet and jazz lessons? What if I had never been schooled in modeling, acting and singing?

What if I had never been chosen Little Miss Miami at age six and awarded with not only a tiara, but the opportunity to sing the National Anthem at the Miami Dolphin's home opener?

And, what if renowned talent agent Monty Simelski had not been sitting in the owner's box that same evening?

What if… What if…What if I had never been born?

"I'm sorry I couldn't do more at the time, Tuesday honey," Uncle Monty said. He laid a Listerine strip on his old-man ghost-white tongue.

Can't you tell Momma "no" either?

"But, I did convince your mother into listening to your demo with me." He pocketed the mouthwash packet. "You had a very soulful, sultry sound. It was definitely a place your voice has never gone before. I was quite impressed. But, not surprised."

Are you trying to schmooze me, Uncle Monty? Zelda was right you are a freakin' picket fence rider.

He scooped up a handful and sand allowing it to spill through the cracks between his fingers. "Your mother and I both agree you are extremely gifted. And, obviously some of that talent of yours is still untapped. Lately, though, you've been a little too sensitive."

Did you ever think there might be a reason for that? Or don't you care to know?

"We know it's part of growing pains, Tuesday. But you are highly creative. In fact, I'd like to help you with your songs by accompanying you on the piano. If…that's all right."

I didn't answer. I didn't know which side of his mouth to believe.

Uncle Monty placed his hand on my shoulder. I sat up straighter. "And we all agree, honey, a new image is imminent. So, I'm here to offer a compromise." His hand dropped to my waist.

I looked out at the ocean that was blanketed in pink from the setting sun's reflection in the west. The finale of the day that I now wore on my defusing face.

What if…Uncle Monty had not shown up when he did?

How many times had Zelda needed him?

"Tuesday, you'll be allowed to select one of your songs with the help of the songwriter. He will make the final decision which one you will perform. And, about the musical arrangements. Okie-dokie?"

My mouth twisted, and my chin sank into my chest.

Should I accept?

"Well?" Uncle Monty squeezed my deflating body. However, I found the strength and pulled forward releasing his everything-is-okie-dokie-now grip.

So, I'm being given the opportunity to share a song. This is my chance.

Perhaps.

WWZD? It's what she had wanted.

## My Mistaken Identity

This is a good thing.

I so hoped.

"Okay, Uncle Monty.

"

# Chapter Eight

## *Reality Check*

You know it's so

So why...

Fight it?

Deny it?

Hide it?

Own up to it.

Release it.

And...

Be healed.

~~~~~~~~~~~~~~~~~~~~~~~~~~~~~~~~~~~~

"So, tell!" Zelda said as she caught up with me wandering down the deserted beach. "I saw Monty return to the house. What did he say? Did you tell them? Did you? Or did you punk-out?"

I turned around and faced her and the ocean that was impersonating a lake. "Yes! I did it, Zelda!" I grabbed her shoulders and sprung up and down in the chilled ankle-deep swell of water burying my bare feet in the sand.

"Shhh..."

I lowered my voice. "I could have never done it without you."

"I wasn't there."

"Yes, you were," I said. "You were here." I pointed to my head. "And, here." I patted my chest.

Zelda smiled that cock-eyed way of hers peeking around her chin length hair. "Glad to hear I'm such an awesome role model for your goody-goody ass."

She kicked a wannabe-wave at me. I struck back. It was a sunset duel in the surf. And this time nobody won. We were soaked and frigid. We rushed back to my white towel I had neglected on the beach. The place where Uncle Monty had found me. The place where I had agreed to one song. My song. And we spooned underneath it.

"Just one?" Zelda said. "That sucks!"

"Better one than none."

"You should have held out, Tu-Tu, for more. M&M's can't afford their martini lunches and fame lifestyle without you. You do know that, don't you?"

I guess I did, but, not really. My whole life I had been told I would not be anywhere if it had not been for the sacrifices my mother had made for me. And, Uncle Monty's connections. And I believed that. I still did. I think.

Do I still need her? Or, him?

"You don't need them," Zelda said as she squeezed my waist.

Huh?

"They need you."

Maybe you're right.

"You know I'm right."

Huh?

## My Mistaken Identity

"Listen, Tuesday, I'm proud of you," Zelda said. "For once you stood up to them."

"Yeah, I did, didn't I?" A smile froze on my face.

Zelda nodded and scootched closer. "Are you really going to go through with their latest prom gig? Pure cheesy. I'd vent if I was you."

I don't think I can do that again.

"Zelda, tell me about high school." I wiped the sand drying to the side of my face and matting in my hair.

"What's to tell?"

"Come on, you know, what's it really, really like?"

"It's school. It's mandatory. Haven't you ever been to school before?"

"No. Not public."

"Maybe you are lucky."

"Please, Zelda."

"Okay, let's see. Teachers, some suck. Some don't. Same with students. Some are torturing. Some aren't."

"I bet you have tons of friends."

Zelda shrugged. "Enough."

"Are you popular?"

"Me?" She laughed. "Not happening."

"What about dances, clubs, homecoming …?"

"I wouldn't know," Zelda said, "I'm not into that."

"Oh." I sighed.

"Sorry, Tu-Tu," Zelda said, "I guess I'm not the all-American-chick-next-door type. Too feral."

My turn to offer up an I-don't-give-a-shit shrug. "It doesn't really matter. I just wondered what it would feel like to be...you know...normal."

"Normalcy. Way overrated," Zelda said. "You are who you are, Tuesday. Stay true. Define yourself. Don't leave the page blank for others to write."

But what if I don't know myself, who I am?

"Don't let constantly-in-charge-Constance, her side-kick Monty, Glissando Records, that song writer dude, and all the rest of the users and abusers of the Tuesday Greenwood world take advantage of you."

"They're really not all that bad, Zelda."

Huh? Wasn't it thirty minutes ago I was ready to end it?

"You really think not?"

Things are better now. They've agreed a little with me.

"Yeah," I said wiping my knees off and sitting up. The moon was full and marking a broad pathway across the ocean's surface. "Momma has problems I know, but she can't help it. She's sick. And she's always put me first. My career. She gave hers up for me."

Why am I taking her side?

Zelda sat up too and shook her head. "Seriously, has she brainwashed you?"

I shook my head in protest. "No, she and Uncle Monty have always taken care of me. They've always done what's best for me. I would never be..."

"Where I am today if it wasn't for them. Right?"

## My Mistaken Identity

I nodded and dug my nails into my palms.

Maybe I'm the picket fence rider.

"And, Tuesday Greenwood queen-of-the-tween-scene, where would they be without your ample paycheck? You're the provider. And they know it."

Yeah, but…

Zelda rapped her knuckles on my damp head. "Hello. Reality check."

I smirked.

"Okay," Zelda said, "I can see it's going to take an epiphany for you to buy into this. So, let's move on. Erase it. What about your dad? Have you asked Constance yet?"

"No, but I will. I promised."

Myself.

The tide was rolling out further and further. I feared finding my father was escaping me too.

My mother called out my name. Time to part before momma caught a glimpse of my forbidden friend. I catapulted up. "I'm coming!" I turned back around to snatch my towel.

Zelda had vanished into the night.

How does she do that?

LL Eadie

Chapter Nine

## *The Truth about Your Truths*

Is it true?

What they say...

About,

Your truths?

Are they really, really,

Just stretched

Little...

Tiny...

White lies?

That only sting for a little while.

~~~~~~~~~~~~~~~~~~~~~~~~~~~~~~~~~~~~~~~~~~~~~~

"Protect your interests," read my mother from the Gazette's horoscope as we sat among the glitter-upped south Floridians in the Seafood Bar at The Breakers for lunch a week later. This was after a shopping for my soon-to-be prom dress, and my mother's, on Worth Avenue in Palm Beach the Rodeo Drive of Florida.

She took a twenty-dollar sip of her chardonnay. Constance-the-cougar grinned seductively at our below-the-legal-age waiter. "I sure hope you haven't mentioned my awesome idea to anyone, Tuesday."

Who would I tell, Momma?

I so didn't have anybody that even resembled a friend. No crew. There were those that I don't even remember their names. They were not really friends. It seemed as if everyone I had ever known had pissed on me. Trust was a luxury I couldn't afford. Those supposed so-called friends all had their own agendas. Or, were moochers. Except, for Zelda. She was becoming my gal pal I hoped.

I shook my head to calm my mother's suspicious mind.

She folded the paper and laid it in the vacant chair next to her. "I just adore the white-frosted taffeta gown we selected for you."

You mean, Momma, the one you picked out for me.

"It should be ready," my mother said, "in a couple of weeks for a fitting. It will make you sparkle and shine when you take that stage. You'll command it, Tuesday!"

I glanced up at her through my thick blonde hair, shook my head and smiled as the waiter served our lunch. She didn't notice – my smile.

"Your onyx colored dress was awesome, too, Momma." And it was.

"Oh, do you think so, Sugar Plum?" My mother waited for more rave reviews.

"Pure hottie," I said and smiled again.

"Thank you, Sugar Plum." Another sip of wine. She reached for her cell phone. "I wonder why Monty hasn't called me. He was meeting with Baldwin today and going over the lyrics for one of your new songs."

Jeez.

"That's nice," I said. I blew bubbles into my water.

"Baldwin Spikes is the best. You should thank your lucky stars that Glissando hired him to help you."

# My Mistaken Identity

I don't need his help, Momma.

"I'm sure he is."

"I wouldn't have anything but the best for my Sugar Plum." She reached over and patted my hand. The one engaged with the straw. "Now, stop that, Tuesday." She popped it.

My hand and mouth obediently behaved.

Why not now? It's perfect. No Uncle Monty around. Just me and Momma.

Ask!

"I read my horoscope, Momma, in one of those teen magazines you subscribe for me. It said for me to travel back in time to get to the bottom of something that has been bothering me about my...uhh...past." I wiped the perspiration percolating on my distilled glass of water, and then, from my forehead. "About my...umm...father."

Oh my God, did I really ask? I reached for my lip. But stopped myself.

"Hmm, him? I wondered when you'd bring up that nasty subject again." My mother sliced into her crab encrusted piece of grouper. "Actually, there's not much to tell, Tuesday. He was, as I said before, someone I met in college."

I sighed. Same-o-same-o story.

She looked up at me.

Did I react? How was I supposed to act?

This is a part of my life that has no part. It never really mattered before.

Why now?

Surfacing Z-moment – "It's your freakin' father! Not hers."

You're right.

I suddenly became aware of several non-native prairie dog heads popping over booths to cell-phone picture me. I appeased them with my courteous parade wave and smile.

Thank God, we drove the presidential-tint car.

"And," my mother continued, "never heard from the likes of him ever again." She waved and grinned too at the cell phones. No such thing as a constantly-candid-Constance. My mother fluffed her hair and turned to her best side before the maitre d' dropped an off-limits' tie-back curtain around our tucked-away enclave in their aw-shucks' faces.

I became very attached to the napkin in my lap folding it over and over as if I was an expert at origami.

God, why did I bring up this mood-altering topic? I should stick with the don't-piss-off-your-momma guidelines. Just a little pinch.

"Stop that!" My mother's hand squished mine away from my mouth.

But, like Zelda said, with Monty hanging out 24/7 there's never a good time to get acquainted with my daddy.

My mother's voice raised an octave as she sharpened her teeth. "He was a nobody!" She snapped off a bite of her fish, crushed, gnawed, devoured, and critiqued my forever after absent father. "Nobody you ever will meet!"

I nodded my head, picked up my fork and attempted to taste my fresh spinach salad encrusted with tofu. I was attempting Zelda's vegan diet. No more food-of-shame on my plate.

"Excuse me, ladies," the chef said, as he carried a tray with two amaretto crème brulees. "I hope your dishes are prepared to your liking, Mrs. Greenwood."

"Miss Greenwood." She lined-up her cleavage with her deep "V" cut silk blouse. Pure boob-assisted. "Delicious. My compliments."

"I hope," the chef continued, "I'm not imposing, but I brought you and your wonderfully talented daughter complimentary desserts. Of course, your lunch is on the house as well."

Not now. Please move on.

"Why, thank you," my mother said. "We shall return."

"No. Thank you, Miss Greenwood. It's all my pleasure." The chef set the dishes on the table, smiled, nodded toward me, and imposed. "I hope you don't mind, but my daughter is one of your biggest fans, Miss Tuesday." He held out the restaurant's menu along with a pen. "An autograph perhaps?"

"Of course, she doesn't mind," my mother said handing over the goods to me. I reluctantly reached for them and signed it.

"Her name is Kasey. With a K," the chef added.

Jeez.

Okay. I owe him that much.

I added Kasey with a K and handed the menu back and attempted a smile. A crooked, brief non-lit one.

"Thank you so much. She will be thrilled." He reversed his steps to the kitchen.

I must be a slow learner because I didn't shelf the risky topic. "Did he...umm...my father ever, you know, ask about me? Or...uhh...come and see me? What about his family?"

"No. No. And no," my mother said, lighting up in this nonsmoking establishment. Her smoke was as intrusive as the patron-photographers. However, no one interrupted her from contaminating me with her secondhand nicotine and stinging truths about my mythical origin.

She looked up at me over her second glass of wine, "You wouldn't be sitting in this restaurant today, Tuesday, and receiving complimentary meals like this one prepared by a world class chef, if it wasn't for me. Believe me there's no such thing as a free lunch."

Yeah, yeah, yeah.

My mother took another hit on her coffin-nail and continued the updated barrage. "Your so-called father was no where to be found when I needed him. No where! And, neither was his think-they're-somebody-important family. Do you hear me, Tuesday?" She sneered. "You were born, my Sugar Plum, in the charity ward of Grady Memorial Hospital in Atlanta. I had no one to call upon." Her fists bounced off the table. "No one! I fought and scraped for you, Tuesday. Don't you ever forget it!"

Can you not? Please, don't go there, Momma. Not here. Not now.

Why did I insist? Damn.

"I'm really, really sorry, Momma." I reached for my mother's stirred-up hands. "I didn't mean to upset you. You're all I have, too."

She placed her quaking hands on top of mine. Tears drooled down her cheeks.

Were they for-real? Or, was it constantly-counterfeit-Constance speaking? Hard to tell. She's still a good actress.

Funny how my pity is slipping away for her.

"You know, Tuesday, you should be grateful for Monty. I know he's not really your uncle, but he's been like a father to you."

He should have been a father to Zelda.

"I lost my parents when I was seven."

Brace yourself, Tuesday, here comes the cricket moment. Again. Maybe, she'll offer it up in a Cliffs Note's version. How once upon a time she was a child star and her parents pissed away her fortune.

## My Mistaken Identity

My mother patted the corners of her mouth, careful not to disturb the liner. "That, of course, ended my acting career, because my grandmother had zero tolerance for the entertainment industry." She took another sip of wine before drawing in more nicotine.

I had her woe-is-me bio memorized. However, I was not moved anymore by my mother's sacrificial story. Was I turning into Zelda and becoming totally anti-Constance?

The Z-moment was loud and clear - "Be careful, Tuesday, she's most definitely your doom and future destruction. She thinks you owe her everything."

I wonder if he ever knew my name.

LL Eadie

# Chapter Ten

## *Over-Sharing*

Share your life,

With someone.

Your pain,

Your guilt,

Your longing.

Is it sorta, kinda, maybe like,

Their pain?

Their guilt?

Their longing?

Or,

Is it sorta, kinda, maybe like...

Their gain?

~~~~~~~~~~~~~~~~~~~~~~~~~~~~~~~~~~~~

"I insisted they change the charity to my new favorite – Saving American Horses," I said, as Zelda took photos of my personal stuff in between the best parts of the movie, The Midnight Hour, one of her favorites a couple of weeks later.

"Did you know, Zelda, that four and half million horses in America are slaughtered every year to be digested for dinner in foreign countries?"

"No way!" Zelda snapped a picture of a pair of my three-hundred-dollar leather espadrilles. "You're such a tag hag, Tuesday." She said and snarkled. "Wish that was all I ever wore were hideously expensive clothes."

I ignored Zelda's comment and continued to try to impress her. "Check this out, Zelda, today Baldwin Spikes, that's the songwriter dude, said I had taken my music totally out of my comfort zone and somewhere really special."

"Smart man. Glad he recognized that fact. It's about time somebody did."

I watched Zelda disappear into my bath and powder room. I raised my voice. "Baldwin also said my songs were a bit left of center, but undeniably commercial at the core. You know, radio friendly. Zelda, are you listening to me?"

"Mmm-hmm, that's awesome. Ecstatic he's on your side, Tuesday. Now, if he could just convince M&M's. And, Glissando."

True.

"Hey, you're missing one of the best parts. The vampire's kiss of death scene." However, Zelda ignored me this time. I got up and shadowed her.

What is she up to? So strange. But, what's new about that?

"Why are you taking these weird-o pictures?" I asked, as I stood in the doorway watching Zelda flashbulb the bath oil ring in my tub.

"You're behaving badly, Tuesday Greenwood. A wannabe-rebel in the making." Zelda cocked her head toward the dirty ring. "Pure James Dean."

"I'm working on it," I said and smiled, as I kicked my thongs across the tile where I had dropped them before my bath.

# My Mistaken Identity

"Did you know, Tuesday, Newton Powers sued his parents for control over his own finances at fourteen?" Zelda asked, as she focused on the bristles of my electric toothbrush.

"Yeah, I think I heard something about it," I said.

"Well, you should most definitely take note!"

I placed my hands on my hips. "Zelda, what are you doing?"

"He's not the only one, you know? Alicia Alexander at sixteen kicked her dad's ass in court after he swept her for millions!" Zelda zoomed in on my bottom lip. "Stick it out, Tu-Tu. Pout for me."

I puffed out my bottom lip and started laughing. Hysterically. "Can you not?"

Zelda could not. She continued to snap pictures of my open mouth.

"Please!" I said, as I escaped the Nikon lens, backtracking to my bedroom and laid down.

"I thought we'd make you one wicked social network page." Zelda followed me over to the bed. "It's time for you to break-out and blog, Tuesday. I know you already have one…but…you don't write it."

"Me? Myself? Really?"

"You're not web-shy, are you?"

"No, but I could never use my real name."

"No one does. You use your plane name." Zelda clicked my toes.

"Plain name?" I spread my toes apart as if I was having my nails painted after an exfoliating pedicure.

"Yeah, the made-up one you use on an airplane when the weirdo next to you asks for it." Zelda headed for my computer in the connecting study.

"All right," I said and shrugged. Then, I too, rushed into the room.

Wow! My own blog!

I hope Momma and Uncle Monty don't find out.

"Now, I know you live by the Just-Say-No pledge, Tuesday, with your self-imposed straight edge limits." Zelda got all cozy at my computer, staring at the wide screen and pointy-fingering the keyboard.

"I wouldn't exactly say self-imposed." I rolled up the other zebra-printed chair.

"No, you're way right, they're most definitely M&M's regulations. God, there's such an over abundance of keep-it-clean issues hanging out here. It so sucks. But, what do you do for fun, Tuesday? Does that celibacy ring on your finger hold you back from all areas of recess?"

Huh?

Zelda turned to face me and continued. "Are you a for-real fun sucker? You don't party, you don't smoke, you don't drink, you don't do drugs, you don't do guys. Or gals," she said and snarkled. "No one's that perfect! What are you? A registered protected specie?"

Zelda opened the palms of her hands and pointed them at me. "Where's the sex, drugs and rock 'n' roll lifestyle? Don't you ever want to do something naughty? You're not up for sainthood, are you? Pure Joan of Arc."

Why does the truth hurt so much?

"That's me all right! Tuesday Greenwood the Queen of the Tween Scene. Former kiddie-channel star of The Jazmyn and Justyce Show. The chick with the goody-goody girl demeanor."

"Damn." Zelda shook her head. "I'm sorry, Tuesday, sometimes I just lose it when I think of what you're going through. It's so not fair."

# My Mistaken Identity

I squeezed my eyes shut, wrapped both arms around my stomach and bent forward. "Owwee."

"What's wrong?" Zelda stared at me through her jet-black rimmed glasses and hair. "Tell me! Are you sick?"

I shook my head and continued to rub my stomach. "It's nothing. I just get really, really bad pains sometimes. Did you bring any junk to eat?"

"Yeah, maybe. In need of some comfort food, huh?" She pulled the messenger bag over her head where it had been draped across her layered T-shirts and handed it to me. It was decked-out in an over abundance of devotional rock band pins. I dug inside and found an empty pack of cigarettes, a ticket stub to a Cinderella Confessions rock band concert, a tube of Chap Stick, black liquorices and, a smashed Hostess Twinkie.

"Hey, look here again," Zelda said. "You've got an eye booger. Hold still." She reached over and thumbed the inside corner of my eye.

My turn to smirk.

Damn, just like momma used to do.

"What?" Zelda said.

I shook my head and licked the Twinkie wrapper. Zelda laughed and smashed it into my shocked face. I snagged the sticky plastic from her and wiped the white cream and yellow cake up and down her unresisting arm. She grinned and lapped it off. I smiled. Zelda was becoming a for-real best friend. I hoped it lasted forever.

"Okay, time to bare all," she said. "Come clean, Tu-Tu. Be dipped into the forgiving waters of the internet and feed me your past crush confessions."

"If only." I said and smacked, as I sucked the Twinkie from my fingers. "Guys don't ask me out. No doubt, they've heard my mom requires a blood and urine test. If not a casting call."

"Or a couch casting one," Zelda teased.

"They really don't, Zelda. Most of my dates are just flash for promos. They rarely take me out again. I'm seriously prone to dating droughts."

"What a constipated love life," Zelda said, and then she added, "I'd totally date you, Tu-Tu. That is, if I was a guy."

I shook my head and smirked. "Gee, thanks."

Zelda socked me in the arm. "Don't get your hopes up." She grinned.

I smiled and rolled my eyes.

"But, don't you meet tons of hot guys in the biz?" Zelda asked, "Like the band? The back-ups? Dancers?"

I licked an itty-bitty-bit of Twinkie from between my fingers. "My mother doesn't like me to mix work and recess. And, she so doesn't trust outsiders."

"What a padded-cornered life you've lived," Zelda said and laughed. "So, you've never ever had a crush? Or a romantic failure?"

I stopped de-gooeying my fingers and paused for a tortured memory. "I thought I knew forever-after once. With one of my co-stars. It sucked."

"I think I hit a sushi nerve," Zelda said, sitting up straighter. "Fess-up the back-stage-pass romance, Tu-Tu."

Then, there was a what-in-the-world-have-I-spilled silence. Pure brain cramp.

Zelda whispered, "Seriously, Tuesday, you can trust me."

You're right. I can. And maybe, no one else.

# My Mistaken Identity

My nails dug into my palms as I forfeited his name. "Ashburn...Ashburn Fitzgerald. He had small acting parts from time to time on the show. His father was the producer."

"That figures. Okay, progress. His name is Ashburn. Did he try to blow that purity ring off your finger?"

I smirked and looked down at my gold band of abstinence Uncle Monty had given me for my fifteenth birthday and twisted it around and around. I smiled. Then frowned and replaced my nails into my clammy palms once more. "I hate Ashburn! And, Stormy Gallagher!"

"Taken advantage of, huh? You so need to end it with both of them. What better way to share your pain than to blog smack." Zelda said. "I so hope you unpacked him first. Divulge your burning drama of he said – she said and bare your soul. Let's get ready to crumble!"

My tears streamed through the cake maze still stuck to my cheeks, as I regurgitated my rejected past on cyberspace. "I thought Ashburn really liked me, you know. He called and woke me up every morning and kissed me goodnight when he left my house at constantly-curfew-setting-Constance's orders on Saturday nights."

"So, what happened?" Zelda asked.

I shrugged. "I think things got really messed-up with us when I divulged all Ashburn's right moves to Stormy."

"Do tell."

"You know," I said, as I turned my head and looked away. "How he would kiss my eyelids, and whisper his secret desires into my ear, and..."

"This is rich!" Zelda said.

"Yeah, well, I guess Stormy wanted a piece of that action, too."

"No freakin' doubt!"

"All of sudden the wake-up calls stopped, and so did the tuck-in kisses." I looked back at Zelda posting my split-up on Tu-Tu's InUrFace page. "I made a gargantuan mistake." I stared at the floor. "I called him."

"Pure desperation!" Zelda shook her head.

"I know."

"God, Tuesday, tell me you didn't. No, you didn't beg!"

I nodded.

"You broke the number one rule in break-ups!"

"Guilty."

"What happened?" she asked.

"Well, unknowingly I confided in Stormy."

"You did what?"

"Zelda, I swear I didn't know she liked Ashburn. I had no idea. So, I asked her to do me a favor and talk to him, you know, and try to find out why he wasn't calling me."

"Shit."

"I know. I thought she was my friend. It was all a lie. I thought the only reason they sat together between takes on the show was because she was helping me out. What an idiot I was. They were obviously laughing at me the whole time."

"What a bitch."

I stared at the computer screen. "No one will know it's me, will they?"

"How could they?" Zelda said. "Remember I used your plane name. So, anytime you want to vent – go for it. It's your page, Tu-Tu."

# My Mistaken Identity

"Cool."

"Hey, Tuesday," Zelda said turning her head to look at me. "Are you really going through with that prom gig?"

My mouth twisted back and forth.

"I guess that's a yes, huh?" she said.

I nodded.

Zelda shook hers. "You're entering a no-bubblegum zone, I hope you know that. It might not be such a good idea."

Maybe, just maybe, she's wrong this time.

I hope.

LL Eadie

Chapter Eleven

## *A For-Real Life*

A life,

I only dreamed about.

A life,

I was told stories about.

A life,

That didn't belong to me.

A for-real life.

~~~~~~~~~~~~~~~~~~~~~~~~~~~~~~~~~~~~~~~~~

Two weeks later the airport limousine drove us through the gates of William P. DuVal High School in Jacksonville, Florida the so-called winning school of my exclusive performance at their spring prom. Because of the expected national attention to be brought onto their campus the prom committee was meeting now at the beginning of the school year.

Oh my God! A for-real high school with sectioned-off plastic lunch trays, way crammed metal lockers, overdue library books, forgotten assignments, graffiti-topped desks, ear-piercing pep rallies, notes of rich gossip, the homecoming monarchy, signed yearbooks, peer pressure – jeez, I only wish I knew what that was, and…a prom. Wow, I have truly arrived. Finally.

A soccer game was in progress to my right as I watched the teams dressed in either purple and gold or red and black chase after a black and white funny-shaped ball.

# LL Eadie

"Free kick," Uncle Monty said looking over my shoulder at the scoreboard. "Tied. Zip to zip. Might go into overtime if he doesn't score. Or it could be decided on a penalty shootout."

I only wish I knew what Uncle Monty meant, and which colors belonged to the William P. DuVal's Muskogee's. And, that I could have been one of the multitudes of students sitting in the bleachers cheering on their team. Or, boyfriend. If only.

We pulled into the brick-paved courtyard by the 1960's-ish retro-contemporary totally glassed front office. The area was empty except for an abbreviated unwelcoming party of three short skirts with snarled lips. Their intimate circle closed-up tight and their glittered-up eyes blinked like a neon sign. Warning! Warning! Warning! Zelda was way right these were not my fanatical fans.

I so wished I could have launched a massive recall on my mother's latest toxic-exclamation-mark career move for me.

A Z-moment emerged. "You know, Tuesday, everyone your age is laughing at you." She had said and then added, "Only fifth graders buy into your music."

I knew we shouldn't have taken a limo. It so screams I'm better than you. If only these girls knew, their disdained pretty faces would melt to sympathetic ones.

"Are we here on the right day?" My mother turned in her comfy seat to take in the absentee legions-of-fans courtyard. "You would think they would be out here to greet us…I mean…greet Tuesday."

What does she expect? The marching band? The dance team? The cheerleaders? The majorettes? Posters and banners? Confetti? And…the paparazzi?

I had so pulled the plug on the last guests, refusing my mother's request for a gargantuan press coverage and ad campaign, instead for a delayed one to her total meltdown.

# My Mistaken Identity

"Monty, go find out where everyone is," my mother ordered, as she panicked in the backseat by layering coats of her lip gloss to her recently filled collagen lips.

"I'll go." I started to scooch forward on the white leather seat toward the now opened door. Our chauffeur stood tall in his dark uniform with matching hat and white gloves, as he waited for our tardy departure.

"Sit still!" My mother shoved me back into my seat. "Monty will go find out what in the hell is going on."

"I don't mind, Tuesday honey," Uncle Monty patted my knee and stuck an insta-mouthwash strip on his tongue. "Perhaps, we came on the wrong day."

"Or, at the wrong time," My mother glanced at her diamond Rolex.

"The prom committee's meeting started over an hour ago," I reminded her. I had not forgotten how my mother had held us up at the airport refusing the black limo for a white one. Of course, her horoscope had warned her against dark colored rides.

"They probably gave up on us, Momma. Just let me out. Please." My fists were clenched as my nails dug deep into my palms.

"I said, don't move, Tuesday!" she repeated, as Uncle Monty exited the limousine with its seclusion screen from the driver, its mirrored ceiling with mood lighting, and its on-the-limo all-you-can-guzzle champagne (of course, with the exception of yours truly.)

Why did I agree to this? I so need to shake this gig. These kids don't listen to my music. They don't even like me. Zelda was way right. I'm just invading their space. And, their prom. Who do I think I am? I so need to end this. Maybe, I'll suddenly be ill, have laryngitis, or have an accident. If only.

Uncle Monty reappeared with more snarled-lipped short skirts. Pure retaliation. God, did they call for back up? Am I drawn to disaster, or what?

Also in the procession were three geeky guys, several in-charge looking teachers and administrators with four of my fanatical fans – their little kids dressed in Jazmyn and Justyce apparel.

"Aren't they cute, Tu-Tu? They're wearing…"

"I know, Momma. Please, can you not?"

"Please, what?" My mother reached for my hair and combed it with her two inch acrylic nails. Sort of like she used to do. Except before I sat on her lap as she brushed my fine hair each night before bed. And, she would recite a for-real fairy tale about how the fairies' hair was spun from the threads of a silk cocoon.

I pushed her hand away.

"Now, listen up, Tuesday, you're just excited and have the jitters," she said. "They love you!"

"No, Momma. They don't."

"Nonsense! This is the high school that raised the most money!" My mother reached for her champagne glass. "They can't wait for Tuesday Greenwood to sing at their prom!"

I seriously doubted that. It wasn't really that much money. And, it certainly helped that there was an equestrian center close by which pitched in the final over-the-top donation. Lucky them. Unlucky me.

Will I come out of this unscathed? They'll probably boo-and-hiss me off the stage that night. Or else knock me off from the pedestal that they think I rest my cushy ass upon.

Another Z-moment surfaced – "Constance is pressed. She'll do whatever it takes to get what she craves, and stomp the shit out of whoever tries to screw her. Pure Machiavellian."

"Remember, Tu-Tu, your new image is on the line," constantly-career-calculating-Constance reminded me with her I'm-warning-you eyes.

# My Mistaken Identity

I offered up my I-don't-give-a-shit shrug and said, "All right, fine, whatever."

Maybe Zelda is right about Momma. I am her status symbol.

The undertow on the sidewalk was growing stronger, and as I stepped out of the limo I lunged forward being sucked down toward the sidewalk, to the delight of the totally T.G.-loathers. I landed on my hands to break my fall. My short skirt became a blouse and my ass a download on the internet for a bazillion months to come.

Note to self:  Warning – make sure the strap on your shoulder bag is not secured around your ankle before exiting vehicles.

"Are you okay?" a deep drawling voice asked accompanied by a bobbing Adam's apple and a gaze of tender awe. And then, I was hit by friendly fire. The geek tripped, too, over his two gargantuan feet that he had not yet grown into. And we collided leaving asymmetrical book-end pump knots on our foreheads.

The paparazzi need not be present. The lose-lose T.G. situation was totally captured. It became a feeding frenzy.

"I'm so sorry," said the geek with the matching bump. He snatched me up from the gravelly pavement like a baby. My knees were skinned. "You're bleeding!"

"Tuesday!" my mother shouted from inside the limo.

He smelled like Old Spice.

Do guys really wear that stuff?

"Don't worry, I got her, ma'am!" He rushed me over to a concrete bench under the walkway's corrugated covering by the office.

Oh my God! This so isn't happening!

A rabid crowd formed around me. Pushing him out of the way.

"Tuesday! Are you okay?"

"Tuesday! Look here!" Click.

"Over here!" Click. Click. Click.

"Tuesday! Can I have your autograph?"

"Get back everyone!" said the principal, Mr. Webb, as he shoved his way through the students and teachers. My mother and Uncle Monty were tunneling right behind him.

Damn. Where's that guy?

"Are you okay, Tuesday darling?" my mother asked me as she plopped down next to me on the bench. Uncle Monty took up residence on the other side. As usual. My M&M bookends.

"I'm fine, Momma. No big deal."

Seriously, where'd he go?

"Here, Tuesday," said my assailant slash hero.

There you are.

"I brought some wet paper towels." He knelt down in front of me like a fairy tale Prince Charming, then he carefully laid the brown moist towels on my scuffed-up knees where there was only a faint dribble of blood.

"Miss Greenwood, is there anything else we can do for you?" Mr. Webb asked. "Perhaps something to drink or eat? We have refreshments inside."

"No thank you," I said as I watched the perfect vision in front of me.

Oh my God! He's so cute!

"Ms. Andrews," Mr. Webb said, "will you please see if the nurse is still here. And, Brady Paul, keep the pressure on, son."

# My Mistaken Identity

So sweet. Brady Paul.

He glanced up at me through his shaggy hair and pressed harder. "Does that hurt?" he whispered.

I shook my head and smiled.

This may not be such a bad gig after all.

"Yes sir," said the teacher as she waddled inside the front office door.

"It doesn't look too bad," Uncle Monty said as he leaned over to get a better view.

"It's just a little scrape," my mother said. "I'm sure it won't scar."

"I'm so happy you didn't hurt yourself anymore than that," Mr. Webb said. "Do you mind, Tuesday, if I take your parents over to the gymnasium before the volleyball game starts?"

"No, please do," I said. "I'll be just fine."

"I'm not her father," Uncle Monty said. "I'm her agent, Monty Simelski."

"Excuse me, Mr. Simelski," Mr. Webb said.

"Are you sure you'll be okay, sugar plum?" my mother asked brushing my hair out of my face.

"Of course, Momma."

"Okay, now that that's settled," Mr. Webb said, "why don't we walk over and I'll show y'all where the prom will be staged while Tuesday is being taken care of."

"That sounds like a fine idea," Uncle Monty said standing up and placing his hand on my shoulder. "Are you sure you're okay with that, Tuesday?"

"Of course," I said, "I'll be fine."

Please go. And take Momma too.

"Constance," Uncle Monty said, "are you coming?"

Thank you, Uncle Monty.

"Tuesday?" She unwrapped her arm from my waist and peered at my face.

"I'm fine, Momma. Go ahead."

Please go!

"Mr. Webb!" Ms. Andrews was swinging a white metal box with a red cross on its lid, "The nurse has already left for the day but I found this medical kit."

"Great," Mr. Webb said, "We're heading over to the gymnasium. Do you mind staying behind and helping Miss Greenwood?"

She nodded. "Not at all."

No, not her! That guy – Brady Paul!

"I have it under control, sir," Brady Paul said.

He most definitely does!

"Well…" Mr. Webb scratched the back of his thick neck. "I guess you can stay here with Ms. Andrews in case she needs something."

Damn.

Brady Paul's turn to nod. He glanced up at me and smiled.

I returned it with a for-real one.

"Okay," Mr. Webb said while directing traffic. His right arm, decked out in a grey suit, made this-way-everybody patterns in the humid air. "Let's all head over to the gym." He loosened the sweat-dam – his striped tie and top button to allow it to drool inside his white collar.

"Daddy, I want to stay here with Tuesday." His daughter pointed toward me with a pout and a matching Jazmyn and Justyce ring and bracelet.

"Me, too," said another little girl decked out in a Jazmyn and Justyce tee.

"No, you come with me," Mr. Webb said. "All of you. Miss Greenwood doesn't need any more helpers."

A few more exclusive bloody knee shots were taken by my T.G. loathers. They snickered, whispered and wisped away behind the welcoming prom committee.

Ms. Andrews plopped down next to me. She was digging through the tin box. And, breathing heavy. "Here, Brady Paul, here's some antiseptic cream, but there's not a single band-aid in here. I'll have to go back inside. I'll be right back." She set the box on the bench and rushed back down the sidewalk to the office once more.

Good. She's gone.

"This might sting." He dabbed the white cream on my right knee. Then my left. All the while watching my face for any evidence that it did. But it didn't.

"Feels nice," I said.

Feels nice? What an absurd thing to say!

He smiled as he wiped his fingers off on the paper towel. I glanced over at the limousine. The chauffer was safely packed into the driver's seat waiting in the air conditioning. I didn't blame him.

"So," I said, "your name is Brady Paul?"

"Sorry. I guess I should have introduced myself. I'm Brady Paul Larson. I'm a junior."

103

"I'm a junior too."

"Really, where do you go to school?"

"I don't."

"Of course, you don't. How stupid of me. You'd be mobbed. You're a star. I guess you're home schooled, huh?"

"Well, sort of. I actually have tutors."

"Here are the band aids!" Ms. Andrews said while hurrying back to my side. Tiny beads of perspiration were forming above her top lip.

"Thanks," I said. I smiled at Brady Paul.

"Ms. Andrews," Brady Paul said, "I think Tuesday could use some ice for her forehead." He reached up and wiped my hair from my bump and winked at me.

I covered my mouth and snickered.

"Oh, my!" Ms. Andrews said. "I'll be right back."

Brady Paul smiled and nodded. "I saw one of your movies, Tuesday."

"You did?"

"Yeah, my mom made me; I mean my sister wanted to go. So, I took her."

It figures.

"I guess it was one of the two Jazmyn and Justyce movies we made, huh?"

Of course, there were many others through the years. I don't even remember how many commercials, TV shows or movies I played character roles in. Maybe that's my problem, I've never played myself. Whoever that really is.

"Yeah," he said. "It was real cute. My sister loved it." He stood up and reached into his front pocket and pulled out his cell. "And speaking of sisters...I just got a text from mine."

I wish I had a sissy. At least I have Zelda.

He smiled as he read it. "She wants to know if you have arrived yet."

"May I?" I asked as I reached out for his phone.

"Sure."

"What's your sister's name?"

"Alley."

"Alley?"

"Yeah, it's short for Allison."

"Cute. How about this?" I said as I read my text aloud. "Hi Alley, I'm here. Wish U were too. Can't wait to meet U! T.G."

"Damn, she's freaking out now!" Brady Paul said and laughed as he sat down beside me.

"Here's an ice pack, honey for your head," Ms. Andrews said. She was gasping tiny gusts of humidity.

"Thank you, but you know what? Brady Paul needs one too." I reached over and smoothed his hair from his matching pump knot and winked at him.

"Oh my!" Ms. Andrews wasted no time again as she headed back to the nurse's station once more.

I bet she hasn't moved like this in years. Poor old lady.

"Don't rush!" shouted Brady Paul.

And then we both laughed. That is, when the teacher's XL polyester pantsuit was concealed behind the tinted glass door.

"May I program my number into your cell?" I asked.

Am I bold or what?

This is so not me.

What's gotten into me?

Zelda?

Brady Paul's head jerked back, and his eyes shot wide. "Of course!"

I looked up as I heard the crowd rounding the corner from the soon-to-be prom destination. The group seemed to have grown. There were volleyball players from two schools in the mix now. Uncle Monty was in the lead. Momma was not far behind with Mr. Webb holding her hand as they walked through the grass as if she needed his assistance.

Damn. Here they come. It seems like they just left.

"Here you go, Brady Paul," Ms. Andrews said as soon as she rushed back to our side. Sweat dribbled down the sides of her flushed temples.

I handed Brady Paul's phone back to him.

Shit, I didn't get his number. Please, God, let him call me.

## Chapter Twelve

### *Throwaway Love*

You try it on,

Wear it for a while.

And,

When it no longer fits,

Cause,

You've out grown it.

Or,

Cause it fades,

Or,

It's ripped.

Just…

Throw that love away.

~~~~~~~~~~~~~~~~~~~~~~~~~~~~~~~~~~~~

"Wake up!" Zelda stood at the foot of my bed. "It's three o'clock in the freakin' afternoon! Enough!" She snagged the duvet off of my way fatigued body.

I rolled over onto my back. "I really, really don't feel too hot," I said, as I retrieved the comforter. "I have a gargantuan stomachache."

"Again?"

I nodded. "Most definitely that despicable time of the month."

"Sorry," Zelda said, "should I come back another time?"

"No! Don't go!"

"Shhh…" Her finger located her lips. "Do you want them to hear us?"

I shook my head. "Of course not."

"I just snuck over here so you could tell me about your prom meeting, but I guess you don't feel like talking." Zelda headed toward the door. "I'll catch up with you later."

"No! I mean…" I lowered my voice. "No."

"Beg."

I clasped my hands. "Please, Zelda, my favorite fan and pretend sissy, don't leave!

"Well, okay, if you insist," she said and giggled.

I sort of laughed.

"Well, tell."

"Not so good, Zelda. I knocked heads with a dork. And, totally showed my ass." Why did I call him that? I guess he was sort of dorky.

But so sweet! And, cute!

"That was a way fierce start, Tuesday," Zelda said and snarkled. "Let's dissect the dork, first. What's his name-o?"

"Check this out – Brady Paul Larson." I sat up and chuckled. "And, he goes by Brady Paul. Can you believe that? It's so south of the Mason Dixon line."

Zelda flopped down on my bed on her back with her arms draped over her head. "Did you cell-pix B.P.?"

"No."

"Sigh, please do," Zelda said, as she rolled to her side and palmed her face. "Is he bitchless?"

"I really don't know too much about him. But, I'll research it." I stuck an organic dark chocolate truffle into my mouth. Yum. Confession: chocolate is my Achilles heel. And besides, my body was way in need of a sugar fix. Totally oversaturated with tofu. I held out the box. "Want one?"

Zelda nodded and snatched several pieces. "He's not the athletic redneck kind is he?" Chocolate drool ran out the corners of her mouth.

"Not at all," I said and laughed.

"He isn't gay, is he?" Zelda sat up and reached for more candy. Her mouth was full with all five pieces. She removed her cream-colored granny cardigan with the pearl buttons to reveal a Back-Off-Or-Else band tee. "That's always such a straight girl let down. Not to mention a humongous waste of time." She shook her head and her over-sized plastic white-hot hoops agreed. And, so did the dark chocolate drool.

"I don't think so," I said while eating another piece of comfort food.

"Look at me, Tuesday." Zelda pinched my chin as she read my face. "You had a moment, didn't you? I can see it in your dreamy eyes. You connected. Didn't you?" She laughed. "You so want him! Don't you?"

I laughed too. "You're such a skanky pig, Zelda!"

"He liked you too, didn't he?"

Someone knocked on my parlor door in the other room. That someone was constantly-curious-Constance. "Tuesday, may I come in? You hoo, Tu-Tu."

"Uh, hold on a sec." I looked at Zelda with sudden fragile fear. No way did I want my mother to discover Zelda. What if I was barred from ever seeing her? I would so hate to go there.

Zelda read my stressed-out eyes. She performed a digital wave then turned on the canvas toes of her shoes and skipped to the bath and powder room.

I walked into my sitting room and unbolted the door. I smiled inside myself. Thank God, I had followed through on my note-to-self, and, gave Zelda and Uncle Monty the only other existing keys.

"I don't care for this lock on your door, Tuesday." My mother pointed at the pewter handle. "What if there was a fire?"

I reintroduced my mother to my I-don't-give-a-shit shrug.

Who were you talking to?" My mother scanned the room with her interrogating eyes. She straightened the six-foot black and white lithograph of me mounted on the wall. I wasn't even that tall in person. Five four and a half in heels if that.

"It was the TV." I pointed at the darkened flat screen on the opposite wall. "I...uh...turned it off."

"Oh," my mother said, and then she made herself all cozy by plopping down and stretching out on the ivory tufted velvet chaise. The brass casters on its legs moved an inch. She was wearing her vintage Audrey Hepburn inspired dusky frock that matched the throw pillows.

"You look thin, Tuesday. I'm worried." She flicked her lighter at the end of her cigarette.

"Could you not?" I said and sighed.

Her turn to sigh. "Fine." She pursed her worst habit. "Monty and I were discussing your problem...your tummy aches and we...I mean...I was wondering if by chance it could be toxic shock syndrome?"

"Do what?" I shook my head. "Please."

# My Mistaken Identity

"No, seriously, Tuesday, I've been concerned ever since you insisted on wearing tampons." My mother reached up and her hand landed on my forehead.

That rare move brought on another relapse of mommy-and-me déjà vu. I was way sick with the flu and my mother had taken up a three-day vigil by my bedside. I must have been all of five. She must have over-dosed her brain on fairy tales. Literally. Absurd that I can even remember it.

"Hmm, you don't have a fever. Have you had a bout of diarrhea recently?"

"Could you not?" I pushed her hand away as it attempted to show for-real concern and make its way through my hair.

She stood up and straightened her flirty skirt that just covered her airbrushed tanned thighs. Shoulders back, chin up. My mother was now instantly an inch taller and percolated. "I see. Okay." She clucked her tongue a couple of times and blinked simultaneously. "I think I'll call Dr. Butler before Monty and I head out for the Bahamas."

"You don't need to do that," I said. "I'm fine."

"Well, I want to be sure," she said, "we'll cancel if..."

No!

"Weren't you listening? I said there's nothing wrong with me!"

Then my mother's mouth and body stalled. Her face, though, was way predictable.

Here it comes. A stirred-up reaction. Again.

"I came in here to talk, but I can see you're not interested in talking to me."

Do I dare move forward on this?

Go for it!

"Okay," I said. "You win. Let's talk. About my future. I was thinking…"

"I already heard your ideas." She smirked.

"Well, let's discuss them some more."

"Nothing to discuss," my mother said. "Monty and I have everything under control."

"That's what I want to talk to you about. I do have my own ideas about how to strive for a newer better me. And I would like to try them on for a change. If you'd listen for once you might like them."

My mother's head took on a not-happening shake as she attempted to make an exit.

"Momma! I was talking to you! This is my life! Not yours! I can't help what happened to you! So, why don't you just get over it?"

Her heels reversed their pace as her face changed: narrowed eyes, lowered chin, and, dark voice. "The spotlight always has to be on you! Doesn't it, Tu-Tu? It's always about what Tuesday wants! Always!"

"Tone it down, Momma. Chill."

It stung and left a scarlet rebuttal souvenir. I gasped and palmed my left cheek.

"How dare you!" my mother said. "You're so damn spoiled!" You have no idea the sacrifices I have made for you! Starting with your birth! And, you have the audacity to ask about your father! That son-of-a-,,,"

"SHUT UP!" I exclaimed. My head pounded with over abundant throbs and I actually thought there was a chance that it would explode all over my self-persecuted mother.

"Get out of here." I whispered and then my voice exploded. "NOW! You…You…BITCH!"

## My Mistaken Identity

My mother was on me in a nano-second. I dropped to the floor and struck a fetal position as she ravaged my deviant behavior.

Tears had no place here. They did not adequately express my pain. I had willingly, knowingly and daringly called up the mommy-monster.

Pure brain-cramp.

LL Eadie

Chapter Thirteen

## *Glances of You*

I glanced over my shoulder,

And...

You were there.

I looked again,

You were gone.

Where?

Tell me,

Where?

Do you go,

When I turn my head?

~~~~~~~~~~~~~~~~~~~~~~~~~~~~~~~

Why did my mother have to disappear again? Did the mommy-monster get her kicks by degrading me one slap at a time?

Appreciation goes out to the first responder, Uncle Monty, for his endless pet-rescue intervention. On a scale of one to ten I extolled upon my mother – an eleven. Her manic episodes were not only earning a higher score but coming on more frequently.

I hugged the shower's slate wall and held onto my lip with the other. I was totally dressed as the water and my soundtrack from my demo Plain Vanilla flooded over...And over. And over. Me. On replay.

You say – the clouds are vanilla,

And, that so am I.

You say – the moon is vanilla,

And, that so am I.

You say – the caps of the waves are vanilla,

And, that so am I.

[chorus]

You say – I'm plain,

Always the same.

A boring, stale, lacking, placid, simple, ordinary flame.

"Plain Vanilla."

Since when did you notice me last?

Am I on today's forecast?

Or, am I just your latest outcast?

Listen up, Migraine, this is my updated newscast:

The clouds may be vanilla,

But they deliver the rain.

The moon may be vanilla,

But in the night sky it reigns.

The caps of the waves may be vanilla,

But they can not be contained.

# My Mistaken Identity

And neither can I…be just plain.

[chorus 2x]

You say – I'm plain,

Always the same.

A boring, stale, lacking, placid, simple, ordinary flame.

"Plain Vanilla."

Since when did you notice me last?

Am I on today's forecast?

Or, am I just your latest outcast?

Listen up, Migraine, this is my updated newscast:


The clouds may be vanilla,

But they deliver the rain.

The moon may be vanilla,

But in the night sky it reigns.

The caps of the waves may be vanilla,

But they can not be contained.

And neither can I…be just plain!


Six blasting shower heads were aimed at my way abused shrinking torso that was curled up on the floor rocking. They were, however, no mystical healing antidote. My left cheek accompanied with my entire back was autographed by the mommy-monster. The chilled water numbed its stinging but could not erase the scene of unrelenting slapping palms.

My teeth chattered, my body quaked, and my mind cracked a little bit more than the time before. It continued to drift into forbidden territory, and I wondered what drowning would feel like. They say burning to death is the worst. So, drowning might be approachable. I opened my mouth. There is such a thing as dry drowning I'd heard.

My fingers matted their way through my hair pulling at the hair plugs glued to my own. I wrapped one around and around my finger into a spiral and yanked it out. Then another. And another. And. Another. I only wished I could have removed the fleshy boob implants as easily as the extensions.

I so needed Zelda at that rough patch time to help me deaden my pain. But she must have taken off to her guest apartment. She was so elusive.

"Are you okay?"

"Zelda!"

Her finger rose to her lips. "Shhh...you look like you could use a hug. Come on out of there." Zelda snatched a white one from the towel bar heater. "But first use some shower tissue, Tu-Tu, and blow your snotty nose. There are freakin' boogers streaming into your mouth."

"Huh?"

"Your hands!" Zelda said and snarkled. "Use your hands!"
Snot bubbled out of my nose as I wiped if off. I held my hands out under the spray while my thawing torso tried now to avoid even a drop. When I had finally turned off the shower heads I said, "Zelda, will you take me with you sometime to one of those clubs you told me about?"

"I smell a road trip." she said and laughed. "I thought you'd never ask for some unchaperoned urban exploration. And, I know just the place. Delicioso vegan grub and up to the microphone tonight are the beastly band – Your Bad Habit."

## My Mistaken Identity

She reached out for my hand and helped me to my feet. My clothes seemed super glued to my body. Zelda helped me strip them from my trembling limbs as if we were engaged in a game of tug-of-war. She tossed them back into the shower and wrapped my vulnerable body in the white-hot bath towel.

"But we're going to have to go thriftin' for club gear before I introduce you to The Tongue and Groove...for Tuesday's plain vanilla life."

"Huh?"

"Nothing, absolutely nothing sewn after the year 1984 is acceptable," Zelda said and smirked. "Not a thing in your wardrobe is appropriate. We have to sweep someone's identity. You could never show up as yourself in a pair of your high dollar labels. Your clothes need to be funkified."

"No problem," I said and smiled. "I don't want anyone to recognize me anyway."

"Don't worry," Zelda said, "they won't."

She held me tight. It so reminded me of another moment in mommy-and-me de'ja' vu land. When my mother would cuddle me in a fluffy towel after my bath until I was fuzzy warm and tell me the tale about fairies emerging from cocoons. Then I would wiggle out of the towel and dance around the room like a just-born fairy trying out her new sprung wings.

I rested my head on Zelda's shoulder while fresh tears dampened it. Some words, you know, can not be spoken aloud but have to be whispered instead, even if no one is actually listening. "Thanks," I said, "for coming back."

"9-1-1!!" Zelda cranked up my music. "Five, four, three, two, one – Dance!"

I defied my mother's strangling cocoon and was morphed into Zelda's cure with a time-framed wingspan. We danced till we were dizzy and collapsed into one another's arms.

I headed for my vanity and sat down. "I'm ready, Zelda."

"For what?"

"To scuff it up." I took a pair of scissors out of the drawer.

"What are you up to?" Zelda shook her head. "You're not going to do it. I double-bitch-dare you!"

"Watch me," I said as I gathered my hair into a ponytail and...

Snip.

Saw.

Snap.

Done.

## Chapter Fourteen

### *How Can I Be Sure*

I'm looking for,

Someone.

A someone,

To run with.

A someone,

To have fun with.

Is it you?

How can I be sure?

That you're the one,

That wants to have fun.

And,

That's not gonna run.

From me.

~~~~~~~~~~~~~~~~~~~~~~~~~~~~~~

"Enough." Zelda said as we sat in the car. "Are we going to hang out, or not?"

"Bye bye Brady Paul," I said, as I pocketed my cell. "Oh, Zelda, he called me!"

"I knew he would. What guy wouldn't?" Zelda said and snarkled. "I just didn't think you'd ever shut up though."

I hugged her neck. "Life is good."

"Life sucks."

I smiled at her. "Uncle Monty filled my wallet tonight."

"Whoa!" Zelda said. "Back up!"

Huh?

"What's wrong?" I asked. "He gave me enough for both of us and I didn't even have to ask for a surplus."

"This is *your* money. You know that, don't you?"

"Well…"

"Hell! Tuesday, come on! Demand your own bank account already!"

She's right. I shouldn't have to ask.

But…

"I told Uncle Monty I was hanging out with Stormy tonight. But my stupid curfew is midnight," I said, as Zelda reversed out of the six-car garage.

"Pure Cinderella," Zelda said. "So, he doesn't know about the cat fight you two had, huh?"

"It never exactly came to that."

"You mean you never even said anything to her about stealing your boyfriend? You just let it go? Really?"

I nodded and grabbed my lip.

"That figures."

How would she know that about me?

I released my lip, changed the subject and asked as she headed for the delivery and servants' entrance before exiting onto the main strip and distancing us from my snobby zip code, "It was really nice of Rosa, your mom, to loan her car to us."

"Cause yeah, well, we obviously could never vacate in your Benz," Zelda said. "Get down!" She pushed my head closer to the floorboard. "You don't want those paparazzi pigs to spy ya, do you?"

"No way."

"You're free at last, tabloid target!" Zelda stuck in the Switched At 15 rock band's CD – The Three D's – Dejected. Depleted. Deranged. Their song – Demented Decoy exploded from the dash. "No parental restraints tonight," she said. "Let's hit the club!"

"Are you sure?" I glanced around. "The paparazzi could be tailing us."

"Come on, Tu-Tu, don't go and get all paranoid on me. Okay?"

Note to self: Warning - don't ever let Zelda have a peek into your window-of-weaknesses. She may be easily repelled.

I changed the subject again, imitated a smile, and said, "Rosa used to let me drive this car inside the gates before I was legit. It has a scratch on the driver's side where I hit the fountain in the courtyard." I laughed, listened for a chuckle from Zelda, that didn't come, and added to further impress, "And, you know the bumpers are way plastered in dents from my botched attempts at reversing. Actually, Monty taught me to drive. Or, he tried."

"It figures," Zelda said and laughed as she tailgated the Beemer in front of us.

Careful, Zelda, careful.

"I guess I owe Rosa some sable hair color that we swept from her room."

The color matched Zelda's perfectly, and so did my whacked off cut. I guess Zelda used the same color. And to think I thought it was natural. At least on Rosa.

Zelda glanced at me and nodded. Then smirked. "I discovered this totally cool second-hand store not far from here. I think I told you about it. We'll most definitely find you some club gear there."

I turned, looked at her, smiled and then checked-out Zelda's other CD's - Mid-Youth Crisis, Low Blow, Laboratory Experiment, Back Burner, and Bare Ass Essentials to namedrop a few.

Will I ever squeeze into this scene? Or, will I always be stuck in bubble gum with ten-year-old groupies?

"Damn!" Zelda exclaimed. "Someone is following us!" Before I could turn around and look she had pushed my head into my lap. "Hold on! I'm going to have to lose them." She made a sharp left, then right, and then left again. "I think I lost 'em. You can get up now."

I turned around to peek. Zelda was right, they had lost our scent. Thank, God.

"Zelda, tell me about this place – The Tongue and Groove."

"Well, it sure isn't going to resemble that lame honky-tonk prom you're attending. And, you sure aren't going to have to navigate around any posh pomegranate flavored two-inch ice cubes in your drink there. Or, juggling bartenders, karaoke time, bikini competitions, V.I.P. private rooms, or T-shirt exchanges." She said and snickered, "And, don't expect any freakin' pole dancing lessons either, Tu-Tu."

"I'm sure it's kid tested," I said and laughed, "and most definitely mother approved."

Speaking of mothers, I didn't care anymore what constantly-combustible-Constance gushed for me. I so had to cut the disease out of my life and move forward. I had to put her behind me. Career resuscitation was my goal. And, Brady Paul. I hoped.

It's my time now, Momma. Step aside. Make room for me.

## My Mistaken Identity

Besides, my horoscope had said: Someone will try to stand in your way. It's time for you to do a little soul-searching and figure out who is on your side, and who isn't.

Duh. Way easy. Bye Bye M&M's. Bye Bye Jazmyn. Bye Bye Stormy. Bye Bye Ashburn.

Hello, T.G.'s Evolution: The Third Day of the Week. Hello, Zelda...Hel-looo, Brady Paul.

"Are you listening to me?" Zelda held out a can of Red Bull.

"Uhh...sorry...what?"

"This is your coming-of-age get-down party. Take a pre-game sip," Zelda said, "I warn you, no backwash either."

My horoscope also said: Be spontaneous and act impulsively.

"Okay." I snorted a smirk and reached for the can. Sipped and winced. "Eww."

Zelda laughed. "What a Barbie moment! It's obvious you've never had an ounce of white lightning before."

"You're most definitely correct," I said and laughed, as I scarfed-down the entire go-directly-to-jail brew.

"Slow go on the lightning, Tu-Tu," Zelda said, "It can turn into cruel fuel, you know."

I wasn't listening. I downed another. And, then another. And, another. It felt good. It felt right. I felt invincible. Totally no inadequacies. No vulnerability. No intimidation.

"I feel a sin coming on," Zelda said with a bizarre twinkle in her eyes.

And, no doubt about it, Zelda was fluent in fun.

Pure head candy

LL Eadie

## Chapter Fifteen

### *Stuck*

If I was,

A piece,

Of

Popcorn.

Stuck between your teeth.

Would you,

Swallow me?

Or,

Spit me out?

~~~~~~~~~~~~~~~~~~~~~~~~~~~

"You have so got to get in touch with your life, Tuesday," Zelda said for the umpteenth time, as we parked around the corner from The Tongue and Groove. "It is your life, you know."

Obviously, we were parking in Goofy. No rock star parking decal on this car.

"I'm really, really making a for-real effort here." I stared in the visor mirror at the newbie. Me. I was totally incognito. Even to myself. My hair was no longer girlified. It now resembled Zelda's – way choppy short and dyed inky black.

I banished my new do under a striped wool skullcap from the second hand store. I looked at the backseat where a nudging-up-the-mommy-monster purchase laid – a skateboard. Something I was never allowed to step upon. I smirked at just the thought of my mother spying it in my room. Didn't really matter if I ever hung ten on it or not. That would be satisfaction enough. There was another rebellious purchase as well – a new-slash-old prom dress. One that most likely hung on the back of Stevie Nicks or Janis Jopling. I glanced back at my reflection. My sapphire ones were visibly masqueraded beneath dark eye shadow and liner.

"What do I need to take in with me?" I flipped the visor up and stepped out of the car into a putrid littered-up puddle on an every-third-street-light-might-be-shot-out street.

"No passport required to this club."

"Tell me again, Zelda what you think about my outfit?" I rested one of my previously-walked-in low top black Converse's on the bumper where Zelda was rocking out Rosa's car with a sticker that said – I'm Just Bitter, Sicko. I would have made the effort to bend over to tie my shoe, but my lacerated super-skinny black jeans made that necessary chore no way an option.

"You rock, Tu-Tu! Pure authentic!" Zelda said. "Now this is how we roll, so take club-notes. It's my way or the lame way, so don't do anything malignant. And reveal as little of yourself as possible. Don't talk to anybody. Not even some scrumptious dork. Unless it's your Brady Paul of course." She said and snarkled.

If only.

"But all others…keep your tits off! Those are all mine! You swear?"

I smiled and said, "Of course. I so won't go there."

"Pinky swear." Zelda stuck out her finger. Our ebony pinkies locked in a promising embrace. "Now, that's legally binding, Tuesday."

I grinned.

"Tweak the smiles!"

# My Mistaken Identity

My lips locked my teeth out of view. "Sorry."

Zelda snarkled and said, "You look like you lost your freakin' granny-gear dentures!"

I two-fisted the crew neck of my heather gray XL sweatshirt over my forbidden outburst. I so didn't want to disappoint Zelda.

"Don't go and get all butt-hurt on me." Zelda said, "Here, I sort of got you something." She handed me a belly-button-length strand of faux chunky white pearls.

"Thanks," I said, lifting them over my head.

"Actually," Zelda said and laughed, "I took a five-finger discount."

I shook my head, rolled my eyes and smiled. "You shoplifted?"

Why am I not surprised?

"They were steal-worthy," she said and then she continued to shout-out her look-like-you-don't-give-a-crap orders even as we skipped up the wooden ramp to the second floor of an abandoned bygone era parking garage. Final order. "Leave your T.G. shit-uation at the door."

I kept my mouth shut and obeyed Zelda's solemn instructions as sexless, coal-eyed, broomstick-thin teen figures in low slung gender announcing jeans crystallized around us. There were no neon signs announcing our destination. We were all being sucked-in by the fierce music.

Fourteen dollars later, and a neon orange glow-in-the-dark bracelet and we were there.

We rounded the corner into another world. Ground zero for alternative rock. One with tons of banging heads and bouncing frantic bodies channeling their emotions along with the song – Sign Off - being sung by the band Your Bad Habit.

"The club's on fire!" Zelda said. "This is the sound you're striving for, Tu-Tu. Pure friction."

I nodded and smiled. But I did feel way out of bounds. "Remember, Zelda, you're my wing-woman." I grabbed her hand. She smirked. Her nostrils flared and her head shook double time.

The soles of my feet tickled as we walked on the vibrating-to-the-beat wooden floor. She led me through the shower-of-sweat chaos.

Don't leave me, Zelda.

Pass knotted hair in ponytails, dreads tangling out of bandanas, baseball bills poking out of hoodies, perspiration-harnessing wool caps, and tattoo-confused arms.

Into the orgasmic vibrations. Where the volume of the drum skins thundered like a sledge hammer on a construction site, the electric guitars growled and hissed like a caged animal, and the lead singer in his pre-nineties pinstriped suit with matching fedora hat whined-out blurry words as he chugged the microphone. "How many of you feel like puking when the night is young?"

Me!

"Remember, you're a tourist, Tu-Tu. But, don't act like one!" Zelda nodded her head and knees to the beat. And then, she smirked again pointing out the club's circumference. "See, I told you so. No dancing poles available."

I shook my head and smiled.

This is way fun. I've missed out on so much! Damn M&M's!

The rabid crowd began to roam around us. A train had formed. The passengers weaved through the crowd faster and faster as the pace of the music picked up. Someone's shoe flopped off; it was saved and handed back to the lop-sided train car.

Then, there was shoving.

# My Mistaken Identity

Did someone just push me? Am I part of this? Where's Zelda?

My gait was no longer my own. There were lewd body acts playing out on my chest, butt and belly as my body was lifted toward the speakers, and their sound absorbers – carpet samples hanging by chains from the black painted ceiling tiles.

Please don't drop me! Let me down! Please!

My head felt disconnected. My body felt galvanized. My teeth felt as if they were turning to gravel as the bile in my gut was shaken over and over and...over.

"ZELDA! ZELDA! ZELDA!"

"Shut up!" Zelda grabbed my hand and pulled me out of the mosh pit. "You totally provided some club-scene antics, Tu-Tu!"

Zelda led me to a nailed-down table that was cluttered with soggy paper plates of leftover BBQ tofu and cigarette butts, as I pulled my woolen skull cap off my perspiring head.

My eyes sponged-up The Tongue and Groove as we sat on a pair of converted bucket-car-seats covered in worn sheep-skin in the back of the club where a sign on the wall read:

IF YOU ARE NOT HERE TO STUDY YOU WILL BE ASKED TO LEAVE.

My brain began to channel the earth's rotation as I watched the retro comic-strips race across the walls. I tried to pin my eyes to the floor, but the kaleidoscope began to pick up speed. I slammed them shut.

But now, I was pirouetting faster. And faster. And faster. And, becoming dizzier.

And dizzier. And dizzier. Pure vertigo.

I looked up at the seemingly swinging metal pipes that were reflecting the yellow bug lights dangling from extension cords twenty feet above our heads, where smoke hung like clouds forming a threatening tornado. The reeling brick walls oozed their mortar and the band oozed its frenzy. And, my mouth suddenly became a spigot and oozed Red Bull and vodka.

Pure boogie-till-you-puke.

"TUESDAY!"

"Uncle Monty?" I whispered as I hung my head in regret between my shaky legs. The stench coming from under the table was nauseating. Then I realized it was mine. My spew. I looked up. "What are you doing here?"

Damn, it is him! How does he always find me? Am I micro-chipped with some kind of homing device that's implanted under my skin?

"Come on, Tuesday." He lifted me up into his arms and carried me away. Away from The Tongue and Groove. And...

Where's Zelda?

The car ride home was a blur. Maybe because my face spent most of the time in a barf bag. And my mind in promises I would probably never keep.

I'm never drinking again. That was so not fun.

"You'll feel fine in the morning." Uncle Monty tucked my sheet between the mattresses and pulled my duvet cover over my limp body.

Where am I?

I lifted my head.

He wiped my face with a wet washcloth. "How's that? Better?"

I nodded.

"That's some hair style you got there, Tuesday."

# My Mistaken Identity

Another nod in slow-motion.

"I'll see what we can do about it before your mother sees it."

I like it! Don't you touch it! And I don't care is she sees it. Let her!

Just not right now.

My eyes felt like I had no control over them as they wandered around my room. Lighting here and there, like a fairy and then spinning off once again. Once they landed on my putrid club clothes dotting the Persian hundred-year-old rug.

My mother would so lose it if she saw that.

I don't care. I hope she does!

I fought the tucked-in white sheet with my right foot for a landing on the floor next to my bed. Finally, it obliged.

Oh, jeez, I feel like crap.

"Sometimes that helps." Uncle Monty walked out of my revolving vision.

I nodded, pinched my lip and dozed off. For a moment.

"Tuesday?" His face appeared next to mine on the pillow.

I opened my eyes. "Brady Paul?"

"Who?" Uncle Monty asked.

"Oh, it's you." I closed my eyes and rolled over.

"Is that the boy from the school?"

"Yeah, that's him. He's so sweet... I wish he'd kiss me," I mumbled. "Don't tell Momma."

"I won't," he said. "And I didn't tell your mother about tonight either. In case you're wondering."

I shook my head this time. No, I wasn't wondering. Nor did it matter if she knew. Or did I? But I was wondering about Zelda.

Should I ask?

No way! Don't be an idiot!

God, I hope he doesn't ask about whom she is and where Stormy was.

"Uncle Monty has everything under control, Tuesday honey." He patted my leg and kissed my cheek. "I'm right here."

I nodded.

Good ole Uncle Monty.

# Chapter Sixteen

## *Are You For-Real?*

You're so honest.

Tell me,

Are you for-real?

You're so nice.

Tell me,

Are you for-real?

You're so yourself.

Tell me,

Am I for-real?

~~~~~~~~~~~~~~~~~~~~~~~~~~~~

The following Monday I was back in Jacksonville. I had so pulled the plug on the limo lease and bodyguard, and opted for normalcy. For once. And, I had a clean bill of health from Dr. Butler so I could attend this prom meeting and not have to travel to the Bahamas with M&M.

Thank God, Uncle Monty swept Momma away to our island retreat before she caught a glimpse of the new me. Not that I really cared. But I guess I owed him one.

Momma totally needed some re-balancing time.

The prom committee meeting was strained, but I didn't care what the others thought of me. Only Brady Paul.

I wonder what he really thinks of me. He's always so nice on the phone. But I feel like I'm just running my mouth. He must think I'm a freak. Doesn't he see I'm just like any other sixteen-year-old girl? Who am I kidding? But I did see him check me out during the meeting. Or, I think I did. And, he could have bummed a ride from anybody there today, but he chose...

"Thanks for the lift to the marina, Tuesday." Brady Paul sat in the passenger seat beside me in my economy-sized rental. Pure incognito.

"That was an awesome idea," Brady Paul said, "about the prom."

"Glad you liked it," I said with a gargantuan smile, as I did my best not to linger too long on his tan arms, nut brown eyes, freckled face, shaggy sun-tipped hair, and way kissable lips. The traffic light would be turning green any moment.

He's so much fun to look at. I wonder if he thinks I'm cute, pretty, hot...

...or ugly.

His eyes dived into mine and all his attention was focused on what I was saying as if it really, really mattered. And, I knew it was possibly a schmooze, but I didn't care because it felt so genuine.

"Getting everyone involved like that," Brady Paul said, "the pep band, the dance team, the audio-visual class, and the chorus. They're all so pumped about being part of your performance. Was it your idea? Or your mother and uncle's?"

That move most definitely improved my varsity-girl-inferiority-complex standings. And, so did disposing of the prom king kiss.

"None of the above," I said as I was being extra careful to follow the rules of the road. I admit I had not had much practice. "The idea was actually a friend of mines."

Am I smiling too much?

## My Mistaken Identity

Note to self: Warning - Keep your roped-and-tied eyes on the road and your paws to yourself on your first playdate. He could delete you.

"By the way, where are they?" Brady Paul asked. "Your mom and uncle?"

"Oh, them. They went on a spa-cation in the Caribbean." I glanced in the rearview mirror. My eyes were still smudged in black. Next, I checked-out my lips, to make sure they were ready for his. If only.

"A spa what?" he asked.

"A vacation. My mother needed some RRR. To relax, renew, and refresh." I chuckled. "At a spa."

I wonder if Brady Paul can forget who I am. And figure out who I really am.

Of course, I'm not sure myself.

My Plain Vanilla demo was playing in the CD player and before I realized it, I was singing along. Brady Paul reached over and turned it up. "Hey, that's you! Isn't it?" His lush hair flirted with his eyes.

"Busted." I shook my head as my tongue stroked my lips wishing they were his. I smirked and white-knuckled the steering wheel.

"You're good." Brady Paul nodded his head to the beat. "I like it."

Is there really such a thing as love at first sight?

Absurd.

I studied every curve of his mouth at the next red light. He could totally pull off his belted pair of Wranglers with the Columbia fishing shirt and accessorized with pointy alligator-skin-looking boots.

"So," Brady Paul said, "this friend of yours, is he a close friend?"

"She." I said, as I took in a quickie of his swoon-worthy view again. "Her name is Zelda."

Is it really possible that he could actually like me? Love me?

Get real.

He grinned and pointed up ahead. "Turn right at the next light."

"Okay." I turned on the blinker.

"I usually have to listen to reggae and Buffet music."

"I totally love Bob Marley. I listen to him all the time. And Jimmy Buffet's so...you know...Florida-ish."

I could hear Zelda now. "You'll lie to kick-in every time, Tu-Tu, won't you?"

"I guess I've grown accustomed to listening to them," Brady Paul said, "down at the marina. That's where I work."

"What do you do?" I asked.

"I'm really just a gopher." Brady Paul shrugged his awe-shucks shoulders. "I do whatever needs to be done. Ya know like swabbing down boat decks, filling 'em up with fuel, cleaning fish, refilling ice coolers, and sometimes, if I'm lucky, I even get to go out with my dad on one of the charters he's mate on."

"The charters?"

"Yeah, haven't you ever been deep sea fishing before, Tuesday?"

"No, but I'd love to go sometime."

Ask me, please.

"Hey, are ya hungry? I've got some spare time before work." Brady Paul pointed toward a roadside restaurant situated under several geriatric oak trees wrapped in mossy shawls with a gargantuan faux pink pig squatting under the take-out window. "This is a great place to stuff your face."

"Absolutely," I said, as my nostrils flared to the unaccustomed vapors of barbecue.

"Do you have enough time before you head out?" Brady Paul asked.

"No problem!" I exclaimed. The pilot could wait. Pure overtime. Money does indeed have a mouth. He could always file another flight plan. Besides, I was his only passenger.

"You sure ya really want to eat here?"

"Most definitely!" I put on my blinker and drove into the right lane cutting off a car. It honked.

Brady Paul waved an apologetic acknowledgement out the window and said, "Only if I can pay."

"Done."

Thank you, Brady Paul, for introducing me to a for-real life. I am so on the mend.

Smoke poured from the Pig-Out's chimney, and up our noses as the scent drew us into the gravel-paved parking lot. The flatbed of an old rusty red truck served as our table and sawed-off tree stumps provided a place for our rumps to rest as we pigged-out. Splinters were provided for free. Plastic forks and our fingers served as our utensils, tin pie pans lined with wax paper as our dishes, and Mason jars held our all-you-can-drink sweet tea.

And, Brady Paul held my total attention.

"Delicioso!" I exclaimed, as I licked my fingers clean of dripping hot sauce.

Brady Paul swiped a paper towel from the roll mounted in front of us and handed me one.

I wonder what kind of girls he likes. Tough? Sweet? Country? All natural? Low-budget girls for sure. Do I even have a chance?

There were several other customers seated at our non-exclusive table. They had greeted us by nods of heads and tipping of caps. Too much pulled pork, coleslaw, baked beans, or sweet potato fries in their mouths for a "Howdy, ma'am."

"Glad ya like it, Tuesday. I know it's nothing like where you're probably used to chowing-down at."

"I'd rather eat here."

"You're nothing like I expected, Tuesday," Brady Paul said. "I mean, damn, that didn't come out right." He looked at the ground and shook his head. "What I meant to say was…"

"You thought I'd be a rich snooty bitch. Right?"

Another shake of his head. "No."

"Well…" A shrug of his shoulders.

"Yeah." A cock of his head and cut of his eyes.

A smile on his lips. "Sorry."

I waved-off his inoffensive comment. "Don't worry about it," I said with a sympathetic grin. "That's what everyone thinks, I'm sure." I wiped my mouth. No telling what was drooling from its corners.

"Hold on," he said. "You missed some." He reached over with his thumb and ran it against my right cheek. "There," he said as he wiped his thumb on his paper towel. "You're all cleaned up. Barbecue is always so messy. I guess this wasn't the best place to bring someone like you."

"No!" I shook my head. "I love it! It's the best! You couldn't have taken me anywhere I would have enjoyed any more. Believe me, being me is not all that and more. You'd be surprised, but it's actually quite boring and lonely."

"That's hard to believe."

"It's sadly a fact."

His head positioned itself into a precious-puppy-dog angle and he looked up at me with a faint smile on his lips. A curl dropped over one eye. "You know somethin', you look different, too."

Does he like my new look? This is the first time he's mentioned it.

I reached for my renovated Zelda-ish short dark hair.

"I didn't mean for it to sound like that again," Brady Paul said, as he tried to apologize.

Shit! He hates it! I can tell!

"I mean, I like it! I really do." He reached out and touched my updated do. Then, he ran his fingers through the fringe that my right eye peeked out of.

Don't stop.

"Thanks." I reached for his hand.

Damn, I missed.

"And, your clothes are nothing like what you had on before either." Brady Paul threw up his hands. "Damn it, Tuesday, I meant that in a good way."

His right hand slapped his right thigh. "They're cool!"

His left hand came down on his left one. "You're cool!

Pointing at self. "I'm the one," he said, "who's not."

My face couldn't hold back its delight. My grin was becoming a habit when I was with him. The for-real person I had only dreamed of meeting.

"I can't believe," he said, "I'm actually sitting here having lunch at the Pig-Out-Bar-be-cue with Tuesday Green…"

"Shhh…" I covered his lips with my right index finger. My eyes circled the table of the other finger-lickin' inhabitants to be sure none were the wiser of my presence.

Brady Paul reached up for my hand. He held it in his. It lingered there in his grasp. I never wanted to let go.

He does like me!

My life was no longer stuck in a holding pattern. For once I felt I was bathed in a for-real life. With a for-real person. Brady Paul had most definitely condensed my world. My eyes led my lips to his. His mouth was the perfect fit for mine. I was mistaken. No way was this his first kiss. Breathing was optional. He wasn't coming up for air. And neither was I.

# Chapter Seventeen

## *Don't Let it End*

Whatever you do,

Whatever you say,

Just please,

Pretty please,

Don't let it…

End.

~~~~~~~~~~~~~~~~~~~~~~~~~~~~~~~

"Are you sure you don't mind watching me work?" Brady Paul asked as we walked along the splintered wooden dock toward the pelicans waiting on a free handout from the incoming fishing boats. We were greeted by a low tide, the smell of fish, anglers' tidying up poles, lines, and nets and offering me up their peg-leg stares.

I reached for his hand.

Am I being too forward? Does he mind?

He doesn't seem to. I think he's enjoying it. And, me. Jeez, I so hope so!

"No," I said, "I can't wait to see the gopher in action?"

We laughed.

The tide was out and you could see the barnacles clinging to the pilings below. The brackish water's scent was carried by the breeze in our direction toward the shore.

He squeezed my hand. "I just can't figure you out." He smiled.

"Try." I cut my eyes through my hair whipping on my face. "I dare you."

"When I'm done I'll take you somewhere nice to eat."

"Not the Pig-Out-Bar-be-cue?" I said and smiled. I shaded my face with my other hand from the late afternoon sun.

"No, I know a local favorite close to here. Some of the best and freshest seafood in town. You do like seafood, don't you?"

"I totally love it! Especially steamed oysters!"

"We'll order a bucket full," he said. "Of course, I'll have to clean up before we leave. I won't be long. They have a shower here." He pointed up ahead to a tumble-down looking building on stilts above the lapping water. "And I keep a locker."

"Perfect."

And so are you.

"If you want, you can sit out here on this screened-in area." He pointed to the green chipped painted porch. "It'll be cooler. I'll get you a cold drink." He disappeared into the Mayport Marina's dock master's shed next to it. Bob Marley's – One Love – wrapped around me from the two speakers hung on opposite sides of the porch. The rusty ceiling fan above me thumped as it churned up the mugginess.

Oh my God! I'm really with him. Still.

I had never felt like this about anybody. I just thought I loved Ashburn. With Brady Paul I didn't care where we went, what we did, as long as I was with him. That had to be love. It just had to be.

And, I'm actually doing for-real people stuff. With him!

"Is a cola okay?" He walked toward me smiling minus a shirt.

"And if you need anything else just have Wes in there..." He nodded toward the raisin-wrinkled tan face grinning at me through the open doorway. "...put it on my tab."

I nodded back, "Hello, Wes." Thank God, no recognition of me on his pirate-ish mug.

"How's it goin', missy?" Wes said from his rickety wooden stool with a rotary fan gyrating on the counter and pointed at his tattoos.

"Fine, thank you." I sat down on a picnic table bench. One of several inhabiting the porch. They were all empty except for leftover beer cans, crowded ashtrays and crumbled-up chip bags.

"Wes," Brady Paul said as he pulled on his work shirt and a pair of rubber waders that sort of looked like bib overalls. "This is a friend of mine. Tuesday."

Girlfriend.

If only.

He yanked neon yellow boots on too.

"Nice ta meet cha, Tuesday." Wes picked up his handheld marine radio and began chattering away on it to an incoming boat.

"Wes is my boss," Brady Paul chucked his sneakers into a metal locker in the office and slammed its door. "He's the dock master."

"I see," I said as I smiled once more.

Brady Paul glanced at me. "Are you sure you're okay?"

"Yes."

I've never been better.

"Brady Paul." Wes spat into a paper cup, wiped his mouth on the shoulder of his Mayport Marina tee and continued, "The Latitude

Adjustment's on her way in, son. She'll need fuel, her decks swabbed down and fish cleaned and filleted."

"What'd they catch?" Brady Paul asked.

"Wahoo, grouper and snapper."

Brady Paul nodded. "That's a mighty fine catch this time of year." He grabbed a mop and a stack of oversized white plastic buckets from the corner and started to head out the door.

"Wait!" I exclaimed as Wes continued his ten-four's on the radio.

"What's wrong?"

I whispered, "You forgot to kiss me."

Brady Paul's boots clopped in my direction and his face and shoulders relaxed as he knelt and planted his lips against mine once more. "Now are you good?" he asked from his irresistible puppy dog angle.

"Perfect." I whispered back. "What are we going to do after dinner?"

He shook his head and grinned. "What am I gonna do with you?"

"I can't wait to find out." I reached up and combed his hair with my fingers.

He pecked me again. "I'll think of something." He winked.

Please do. Don't let this fairy tale romance end! Pure happily ever after.

I hope.

I stood up and walked over to the screen and watched him swing the buckets as he hustled down the ramp to a lower floating dock. He looked back and waved the mop at me. I blew him a kiss. He shook his head and laughed. My fingers rested against the rusty screen as it bubbled in his direction. "Brady Paul!" I called out. "Can I... help?"

Brady Paul stopped on the dock and turned back around. "Are you sure, Tuesday?"

I nodded in ultra-fast motion. "Yes!"

"Okay, I guess it'll be all right for you to help. I'll find something for you to do. But what are ya gonna wear?"

"How 'bout buyin' one of these T-shirts?" Wes pointed to the stack on the counter. "I can hardly give these suckers away. And grab ya pair of them there shorts too. I'll give ya a good deal. Two for one!"

"Sold!" I said.

After I was outfitted in my newly purchased Mayport Marina duds Wes handed me a pair of rubber boots. "These here will come in handy, missy."

"Thanks." I sat down and struggled with the boots. Or, was it their stench? Pure fishy. Eww.

"Now I ain't gonna pay for both of yous," Wes said.

I'll pay you, Wes, to hang with Brady Paul.

"No," I said, "I don't expect you to."

I found Brady Paul tying up Latitude Adjustment to the metal what-cha-ma-call-its fastened to the deck. "Throw out your fenders!" he yelled. The crew obliged throwing long rubber looking thingy's attached by a short rope over the sides. I soon discovered why when the boat rubbed up against the dock.

"Tuesday!" Brady Paul called out, "Catch the other line. And hold on!"

Oh my God! Do what?

I actually caught it and held on.

"Good catch!" Brady Paul shouted and then winked.

I smiled really, really big.

Yay, me!

Brady Paul scurried around to my side of the boat slip and snatched the rope from my hands. In no time he looped it into the what-cha-ma-call-its he referred to as cleats. The boat was parked. Then the real fun began. Brady Paul jumped into their boat and opened the fish well. He and the vessel's captain talked about the day's catch as if it were some kind of freakin' miracle.

Hello, I'm over here. Don't you see me?

I could hear her now. Z-moment reality check – "Get over yourself!"

Am I really, really that needy?

Again. Z-moment head game – "Yes. You. Are."

"Tuesday," Brady Paul said, "If you don't mind could you fill those buckets with ice?"

Yay! He noticed me!

"No problem!" I hurried over to the three stacked buckets, stood still and looked around.

Where's the ice?

Brady Paul pointed to an ice machine on the dock as if he read my mind. He continued to talk fish with the people on board. The stories captured him from me.

I have to be careful this time. I don't want to scare him off. That always seems to happen to me with guys. Why do I need so much attention? Over possessive and clingy is what Ashburn had called me.

# My Mistaken Identity

One at a time I hauled the three ten-pound bags of ice in each bucket back to the Latitude Adjustment. I was beginning to need an attitude adjustment.

Damn. This sucks. Maybe momma was right about me never really lifting my hand before. Maybe I should have stayed parked on the porch.

Brady Paul was emptying the well onto the dock. The frozen fish stared but never moved. I shaded my face from the direct hit of the sun's rays as Brady Paul slipped a knife from his back pocket and began to slice the dorsal fin off the top. Eww. The sharp blade continued its journey down the fish's fleshy side. He peeled away the skin and bagged the filet.

I turned around and watched the three passengers hop over to the docks, clink their beers and cheer. Wes showed up along with other fishermen to admire their catch, offer-up congrats and drink Buds.

I totally don't get it.

"Tuesday, could you grab the hose and spray down the boat's deck?" Brady Paul pointed his filet knife toward the green hose coiled up like a snake on the dock. "Thanks, you're really a big help you know that?" Another wink.

I sure hope there's a kissy-face award at the finish line.

I nodded, snatched up the hose, and stared at the boat.

How in the hell do I get over to it?

Any yacht or ship I had ever boarded before had a walkway thingy with handrails.

The Latitude Adjustment never stilled. The fishing boat rocked, rolled and pitched. It was no where close to one step away. I eyed it suspiciously as I gripped the nozzle of the hose and leaped.

"SHIT!"

# LL Eadie

The water was colder than I ever imagined as I sunk like a boat's anchor toward the bottom. As hard as my arms and legs struggled to swim to the surface I couldn't. The littered sandy bottom was coming up fast.

What's wrong? What's holding me down? Am I caught on something?

Did anyone see me fall in?

Oh my God! I'm drowning!

Then Brady Paul was by my side under the murky water. I reached out to him. He shook his head, fought to release my hands and tugged at my boots. They were the reason I was sinking. They had filled up fast and were weighting me down. But so were Brady Paul's. He pulled mine off before his. I swam cowardly for the surface leaving him behind.

# Chapter Eighteen

## *Believe*

Don't believe,

Everything,

Or

Everyone.

But do believe,

The ones...

You love.

That...

Love you,

Back.

~~~~~~~~~~~~~~~~~~~~~~~~

"OH MY GOD! BRADY PAUL!" I screamed as I surfaced. I held onto one of the pilings as the salty water slapped against my shocked face. "Somebody help him! Please! He's still down there!" I looked up at the dock above me and watched Wes dive in as another person above me grabbed my wrists and jerked me up to the dock as if I were a fish that had been gaffed. "No! Help Brady Paul! Please!"

I stared back into the brackish water that almost buried me alive and was now holding Brady Paul hostage and collapsed to my knees. My arms were extended toward the nightmare happening beneath me.

"He's right there, ma'am," said a gravelly voice kneeling on the dock next to me and pointing toward the depths. "See him?" It was the captain of the Latitude Adjustment.

I scooted closer to the captain and reached out for Brady Paul's hands as his head broke free. "Oh my God, are you okay?"

"I'm fine." He coughed and spat as Wes surfaced too and held onto one of the other boat's fenders.

"Son, you scared the mess out of me!" Wes exclaimed as he attempted to slap Brady Paul's back.

Brady Paul nodded, coughed and spat some more.

"I'm so sorry!" My tears which had been held back by my fear now flowed with relief. Multiple hands including my own were reaching for the two bobbing bodies in the narrow space between the hull of the boat and the dock. That varied from inches to two feet depending on each wave that caused each roll of the boat.

"It's not your fault," Brady Paul said as he was snatched out of the water to my side. He no longer wore the boots or the waders. My arms could not wait to absorb him. I sobbed into the small of his neck. He held me tight. Really, really never-want-to-let-you-go tight. "I should have known better, Tuesday. You've probably never boarded a boat like that before. I don't know what I was thinking. I'm so sorry."

"Hey!" Wes said. "What about me? Ain't no one gonna welcome me back from the deep?" He laughed. "I saved your scrawny ass! And, lost a perfectly good pair of bib waders and two pair of boots while doing so."

I turned and flung my arms around Wes. "Thank you! Thank you! Thank you!"

"That's more like it," Wes said and laughed. "Okay, you two slackers, back to work! You owe me big time."

"Tuesday," Brady Paul said. I spun around. We stood only inches apart. "You go shower. I won't be much longer."

## My Mistaken Identity

No way was I going to disagree. I had some damage control to take care of – my hair, make-up and a check to write to Mayport Marina. For saving the one thing that felt for-real in my M&M controlled life.

# Chapter Nineteen

## *How Close is Too Close?*

You can never be,

Too happy

Or

Too close.

To the one,

You love.

~~~~~~~~~~~~~~~~~~~~~~~~~~~~~~~~~~

Brady Paul drove my rental car into the empty lot. The sign posted in front of us read – Atlantic Beach Public Parking 8AM – 8PM Cars will be towed at owner's expense.

Promise?

"Don't worry about it." Brady Paul's head pointed out the warning.

I shrugged and smiled.

I won't. Stranded on a deserted beach with you. If only.

His conversation picked up where it left off at the Rusty Pelican restaurant. "As I was saying, the next day of the fishing tournament dad used the best fishing line available. We weren't going to take any more chances."

And neither am I.

# My Mistaken Identity

I knew he wanted to kiss me. He kept glancing at my lips all evening as he talked endlessly about how to land a seventy-pound king mackerel.

I wonder if my breath smells bad. I can still taste the steamed oysters. Eww.

I tried to act interested to his description of the weight of the test line, the position of the down riggers, the fish in the chum line, and the one that got away. I nodded. I smiled. I sighed inside.

Be quick, Brady Paul, or else it might be me.

Who am I kidding? I'm not going anywhere except closer to his hip.

We kicked off our shoes by the car and hiked across the sugary sand dune toward the spotlight of the moon rising over the ocean. A sudden breeze caught my hair and caused my eyes to water.

"I fought that fish for forty-five minutes before my dad gaffed it!" Brady Paul exclaimed, as we made our way closer to the water. I could still smell the tangy cocktail sauce on his breath.

Sweet. At least we're in it together.

I felt his fingers teasing mine. I refused to be played with. I reached for his hand and our fingers locked. I never liked holding hands with guys before. It always seemed like a dumb thing to do. But this time I didn't want to let go. I understood the urge. It felt safe. It felt intimate. It felt like a promise.

Our numb feet stopped shuffling in the surf. I'm not sure whose did first, or maybe they were in sync. His trophy fish story had ended too. I could only hear the waves rushing toward us. I watched the chilly foam leave bubbles balancing on top of our toes. That's when I noticed his feet turn and face mine. His so much larger and bulkier sinking into the sand as the tide rolled out. But mine were sinking fast too. Our feet made a sucking sound as we lifted them. We laughed. So silly. Why was this so funny? It didn't matter.

"I thought I had lost you," Brady Paul said as I took a step in his direction. Now only inches apart. "I'm sorry."

"Shhh…" I whispered as my finger patted his irresistible mouth. His soft whiskers above his top lip tickled my fingers. "Not your fault."

His chest was heaving against mine. He rested his chin on the top of my head and held me close.

Please, God, I don't want to lose this feeling. Ever. I am so in love.

Our embrace broke and we walked back toward the dunes. I sat down and eased Brady Paul next to me with the coaxing of my hand. We stretched out on our sides facing one another. He spoke to my heart first. Then my lips. I could feel his moving against my quivering ones.

As close as we were snuggled, I could still feel the cool night breeze off the ocean. A north wind was picking up and causing the waves to crash against the shore. The moon shined like a giant spotlight across its white caps up the wet sand to the dunes where we lay.

"I thought I had lost you too," I said. "Thanks for saving me."

His breath and lips found my exposed cheek. "You don't have to thank me."

"I've never been so frightened before." I tilted my head so my neck would be available too.

"Me either." His hands palmed my back pulling me closer to him. Mine answered with the same request.

Is it possible to be any closer?

"Um, Brady Paul…"

"Yeah," he answered into the collar of my shirt. The fingers of his right hand moved up to my face and felt it as if they had never been there before. They next moved around my neck and tight-roped down my spine.

## My Mistaken Identity

"We are safe here, aren't we?" I glanced around me. The sea oats were leaning as the cool ocean breeze hit them. I saw no other signs of life. I snuggled closer to him.

"You aren't afraid of rats or snakes, are ya? The dunes are full of 'em."

My body stiffened. "Rats? Snakes?"

Brady Paul kissed my fear away. "I'll protect you."

The kiss started somewhere around eight o'clock and ended somewhere around midnight.

Pure making-out. Big time.

LL Eadie

## Chapter Twenty

### *Fess-Up!*

It's all your fault,

I am…

Misunderstood.

It's all because,

Of your own screwed-up,

Childhood.

I will no longer be,

You.

That was so not me.

Admit it.

Divulge it.

Fess-up!

I totally

Outgrew…

Mixed-up,

Dried-up,

Washed-up,

You!

~~~~~~~~~~~~~~~~~~~~~~~~~~~~~~~

"I'm very disappointed in you," my Economics' tutor said a week later, as she repacked her briefcase. "This isn't like you, Tuesday, not to have your assignments."

We were in the contemporary living room with its black and white décor. Positive and negative. Ying and yang. North and south. A bipolar color scheme.

I shrugged and attacked my lip. "Sorry." But, I really, really wasn't.

Not everyone was disappointed in me, though. Not my guitar teacher – Mr. Tork, the song-writer dude – Baldwin Spikes, Glissando Records, Uncle Monty, William P. DuVal's prom committee, Brady Paul, or Zelda.

"Excusar," Rosa said, as she knocked before entering the library. "Senorita Tuesday, the telepfono is for you."

It must be Brady Paul! I knew he'd call me back.

But why didn't he call my cell?

"It's your tio." Rosa handed me the portable. "He says it's importante."

"Hello," I said, as Rosa dusted her way out of the room. I know she must have hated this black furniture as the escaping fine dust particles floated above it in the stream of sunlight.

"Your mother is on her way home," Uncle Monty said. "Without me."

"Really?" I said.

"Yes, well," he said, "she hopped an earlier flight. Before I knew it, she was out of here. Sorry. Do you want me to call Dr. Butler perhaps to be there when she arrives? She might be upset and…"

# My Mistaken Identity

"Don't worry about it," I said. "I'll be fine. Later." I hung up.

"As I was saying, Tuesday." My teacher – Ms. Disappointed said, as she handed me my failing exam. "If your grades don't improve…"

"Can you not?" I said, "Please, chill."

I closed my eyes. My head pounded. I was exhausted. Tired of being Tuesday Greenwood. I so needed to escape. Me. And be back in Brady Paul's arms. I couldn't stop thinking about our night on the beach. How he kissed me, touched me, whispered to me, and saved me. And to think, before that, I actually wanted to die. What a total idiot I was.

"Excuse me?" my teacher said.

"Don't go and get all butt hurt about it." I opened my eyes. Ms. Disappointed was wearing an I-can't-believe-that-just-came-out-of-your-mouth look. "All right, whatever," I said, "I'll study. Okay?"

Why doesn't she leave already? And why hasn't Brady Paul called me? Texted me or something, damn it! What's up with that?

"Well," she continued. "I would like to talk to your mother about your grades. I understand from your other tutors, Tuesday, they're experiencing the same resistance as I am."

"Didn't you hear me? I said I would study!"

She stood up. "Yes. I heard you." And picked up her satchel. "Loud and clear."

"Sorry," I said. But, I really, really wasn't.

She nodded. "Till next week then. Good-bye, Tuesday."

"Bye." I stretched out on the couch and reached for my cell. But then the phone call from Uncle Monty brought me back to reality. My mother was arriving home early. And without him.

That sucks.

Is that her?

I sat up and listened.

"Ms. Greenwood," Miss Disappointed said. She was not leaving disappointed after all. Momma had arrived.

Damn.

"Thank you for informing me," my mother said from the hallway. "Of course, I will see to it immediately." Her stilettos stabbed the marble floor announcing the coming of the mommy-monster.

Should I take cover?

Snatch a hose to spray her down with?

Disappear? If only.

"So," my mother said, as she fired her Louis Vuitton travel bag and matching purse onto the white leather chair next to me. She stood posed in the doorway with one hand on her hip and the other reaching for the pewter knob. The door slammed and locked. "You're failing your classes. And, to top it off this is your new look, huh?" Her head nodded with disapproval.

"Yeah," I said looking down at my no-way-designer-digs – my mothball smelling tweed blazer covering my band tee Hell Bent, my skinny black distressed jeans, and previously who-knows-done-what-in Converse high tops. "How do you like it?"

That should do it. No wait one more how-do-ya-like-it to feed to the hungry beast.

"You haven't said anything about my hair." I combed the flat-ironed fringe with my stubby fingernails over my right eye.

She circled me as if she were a lioness stalking her soon-to-be devoured prey. Constantly-correcting-Constance's familiar narrowing eyes, lowered chin and dark voice couldn't hold-back from the disapproving process. "So, this is what you think is hip and cool? The

162

rebellious look. Well, you certainly have the raunchy-grungy-look down, Tu-Tu." She snatched open my jacket's lapels and studied the devil on my tee.

"Like it?" I said. "I can order you one."

She smirked. "You think you're so damn funny, don't you?" She let go, slithered around to my back and yanked my blazer to my wrists. "I'm surprised you haven't invested in any tattoos yet." She stared at my bare arms as she continued to corral me. She planted her four-inch heels in front of me and continued, "Aren't they part of this in-your-face-momma attitude you're launching?"

"How do you know I haven't?" My turn to snort a smirk. "I could have a tramp-stamp on my..."

My head snapped. My eyes rolled back. I tasted blood. I palmed my face.

Shit.

"You're handicapping your career!" my mother exclaimed. "And blowing everything I've worked so hard to create for you!"

Grateful? Yeah, right, Momma. You did it all. I had nothing to do with it.

"Your horoscope said, Tuesday, your past was your passport to your future. I'm not so damn sure anymore."

I don't need your stupid reading to tell me what I want in my future.

She strutted over to her XL purse and snagged a photo and The Grapevine from it. "It seems you're taking up a lot of space in the tabloids lately." She tossed the newspaper at me. It landed at my feet. There staring back at me was the puke at the Tongue and Groove and the kiss at the Pig-Out.

I shook my head in disbelief.

Z-moment – "You're just freakin' fooling yourself, tabloid target. You're never really, really safe from your soap life."

"Tell me about this pitiful boy you've chosen as your newest charity." My mother stepped closer to me. "What does he have to offer you?" She answered her own question. "Absolutely nothing! And, he never will amount to anything!" She shook her head and laughed. "How could you even think the two of you would work out? You're such a fool, Tuesday, to believe this indigent boy is in love with you. He's only after your money! A good for nothing gold digger!"

"He's none of your damn business!"

"You don't think so?" Her weapons were planted on her hips. "That's where you're wrong, Tu-Tu. I decided to help out with your goodwill gesture. I bought his family a fishing boat while in paradise." She held out the wrinkled For Sale flyer with a snapshot of an enormous boat. She flung it at me as well. I reached out and caught it. "I've already contacted them. They accepted. Of course, there was a little string attached to the wrapped-up gift." Her grin was sly. Too proud. "And, they agreed that this relationship will not go any further."

"You did what?" I dropped the picture stamped SOLD as my stubby slate colored nails attempted to dig into my palms. My head shook uncontrollably as my mother's only nodded in silence. "You didn't! You wouldn't!"

But her wicked cunning eyes vouched for her actions. Pure nefarious.

"How could you? I hate you! I hate you! I hate you!"

# Chapter Twenty-One

## *Change*

Aren't we all?

You,

Me,

And…even them.

Only one,

Not two,

Or,

Even three,

Freakin' steps,

Away

From doing something,

or

Saying something,

That will

Totally,

Change

Our life?

~~~~~~~~~~~~~~~~~~~~~~~

Two hours later I was laid-up in my sanctuary. Or, was it only an hour later? Or, thirty minutes ago? Or, was it the day before? Pure time-traveling. I was licking my mommy-monster wounds again. At least I had fought back. That was a first.

"Pop culture, what a fascinating beast." Zelda knelt over me as I sought comfort under my quilt. "When was the last time you took a bath or washed your hair? You stink." She chuckled.

"Zelda!" I said, as I squinted through the bruising. "You came!"

"Shh....Is this like a bad time?" She slid in next to me with an opened can of Spaghetti-O's and a school-sized carton of milk. "I guess it's been one of those sucky days around here. Pure fight-night." She took a sip, set the carton on the nightstand and wiped her mouth on my bleached pillowcase. "So scene."

"Most definitely," I said. I could taste blood. I sucked my lip.

"From what you posted on your blog, it was a way amazing WWE smack-down." Zelda took a bite. "Sorry I missed it. Ticket Master was totally sold-out." She smirked as a round piece of pasta fell onto her Screw-Ups band tee. She retrieved it with the spoon. "Want a bite, prize fighter?" she asked, as she scooped out another spoonful.

I shook my head and grimaced as Zelda said, "A blackened-eye for a blackened-eye, a snatch-your-freakin'-hair-out for a snatch-your-freakin'-hair-out, and a slap-in-the-face for a slap-in-the-face! Pure Hammurabi."

I covered mine and nodded.

"Sigh. I guess the yoga and meditation classes offered-up at the spa didn't help-out with her anger management, huh?" Zelda said and snarkled. "I'd say Constance must have lost it after she caught a glimpse of your new look. My guess is she didn't appreciate the changes. Don't you just love it when she comes at you overly caffeinated?"

"Tell me something." I tilted my head back and rested it on her shoulder. "Something really, really good."

"If it helps," she said, "your mom's knock-down-drag-out look is way more abused than yours." She snarkled.

"Is anything truly possible?" I rolled to my back and closed my eyes.

Zelda rolled over, too. "Only if we pursue project cast-off Constance."

"You know what she did?" I fought back the tears, but the tears won. "She paid-off Brady Paul's family with a fishing boat so he'd have absolutely nothing what-so-ever to do with me." I shoved the boat flyer off the bed. "I'll never be with him again. I'm in love with him, Zelda. And, I believe he's into me too. I feel it!"

"Pure Montague and Capulet," she said and sighed.

"Why did Momma do that? I'd only hung out with him a few times. Please, Zelda, help me."

"The bitch is certifiably crazy all right. But you can't say she's stingy, though." Zelda said and laughed. "I wonder how much she'd give me to stop hanging with you." Zelda socked my arm. "That was the laugh-out-loud part, Tu-Tu."

"Come on, Zelda, help me. The sharp side of a razor is starting to sound more and more comforting. And inviting. Can't you see I'm crumbling here?"

"Tuesday, do you really, really want the SOS truth?"

I nodded my head as I choked and coughed on my own blubbering saliva.

"Constance is scared shitless!"

"Huh?" I hiccupped. "I don't get it. What are you talking about?"

"It's so obvious, Tuesday, she's paranoid you're going to leave her." Zelda shook her spoon at me as the tomato sauce splattered across

167

the silk duvet cover. "And where would that bitch be then? Without you? She depends on your soon-to-be nine-digit income. And, she enjoys the spotlight too much not to be in control of it. You're growing-up and all she has to look forward to is incontinence, assisted living, lost metabolism, stool softeners, and her own expiration date." Zelda laughed.

I felt a hint of a smile touch my lips. "Zelda, what would I do without you? You're my best friend ever. You're like my for-real sissy."

"I'd say," Zelda said setting down the Spaghetti O's, "we most definitely need a 9-1-1!" She snagged my arm and pulled me to my feet. "Five, four, three, two, one! Dance!" We jumped and jived till we collapsed, and our lungs were pressed for air.

Then she held me spoon-tight and hummed Dance of the Sugar Plum Fairy into my right ear. The song of my childhood. The one sung by another mother. A loving momma. The one being erased daily from my memory. How did Zelda know? My eyes closed and sleep was welcomed by my exhausted beaten-down frame and mind.

"TUESDAY!" My mother screamed from outside my locked door sometime after midnight. "Please, open your door! TUESDAY!" She hammered the cherry wood with her fists till my swollen eyes opened. "Please, forgive me, Sugar Plum! I love you!"

I sat up and stared into the other room where the begging door pleaded its case.

You love me?

"Tuesday, please help me!" My mother's hysterical voice revealed its grief. It tugged on my empty ache, pulling me closer and closer through the emotional mind-field. My pride checked-out.

"Momma?"

"Tuesday! Oh God, Tuesday, please help me! Monty is calling Dr. Butler! They're going to lock me up in some kind of sanitarium! And perform some new brain electrical stimulation on me! Please, Tu-Tu, don't let them take me away! Please, Tuesday! Please, open up!"

# My Mistaken Identity

"Don't do it, Tuesday." Zelda stood with her back against the vibrating door as my quivering hand reached for its bolt lock. Zelda's head shook in defiant slow motion. "This is your chance to be rid of her. She's too far gone. Let go of the pain. Shelf it. Unpack her. End it."

"But...but...didn't you hear what she said?" I laid the side of my face against the pounding door. The intersection of love and hate.

"She's ruthless and you know it." Zelda's voice was rising. "Don't be fooled. She's carved an abyss in you that can't be filled with truth or lies. Accept the obvious, Tuesday. Constance has never played by the rules. Those fundamental laws require a conscience."

"TUESDAY!" my mother hollered. "Please help me! Open the door!"

"You don't understand," I said.

"Have you forgotten about your little burn she delivered earlier?"

"I know...but..."

"Who are you talking to, Tuesday?" my mother asked.

Zelda shrugged. "Maybe she needs some freakin' treatment."

"Don't you see," My hands thrust to my chest. "...she needs me!"

"It's up to you." Zelda stepped away as her voice began to shrink. "I can't make you. But, remember..." She pointed at my black and blues. "...this...and this....and this.

"And...," she said, "B.P."

LL Eadie

# Chapter Twenty-Two

## *What a Pain*

Fame-game,

What a pain.

I sometimes wish,

I could stop the reign.

Stardom will,

Drive you insane.

Where's the damn

Novocain?

To block and restrain,

Me.

~~~~~~~~~~~~~~~~~~~~~~~~~~~~~~~~~~~~~

"How is she?" I glanced up from my guitar. The tips of my fingers were sore. Calluses were forming from hours of practice. Enough. My thumbs rubbed them.

"Has she asked about me?" I set the guitar down in the stand in front of me.

"I told you not to worry." Uncle Monty glanced at me over the ebony grand piano. The one he bought me for my twelfth birthday. "Your mother is in good hands. The doctors are optimistic with her progress thus far." He played a few new notes, scribbled something on the sheet music and then added, "The psychotherapy sessions and the treatments seem to be working. In a couple of weeks or so, she should be able to come home. Now, let's start back at the top." He began playing the prelude.

It's already been two weeks. What are they doing to her?

Hey! But what about Brady Paul? Why hasn't he called? Damn her! Why do I even care what happens to her?

"All right, fine, whatever." I picked up my guitar and began to sing.

"You say,

I've changed.

Not yesterday,

Or,

Today.

But, somehow,

Someway,

Some unknown reason why,

I've changed.


How?

You say,

Is it my name?

No, it's sorta the same.

But...you got it,

I've changed.

# My Mistaken Identity

How?

You say,

Is it my face?

No, it's still in place.

But…you got it,

I've changed.

"Maybe…" I set my guitar down before the next verse. I readjusted my butt on the stool. "I should go see her."

What's wrong with me? How could I forget what she did to me? And Brady Paul!

"No." Uncle Monty shook his head. "That's not such a good idea. So let's get back to the work at hand. And later we'll have a root beer float just like old times and watch an oldie-goldie movie." He played a couple of chords. "Now, from where you left off, Tuesday honey."

"How?

You say,

Is it my heart?

Yes!

It's fallen apart.

Yes! Yes! Yes!

That why…

I've changed.

{chorus 2}

Not yesterday,

Or,

Today.

But, I've changed.

How strange,

To be deranged."

"Well," I said, "maybe then, I'll call her."

He slammed the piano keys. "That would only set her back!"

My head whipped around. This was totally new. Long-fused Uncle Monty had never raised his voice at momma or me.

"Get a grip!" I said. "Chill."

"I'm so sorry, Tuesday." Uncle Monty stood up. I distanced myself. He reached out for my hand. "I've been under a lot of pressure. Please forgive me. I'm just as concerned and upset about your mother as you are. And, I only want what's best for her. And, you."

I'm so out of here.

He walked toward me. "I shouldn't have raised my voice. That's not fair. I would never do anything to hurt you. It's the doctors' wishes that she not receive any visitors." He tapped his chest. "Only me. Please understand, Tuesday."

# My Mistaken Identity

And who are you for God's sake? You're not my uncle. You're not my father. And you're damn sure not my mother's husband either!

"Forget about it." I turned and walked toward the recording studio's door.

Maybe it's for the best. Of course, it is. She totally screwed-upped my relationship with Brady Paul. I haven't heard anything from him since. I hate her.

"Wait!" His voice was different. It rung anxious. I glanced over my shoulder. "I have some good news. I was waiting to tell you later when your mother came home but…

"Well," I said, "what is it? Spit it out."

"Glissando has decided your solo debut album will feature all your songs!" Uncle Monty exclaimed. "And they love the name The Third Day of the Week."

"Really?"

"Yes, Baldwin convinced them. He's very taken with your talent. Aren't you proud? I am. Your album's sure to explode!" Uncle Monty smiled at me. I looked away. I felt embarrassed to be so happy for myself. "Baldwin will be back tomorrow. He's been working with the high school kids on their part of the production. And, I promised him while you were, you know, recovering…"

"What you meant to say was while my bruises faded from red to purple to pink to yellow." Our eyes met. I shoved mine in a different direction.

"Well, like I was saying," Uncle Monty said, "I told Baldwin we'd…"

"Practice," I said reaching for the handle. "That's all."

"Yes, but…" Uncle Monty said, "I'd like to talk to you about…"

I turned around. "About what?"

"About…" He stepped closer to me. My shoulders reversed. "About the prom gig."

I don't care about that stupid prom.

Or, do I?

Damn, why hasn't Brady Paul tried to contact me? Does he have a girl friend? Did he laugh behind my back? Maybe, Momma was right. I was being used.

Or maybe he just couldn't take the boat away from his family. How else could they ever afford to buy one? It would be greedy on his part.

But was it really worth it?

I must not be.

Or, did his parents make him?

I wonder if he cried over me like I did for him.

"Okay," I said. "Talk."

"Let's sit down." Uncle Monty took my hand. "Okie-dokie?"

I snatched it away, shrugged my whatever-shoulders and followed him to the leather couch. I parked myself in the opposite corner. My bottom lip pulsed as I squeezed it. Uncle Monty sprayed his habit-forming fresh breath pocket-pack into his mouth. I tucked my legs underneath me while my arms shielded my funkified Alice in Wonderland tank.

"The prom is still a go," he said, "and like Baldwin said you have the chops to sing these songs, but…

"But what?" I asked frowning.

# My Mistaken Identity

Here it comes again my T.G. lose-lose situation. Will you and momma ever let me be me? Whoever it is I am. Just let me figure it out on my own.

"I'm not sure you're on the right track with your new, umm, look."

"I see." I unhinged myself and stood up, balled up my fists and attempted to dig my stubby nails into my palms. Botched effort. "So, you're taking sides. Momma's side."

"Please, sit down, Tuesday honey, and listen."

"I am listening," I said, as I continued to take my stand.

"I understand you're experimenting. I did so myself as a young man. Everyone needs to discover who they truly are." Uncle Monty reached out for my hand and gave it a sluggish tug in his direction. It felt dry and fossilized.

I caved and sat down next to him. "Then you should totally understand," I said, as I hugged my knees. He patted my shoulder.

"I do, Tuesday honey. He sat up taller. "I really do. It's just…"

"Just what?"

This is so not fair. But I'm not going to lose it. Strike a poker face. Now!

"Well, I spoke to Glissando Records and they're really excited about your crossover pop-soul sound and style. They said it was very innovative."

"Really?" I looked up with hopeful eyes.

"Yes, and they're sending over a professional hair stylist of the stars…"

I jumped up. "Why?"

"Come on, Tuesday honey," Uncle Monty reached out and snagged my hand. He pulled it oh so slowly toward him. I sat down again.

"What's wrong with my hair?"

"I'm truly getting used to it."

"Then why the make-over?"

"Come here." He wrapped his arm around me. "I won't let them do anything you don't agree to. Okay? And I have a surprise for you!" He released me and walked around the couch and picked up a new guitar. But not just an ordinary one. This guitar was personalized with my album cover's name The Third Day of the Week with a fairy wings' motif – white wings intricately outlined in black.

"Oh my God, Uncle Monty, it's…it's… unbelievable!"

"You really like it?" He handed it to me. "I had it made special. Baldwin helped me hand-select the wood and the finish."

"I don't know what to say." I shook my head.

"Just say you like it, Tuesday honey."

"I love it!" I held out the most awesome guitar I had ever seen and hugged the most awesome uncle anyone ever had. "Thank you!" I started to cry. And so did he.

"Let's sit down and maybe you'll feel like singing something," Uncle Monty said as he wiped his tears before taking my hand and leading me back to the black leather couch.

I sat down next to him and strummed the guitar a few times. It was perfect. I turned and faced Uncle Monty. Pure joy on his face. And I'm sure on mine as well. I set the guitar to the side and my head dropped onto his shoulder and my legs found their way to his lap. I curled up. He held me tight.

"I'm sorry," I said, "that I lost it earlier."

# My Mistaken Identity

"Don't worry about it. I know you're worried about your mother."

"Momma and I are so lucky to have you, Uncle Monty."

"I'm always here for you, Tuesday honey." He kissed the top of my head, then my cheek and whispered in my ear, "I love you."

Good ole Uncle Monty.

But what had he ever given to Zelda?

LL Eadie

# Chapter Twenty-Three

## *Misplaced*

I've misplaced,

My heart.

Have you seen it?

You were there,

The last time,

I felt it.

~~~~~~~~~~~~~~~~~~~~~~~

"Added some layers, huh?"

"Zelda!"

Her finger rose to her lips. "Shhh...I like it. The spiky pieces on top add some swag to it too. Maybe I'll add some to mine."

"Thanks." I glanced into my mother's mirror above her dresser. Uncle Monty was right. The hairdresser thingy did work out. I especially liked the thick old school bangs.

"Why are you hanging out in Constance's bedroom anyway? Looking for the evidence we talked about?"

"Not exactly. I fell asleep in here last night."

And the night before that and that. And that. Maybe for the past couple of weeks.

Zelda walked across my mother's room and picked up the newspaper folded on her nightstand. "Once you've made a decision,"

Zelda read from the Hollywood Gazette horoscope, "the changes will come easy and you'll wonder why it took you so long to fine tune your life."

"Sounds way simple," I said. "Doesn't it?"

"Way." Zelda tossed the paper across my mother's suite. She pointed at a bulletin board leaning against the wall by my mother's closet. "What's this?"

"That's what momma and her soothsayer calls the vision board," I said. "It's all about what's delicioso in my mother's future life. It was supposed to weave magic. It psyches her up. Or, it used to." I stared at the collage of pictures. Of me.

"You were her freakin' prodigy!" Zelda said and snarkled. "She most definitely was overdosing on you, Tu-Tu. Did she really wrap her mind around this crap?"

I lifted up the corkboard and stared at myself. "Yeah. Sad, huh?"

"That is just wrong." Zelda vanished into my mother's closet. "No wonder she's held up in the kooky psyche ward."

Zelda reappeared zipped-up in one of my mother's designer dresses and a pair of her shoes. She laughed as she mocked my mother strutting her bimbo-butt down an imaginary catwalk. "What a gluttonous wardrobe. Constance is such a lush." She shook her booty at me. "I only wonder if the straight jacket she's wearing comes in a designer label." Zelda elbowed me.

I smiled. Sort of. My mother's perfume still lay heavy in the room. "Come on, Zelda, let's forget about it." I felt a pang of guilt about sifting through her personal stuff.

"This is sudden. Why the shift?" Zelda swept a smoke from the pack on my mother's nightstand and lit up. "Come on let's scope it out and locate what we talked about. You know, the core of who you are, Tuesday." Zelda kicked off the high-rise heels and slithered out of the jet-black gown. She coughed a couple of times before blowing a perfect smoke ring in my direction. "You go for her dresser and I'll tackle the desk. We don't have much time. Monty will be back soon."

"Okay, fine, whatever." I dished out my I-don't-give-a-shit shrug as I pulled out the top drawer. But I was way digressing. And my voice revealed that. And so did my lack-luster effort.

"Hey," Zelda said, "if you don't want to know, just say the word, and we'll ripcord. I don't give a crap. This is for you! Not me!"

I shook my head. "No." Then nodded. "I do want to know." And, whispered. "Who my father is."

"Well, crank it up!" Zelda swung around and dug through the next drawer. The cigarette was dangling from her lips.

It's my right to know.

Quit acting like a demented sugar plum fairy.

Momma-and-me de'ja' vu was unleashed in my mind. A picture of her and me sitting on a park bench. Momma mad because I had picked a forbidden bouquet from the Garden Club's wildflower display.

"Don't you understand, Tuesday," my mother had said, "fairies make their homes inside the petals. And now ten of them have no place to sleep tonight."

I had cried when I discovered I could not replant the stems. But momma came to the fairies' rescue and placed the daisies in a paper cup filled with water.

"Clean-up on aisle two!" Zelda said and laughed, as she emptied a mirrored drawer onto the ebony marble floor. "Hey, Tuesday, get your cushy ass over here! I think I actually found something!" Zelda pointed at an envelope taped to the bottom of the drawer.

I tore it off, opened it and folded inside was the combination to my mother's safe.

"Well?" Zelda said as she flicked the cigarette butt and smudged it out on the floor. "Do you know where the safe is?"

I nodded, pointed at my mother's R-rated portrait hung above her white-padded headboard. Her nudity matched her Las Vegas style round bed. Zelda and I floored the exaggerated amount of safari-animal-printed throw pillows and climbed onto the cushy mattress. It had been a long time since I had been on momma's bed up until a few nights ago. But it had been an even longer time since my mother had recited a fairy tale to me.

"Come on!" Zelda lifted the oil painting from the wall. "Pure Lady Godiva." She dropped it behind her on the comforter, as I worked the sequence of numbers on the lock and swung its door wide. "Jackpot!" Zelda bounced on the bed.

I dragged out velvet box after velvet box of jewels before I found a copy of my birth certificate, a handwritten letter, and a cashed check.

"Does she pay everybody off?" Zelda stared at the receipts of my life as we sat on the edge of the bed.

"Nigel Burnett," I said out loud for the first time ever. My father's name. The same name on the birth certificate, endorsed to on the check and signed on the back. And, the same one that wrote a you-better-pay-up-or-else letter:

Constance,

I did not appreciate the way you tore into me on the phone. You thought I'd never figure it out, didn't you? I'm not as stupid as you'd like for me to be. So, if you don't want me in your life, or our daughter's, you'll send that damn money! If I don't get it by this Friday, I will be contacting my lawyer. That's a promise, Constance!

Soon to be sipping on Margaritas somewhere in paradise, Nigel

# My Mistaken Identity

"Half a million dollars," Zelda said and smirked, "Sigh. He should've most definitely held out for more. Brady Paul got a million plus. Of course, we have to consider inflation." She slugged my arm. The one gripping the letter. "That was the laugh out loud part, Tu-Tu."

My vision blurred as my eyes dewed-up.

Zelda pointed. "Look, Tuesday, at the date on that check."

I blinked. Tears dropped. Vision restored.

"That was only five years ago," Zelda said. "You would have been…"

"Eleven," I said. "And just the beginning of the pop princess piggy bank."

"Pure porky black mail." Zelda shook her head. Her black eyeglass frames wobbled. "That sucks. Sorry, Tuesday."

I shrugged and then read the letter again. And, I read it again. And, again. And… again. Then I tore it up into a bazillion pieces.

"Blow the blahs off, Tu-Tu," Zelda said, as she weaved her fingers through her black fishnet stockings, stretching the holes. "I know it's a rough patch for you. But, jerks like him aren't worth our tears."

"Momma was right," I said, as I stared at my broken heart scattered across the cold marble floor. I had envisioned the fairy tale, kiss-you-good-night, buy-you-cotton-candy, teach-you-to-ride-a-bike, take-you-to-the-circus, walk-you-down-the-aisle daddy. If only.

"Right about what?" Zelda asked.

"About every freakin' person just out to get my money!"

"9-1-1!" Zelda exclaimed, as she snagged my arm and attempted to pull me up on the bed. "Five, four, three, two, one…Dance!"

I snatched my arm from her grip. "Could you not? Stop it!"

"Don't go and get all butt-hurt on me." Zelda leaped from the bed. "It's not like you knew him or anything. Better to find out now what a piece of shit he is. Be glad he's not in your life. Constance did you a favor."

"Just leave me alone!" I stood up and glared at her. "It's all your fault! You're the one that kept insisting I find out who he was! Are you satisfied now?"

"Having an itty-bitty-pity party, are we?" Zelda took a couple of steps closer toward me. Her slip-ons squeaked on the marble floor. "Poor little Sugar Plum is all upset about her daddy, huh? The daddy she thought had no idea she existed. The one she believed her mother kept from her all these years."

Zelda took another step. I could almost feel her breath on my fuming face. "The freakin' daddy that doesn't care to ever read her a bedtime story, mop up her tears when she's all sad, or even send her a birthday gift. Just a letter of blackmail. The truth sucks doesn't it? Welcome to my whacked world, Tuesday."

My eyes narrowed as I shook my head. "Shhh!"

"Don't you shush me!" Zelda pointed her index finger inches from my nose.

I shoved it away. "Shut up, you…you…"

"So, it's my turn now, huh?" Zelda said with a teasing smirk.

"What are you talking about now? Just get the hell out of here! Leave me alone!" I didn't back down, or back up.

"Don't worry, Tuesday, I won't bother you anymore."

"Good! I'm tired of you anyway! You think you're always right! You're always telling me what to do! Well, I'm not listening to you anymore, Zelda! You think you're so smart and funny! I'll tell you what you really are! You're just a stupid, ignorant smart-ass liar that's always interfering! In my life! So just leave me the hell alone!"

# My Mistaken Identity

Zelda clapped in slow motion and smirked. Her nostrils flared and puffed as her head did the familiar double shake. "Wow! That was quite a performance, Tuesday. That so would have snatched away that acting award from Stormy you lost." She sat on the bed and leaned back on her elbows. "Good timing though, Tu-Tu, cause I'm tired of trying to be your friend anyway. Trying to help you to be original. Be spontaneous. Be unique. Be daring and bold. To be…yourself. It was all a big mistake."

"How can you even give yourself credit for my life, Zelda? You're obnoxious! You're way crazy!"

"You didn't appreciate any of it. I can see that now," Zelda said. "I'm as dispensable as the rest of your friends you've ever had. It's true. Whenever anyone gets too close, you end it. That's why you don't have any friends. Admit it!"

"That's not true! People take advantage of me! You have no idea what it's like!" I could feel my eyes filling with my misery.

"I don't believe you." Zelda shook her head. "I know how your mind functions. You think just because you're Tuesday Greenwood everyone should be grateful to be in your presence. And they damn sure better give you exclusive rights to their friendship! Or else you're checking-out of it!"

I covered my ears and closed my eyes.

I will not listen to this shit! You can't make me!

"SHUT UP!" I screamed and stared Zelda down.

"Do you do it, Tuesday, because you get bored with us?" Zelda stood back up. "We're no longer any fun to play with, is that it? Or, is it because you're afraid you're the boring one and we're going to unpack you? So, you dump us first. Does it hurt less that way? Tell me, why do you…"

"You LYING BITCH! I hate you!"

Zelda spun on her canvas heels, headed for the door, and shouted just before the back of her head was no longer in view. "FUCK YOU, TUESDAY GREENWOOD!"

Chapter Twenty-Four

## *I Should Have Seen It Coming*

I should have,

Why didn't I?

Did I really, really think?

You would change?

Back to who,

You really are?

I should have seen it coming,

Straight at me.

In my face!

In my space!

What a waste!

I should have seen it coming!

Why didn't I?

~~~~~~~~~~~~~~~~~~~~~~~~~~~~~~~

"Momma, it's me!" I held the receiver tight to my ear and my thumb and index finger snug on my bottom lip after I woke up in her bedroom the following morning. This was a head-down, tail-tucked phone call. But most definitely a necessary one. Maybe I would ask her about Zelda. And then…maybe I wouldn't. I just couldn't risk the chance that Zelda would be banned from ever visiting again. Even though I wasn't sure if Zelda even wanted to now.

Why did we have to have that argument?

I don't care who she says she is.

I just want her to be my friend.

"Who is this?" asked a voice that didn't sound familiar.

"I'm sorry, this is Tuesday Greenwood." I glanced down at the hospital stationery I swept from Uncle Monty's dresser. My mother's private number scribbled at the bottom. "I want to speak to my mother – Constance…"

"I know who your mother is," the same strange-to-me voice said. "Hold on, I'll check to see if she feels up to receiving any calls today."

What does that mean?

I looked around my mother's bedroom. My far-from-eight-hours-of-sleep eyes focused on a framed photo of Momma and me at the beach. We were so happy. So satisfied. So agreeable. So healthy. So long ago.

"Miss Greenwood, your mother will be right with you."

"Thank you," I said to the stranger. The one that now held vigil over my mother – making the decisions whether she could walk, gawk or squawk.

"Hello," said the face in the picture. Twenty years my senior.

"Hi, Momma!"

"Who is this?"

Huh?

"It's me! Tuesday!" I stood up. Reached over and puffed-up her pillows on the Cleopatra lounge I had been stretched out on. I knew just how Momma liked them.

# My Mistaken Identity

"Yes?" she said. And nothing more.

"Momma, it's so good to hear your voice!" I walked over to our picture and picked it up. The one of the day long beachcombing. Momma in her two-piece she had saved up for and me in a matching one piece. "Momma, are you there? Momma?"

"Yes, I'm here," she said, "What do you want?"

"I just needed to hear your voice." I held the photograph closer to me. I could feel the pumped-up rhythm of my heart beating. "You know, make sure you are okay."

"Why?"

I set the picture back on the glass shelf. "I love you, Momma." Tears took hold of my eyes and refused to back off. I sat down on the floor, tucked my knees to my chest and covered my bare feet with my mother's black nightie that I wore. And rocked back and forth. "Momma? Are you there?"

"Yes, I'm here. What did you say you wanted?"

"Momma, didn't you hear me?"

"Of course, I did. Do you think I'm deaf, too?"

"No, Momma." I pulled the sheer nylon up to my face and wiped my eyes. "Are you okay?" I could smell her sweet scent.

"Why do you care?" she said.

I closed them, tilted back my head, sucked air through my nostrils, and exhaled through my mouth, "I love you, Momma."

"I seriously doubt that."

This was way more difficult than I thought it would be.

Why isn't she happy to hear my voice? Doesn't she want to find out what I've been up to? How my album is coming along? Or, even the prom?

"I'm almost through recording the twelve songs for my album. Baldwin says my penned lyrics will have off-the-charts popularity. Their fresh melodies, he said, spell out hit!"

"Don't cash in your songs, Tu-Tu, before they're sung."

"Of course not. But listen to this, Momma, Glissando Records is already planning a fierce ad campaign for me and…"

"I have to go now."

"Why?" I stood up.

"Hello, Miss Greenwood, this is your mother's personal nurse again. She's not feeling well at the moment and needs to lie down. I'm sure you understand."

"No! I don't! Please put my mother back on the phone! I need to talk to her! Now!"

"I'm sorry…"

"No!"

"Miss Greenwood, if you don't calm down…"

"I'm sorry, please try," I said, as I collapsed onto my mother's round bed. I stared up at her Lady Godiva portrait. Mommy and me de'ja' vu poured over me from the broad-brush strokes looming above my head.

"Fairies don't wear clothes either," my mother had said. "Why not, Momma?" I had asked. "It's not necessary because they're so tiny, Sugar Plum. You can barely see them."

# My Mistaken Identity

I smiled up at her. And shook my head. Did she ever really answer my questions truthfully? I doubted it. Maybe, I thought, Zelda is Uncle Monty's daughter.

"Ask my mother again for me," I said to the nurse. "Please."

"Hold on, I'll see if she's feeling up to a few more minutes."

Momma don't punish me like this. I love you. I would have come to see you, but Uncle Monty said...

"Hello," my mother said.

"Momma!"

"Yes?"

"Please, don't hang up. I so need to talk to you. I need to hear your voice. Know that you're okay. I would have come but..."

"Tuesday!"

"I miss you, Momma! I have the most awesome idea, why don't you tell me a fairy tale. What about the one when Sugar Plum got lost because the evil fairy led her into the woods and her mommy-fairy had to find her."

"Tuesday!"

"Momma, I read your horoscope today." I stretched out on her bed and hugged one of her safari pillows. "It said you have so much to gain by being open minded."

"Tuesday!"

"Mine said to show a little affection for the one you love. I love you, Momma. Don't you love Sugar Plum?"

"You're not my Sugar Plum fairy!" My mother said. "Sugar Plum would have never allowed this to happen to her Momma! Don't you think I needed to talk to you too? And, hear your voice? But you didn't call! Or, come to see me! You don't give a shit whether I lived or died!"

Click!

"Momma! Are you there?

MOMMA!"

Chapter Twenty-Five

## *Don't Set Me Free*

I'm all yours,

That's the way I want it.

The way it should be.

Don't set me free.

Not for a moment,

For anyone,

Or anything.

I'm not for rent,

Not for lease.

I'm yours forever after.

Please! Please! Please!

Don't set me free.

Fan my fantasy,

And adopt me!

~~~~~~~~~~~~~~~~~~~~~~~~~~~~~~~

"You called your momma, didn't you?" Zelda walked up behind me in the main kitchen a few boring weeks later. I was in search of some midnight carbs. She snarkled.

I whipped around. "Zelda!"

"Shhh…Who else would it be?" She snatched the bag of Doritos out of my grasp and made herself at home.

"I was beginning to think I would never see you again."

"Why's that?" she asked. "Because you totally took your disappointment out on me the last time we hung? The truth is your loose-lipped venting only bothered my butt for about five minutes."

"I'm…really, really…sorry," I said. "I guess I just lost it."

Why don't you say you're sorry too, Zelda? You never apologize anymore.

"I'll say." Zelda reached into the bag, snagged a chip and stuffed it into her mouth. "Oh well, it's in the past, but next time you might not be so lucky. I just may not return and bless you with my exclusive company." She reached out and kicked me in the shin. "That was the roll your eyes part, Tu-Tu."

I smiled, rushed over and hugged her.

"Whoa! What's up with that? Have you gender-bendered on me?"

I shook my head and laughed. "No way! I'm still too addicted to…"

"B.P.!" Zelda threw the bag above her head. We were showered with cool ranch chips as it poured outside. Lightning lit the sky, followed by a rumble of thunder.

A momma-and-me de'ja' vu released into my mind. Her telling me a story about how the thunder and lightning were the rejoicings of fairies when a baby one was born. Which always calmed my fears during the rainstorm. Momma and I would light sparklers and join in the birth celebration by dancing around the screen porch. We would make up names for all the baby girl fairies born with each crack and boom.

Reality settled. Along with the rain.

# My Mistaken Identity

Zelda is Uncle Monty and Rosa's daughter and there's no such things as fairies. Or...Brady Paul in my life.

"Where were we?" Zelda said. "Oh, yeah, you rang-up the way insane bitch."

I nodded as I sat on a stool. I had not thought about that call-in days. Why would I? My focus was back on the loss of Brady Paul. The one my mother had created.

"What did you expect? That she would be magically transformed into your favorite fairy-tale-telling Momma once again? She is who she is, Tu-Tu. Pure psycho." Zelda wiped her mouth on her stained sleeve. "Don't go and get a heavy convenient case of amnesia on me. You know how constantly-Kamikaze-Constance has made every outrageous effort to squash your desires."

I nodded again. A momma and me de'ja' vu moment popped into my groggy head where a throb was doing its best to resurface. Momma painting my wee little piggies. "Fairies wear pink glittery polish on their fingers and toenails, too, Sugar Plum," she had said. "That way they blend in with the posies so the ugly troll can't find them."

"You're most definitely her compensation-earner," Zelda said. "And, Monty's."

"I know." My body began to fold in half. Tears glued my face to my lap as I collapsed.

Why am I crying for her?

I hate her!

Sometimes.

"Don't go there," Zelda said. "Refrain yourself. Get a grip. End it with her. Now!"

Shhh, Zelda.

"The sooner you do, the better off you'll be."

I wiped my eyes on a napkin. Two coal black smudges were left behind.

"Well, tell," Zelda said, "what happened between you and B.P.?"

I sat up. "I haven't spoken to him."

"Did you check out the picture of the boat in The Grapevine that Constance bought for his family?"

"Yeah," I said, as I watched Zelda forage chips off the slate colored marble.

"It looks like a mega yacht!" Lightning flashed. "Damn, I wonder how those paparazzi pains found out about it."

"You were right about my mother," I said. "She does deserve some freakin' treatments."

"How could you have ever doubted your sissy?"

I smirked and shook my head.

Thank God, you came back Zelda. I missed you.

But then my grin faded. "Why didn't you return my calls?" I asked. "I emailed and texted you a bazillion times."

"God, text pest, are we in some kind of weird-o relationship? I'm not your boyfriend."

I shook my head. "You never answer when I call you."

"Get a grip. Do you think I'm at your beck and call? I do have a life."

Note to self: Warning – Don't pull an exclusive on Zelda! Chances are she'll ripcord.

# My Mistaken Identity

I stood and stared out the window at the rainstorm. "I'm sorry, Zelda. I know you probably have a ton of friends. And, go out with them all the time. I'm just a charity case to you."

"Yeah, you are," she said and laughed.

"I swear, Zelda, I'll never hurt you again."

"Pinky swear." She stuck out her finger. Our pinkies locked in an I-promise-you embrace. "Now, that's legally binding. Hey, I've got an idea!" Zelda exclaimed as Doritos puffed out of her mouth. "Why don't I call Brady Paul!"

"What? No! Most definitely not!" My head shook and my arms flapped back and forth.

"Why not?" Zelda hopped up onto the dark granite countertop and sat with the half full bag of chips. "It would be perfect. It's not like you're calling and begging him to come back to you or anything. I'll just call and feel him out. You know see how he feels about all this. What can it hurt?"

"I don't think it's such a good idea," I said. "Zelda! What are you doing?"

"Speed dialing the reason for your heartache." Another thunderous boom.

"Oh, my God! You've had that phone!"

Zelda shrugged her oh-well-get-over-it shoulders as she held my cell to her ear.

"At least put it on speaker phone." I leaned against the counter next to her and listened to his number ringing over and over. "He's not going to answer. Just hang up." I tried to reach for the phone but Zelda smacked my hand just as...

"Hello."

"Hi!" Zelda said. "How's it going, Brady Paul?"

"Okay." The rain began to slack up.

"This is Zelda."

"Who?"

"You know, Tuesday's friend. I'm sure she's told you all about me. How awesome I am and talented and…"

"Oh yeah…Zelda."

"Well, I just called to see why you haven't called her? Don't you think you owe her some kind of explanation? I mean, don't you care what she's thinking about all this crap?"

My mouth dropped open and my head shook. "NO!"

"Is that Tuesday?" Brady Paul asked.

"Yeah, it is," Zelda said. "Do you want to talk to her?"

"Does she want to talk to me?"

"I'll ask her." Zelda turned to me grinning and said, "Well? Do you? Or, don't you?"

I reached for the phone. "Hi, it's me." And took it off speaker phone.

"It's good to hear your voice, Tuesday. I'm really sorry about all this. I don't know what to say. I'm…"

"You don't have to…" There was barely a sprinkle outside now.

"No," Brady Paul said. "Zelda's right. I do owe you an explanation. This is a really embarrassing situation for me. I've never had to face anything like this before. It's hard for me."

"Then don't."

"No, Tuesday, I need to do this. I should have already done it. So, please just listen. First, I want to say I've never stopped having feelings for you. I've missed you."

"I've missed you too, Brady Paul." I covered my eyes with my other hand.

"Your mother was insistent, and I guess you know that already about us not seeing each other as part of the bargain for the sports fisherman. And...I guess my parents must be pretty greedy because they agreed. But...of course...I didn't stop them. I'm sorry."

"It's okay. I don't give a damn about that boat. They can have it! I just want you!"

"I want to be with you too. I feel really ashamed. You shouldn't forgive me. I shouldn't have believed everything my parents told me about you." It started to rain again.

Huh?

"What did they tell you?"

Zelda jumped off the counter and stood next to me with her ear plastered next to mine. I attempted to push her away. She refused.

"Well, it's not something I need to repeat."

Oh my God!

"You have to tell me, Brady Paul!" I shoved Zelda again. Again, she refused. I gave up and put it on speaker phone.

"Well, I shouldn't have believed it! I'm sorry."

"Brady Paul!"

Zelda rubbed my back.

"Okay, but don't repeat this, okay? I don't want you to get into an argument with your mother. I'm sure she just said this stuff because she didn't want us to be together. And I understand. I'm not exactly the kind of guy she would like for…"

"Brady Paul! Just tell me!"

"Okay…Your mom…sorta…told my folks that I was just one of…you know… many guys you had played around with. And in the end you would…ummm .reject me and move on…Just like all the rest." Lightning lit the room.

"Damn, Tuesday," Zelda whispered. "I had no idea you were such a slut." She grinned and punched me in the arm. I slapped at her as she dodged my frustration.

"My parents" he continued, "think you're not right for me either. Because of…you know…who you are and all." Thunder followed.

"Brady Paul," I said, "thanks for telling me all that. But, you see, my mother is so screwed up that my Uncle Monty had to lock her up in mental institution. So, don't believe what she says."

"I didn't know. I'm sorry, Tuesday."

"Me too, Brady Paul."

"Will you still go with me to the prom?" Lightning!

"YES!" Thunder!

Thank you, Zelda! I totally owe you!

# Chapter Twenty-Six

## *It Hurts*

It hurts…

Sometimes.

Like only when I laugh,

It hurts…

Other times.

Like only when you're beyond

My reach.

~~~~~~~~~~~~~~~~~~~~~~~~~~~~~~~~~

"I was thinking, Zelda…" I said, as I walked over to the counter after getting back together with Brady Paul that same evening. I poured some cola into a glass, "…maybe you should go along with me and Brady Paul to the prom. That would be way cool."

"I don't do proms. And, I'm not a hop-a-long either." Zelda reached for my drink, added some white lightning from her hoodie's pouch. She stirred it with her finger, took a swallow, handed it back to me, and burped in my face.

I laughed. How could I not?

"So not interested in being your safety date, Tu-Tu."

I shook my head and took a sip too.

"Well," Zelda said, as we climbed the private staircase to my suite. The one Rosa used. "I've been thinking too, and I have a scrumptious idea."

"What?"

"About texting. Or, sexting-up your boyfriends' past and present," she said and then chuckled. "Pure sext-pectation."

"Doing what?" I asked, as we entered my room. I locked the bolt behind us.

Damn, I wish I'd gotten that key back from Uncle Monty.

"Get naked!" Zelda exclaimed.

"Huh?"

"You heard me." Zelda pulled my cell from her jeans' pocket.

"You are crazy, Zelda!"

"Maybe." She shrugged her oh-well-get-over-it shoulders. "Strike a pose, Tu-Tu!" She held up my IPhone. "We'll send out to Ashburn – what-you-missed-out-on. And to B.P. – what-you-have-to-look-forward-to pictures."

"You are one crude chick, Zelda." I pulled my tee over my head.

"Brilliant! You're a natural. Pure hooker!" Zelda cranked-up Rock-On-Videos music and entertainment station while clicking away. The girl band Three and a Half Sisters was singing their recent hit Details. "That's it, Tuesday, romance the nerds!"

I sat in the empty tub and dangled one leg over the side, then one arm, then exposed my bashful bare back.

"Work it! That's it, Tu-Tu, play hard to hit!" Zelda said and laughed as she continued to cell-pix me. "Get your flirt on! Careful now, the nipple may make an appearance!"

# My Mistaken Identity

"Hold on a sec!" I pointed at the television. Stormy Gallagher's reality show was coming on. I took a sip of the spiked cola, climbed out of the tub, and wrapped myself in a robe.

Zelda and I stretched out on my bed in the other room to critique Take the World by Stormy on the flat screen.

"She looks hot," I said, "doesn't she?"

"Yeah," Zelda said and laughed. "Especially in the hot tub."

"Did you hear?" I said. "She's written a children's book and going on a book signing tour."

"What's new?" Zelda said and smirked. "All the stars are doing it."

"Did you catch that? She just said something about me." I cranked-up the volume.

"Have you seen Tuesday lately?" Stormy held up The Grapevine tabloid newspaper. "It says her new look is debatable. I say totally punkified! What's up with that? And, that prom gig of hers? What a lame publicity stunt. No doubt it was her mother's and that agent of hers." Their laughter stirred up the steam. "And, who's that dork she's lovin'-up on now? Did you see the yacht she bought his family?"

"Dork?" I leaped to my feet on the bed. "How dare she call Brady Paul that!"

"Check out his rust-standard residence." Stormy held up the paper again. "Park of Palms Subdivision? I so don't think so!" she said and laughed. "It's more like a park that's been seriously bombed!"

"Oh my God, how seedy!" said one of her hot tub buds.

"Let me see," said another chick snagging the paper. "Eww. So trashy."

"Don't let Stormy and her bitchy friends get to you," Zelda said, as she tugged my hand pulling me back down next to her. "Brady Paul's the best thing that ever happened to you."

And so are you, Zelda. I promise I'll never hurt you again. Even though...

"That guy is kind of cute," fessed-up one of Stormy's hot-tubbers.

"He looks gay to me," said the bed-head chick. "Way too pretty."

Stormy snatched the newspaper back and stared at Brady Paul's picture. "Yeah, he is kind of yummy, isn't he? She added a capful of scented oil to the tub. "Hmm, maybe I'll try her new boyfriend on for size. I like variety."

"I despise Stormy!" I tossed a pillow at the flat screen.

"She's most definitely a she-bully," Zelda said.

"I can't believe I actually had the delusion that I wanted to be her! How absurd! I craved those almond-shaped eyes and her freckles sprinkled across her perfect nose and high cheek bones."

Zelda lit a cigarette. "Hey, Tu-Tu, Stormy will never be the singer you are." She blew a smoke ring in the direction of the TV. It formed a noose around Stormy's neck.

I smiled, nodded and focused on the show once again.

"And," continued Stormy, "I've heard from a credible source that her mother is locked-up in a for-real nut house! Why am I not surprised?"

"This is the part," Zelda said, "where you choose to wallow in your tears, roll your eyes or hold your hands over your flame-red ears."

I leaped to my feet again, but this time I snagged Zelda's hand and chose to blow the blahs off and jump and jive. "9-1-1!"

# Chapter Twenty-Seven

## *Desirable Dream*

You started out,

As a distant

Dream.

Untouchable.

Unattainable.

Unbelievable.

Just a

Premeditated,

Recognizable,

Unconceivable,

To be acquaintable,

Desirable

Dream.

~~~~~~~~~~~~~~~~~~~~~~~~

"Well," said Mr. Webb, the principal of William P. DuVal High School a couple of weeks later. He massaged his prickly chin just before he read the results of the committee's vote from the short list. "The theme of this year's prom is..." He glanced up and ran his concerned eyes around the eager faces seated at the cafeteria-sized table.

The students leaned forward while their chests swelled from holding their breath with expectation. Mr. Webb's mouth twisted to the left and then right, another irritated twist back to the left, then right, then opened and announced almost under his breath, "Bitten."

Cheers, high fives and standing O's erupted from all around in the vacant front office. The Pirates of the Caribbean was totally squashed along with the other theme The Wild, Wild West, by the vampire's nighttime activities.

I smiled at Brady Paul. He squeezed my hand under the table.

I should visit more often. I can always lie about the meetings. Just like the little white tale I told today, "No need for you to come, Uncle Monty, Baldwin's going to be there."

"Hold on!" The principal waved his arms as if he were directing a plane onto the runway.

"Tuesday!" said one of the short skirts. "Thanks so much for that awesome idea!"

I'll tell Zelda you said so.

Brady Paul rubbed his calloused thumb across the smooth surface of my palm.

A momma and me déjà vu hit me. "These are your lifelines," my mother had said as she studied my palm. "Fairies don't have these. They will live forever, even the evil fairy, as long as the troll doesn't find them."

"Yeah! I am so looking forward to it!" said another student.

"Me, too!" shouted one from the far end. "I can't wait to get online and check out all the vampire stuff!"

"I'm not done yet!" exclaimed Mr. Webb. He slapped out each cautioning word on the table. "There will be absolutely no vampire masks, blood, or gore permitted."

"The prom will be the coolest yet!" another student added. "I know an awesome website for gothic clothing!"

# My Mistaken Identity

Brady Paul squeezed my hand tight.

*Please don't ever let go.*

"I hope you all are paying attention to me," continued the exasperated principal. "If any student shows up dressed-up like it's Halloween," he slammed the table again, "they won't be permitted to attend!"

Brady Paul's body gravitated toward mine. And mine toward his. I turned my head. He turned his. We smiled at each other. We had talked every night on the phone since Zelda had hooked us back up.

*Don't screw this up.*

"No one will dare miss it!" a girl to my right said.

"This prom totally rocks!" said the guy seated next to her with the buzz-cut.

"Thank you," I said. A grateful smile in their direction overwhelmed my face.

*Thanks, Zelda.*

I took a gulp of congratulatory air. It felt good. Really, really good. I almost felt accepted. Almost.

A teacher-sponsor spoke up as she flipped through a magazine. "What type of decorations should we use?"

"We could get coffins!" said a girl with spiked hair.

"Yeah," her friend added, "Lynsee's dad owns a funeral home."

"No coffins!" Mr. Webb shook his blood-pressure-is-on-the-rise head.

"There's not anything in this catalog listed under that theme," the same teacher said. "But there are plenty of ideas for pirates. Look at this darling ship! You walk the plank into the prom entrance hall." She held up the page. "And just take a gander at this cardboard red barn on the next page. There are even three black and white dairy cows to assemble. And it says here that they moo when you walk past them!"

Brady Paul spoke up next, "Excuse me for interrupting, Ms. Andrews, but I don't think you need to worry about the decorations. Tuesday's already checked-out what there is available."

I kicked him under the table. He grabbed my leg. Oh my God, a pure thrill-up-the-appendage moment. He winked at me.

*Let's hit the beach. Tonight!*

"And," Brady Paul continued, "she's come up with some mighty cool ideas for Bitten – the vampire prom."

"All right!" exclaimed the same guy down the way.

"Let's see 'em!" another student said balancing-his-butt on the edge of his seat.

"With the committee's approval," I said, as I glanced around at all the former T.G.-loathers' stoked faces. And then, at the adults' lack-of-approval sideway glances. "That is…if everyone is really…interested…in taking a look."

My horoscope had warned me to stay low key and let things unfold naturally. So far it was working. Wow, was it ever working!

A unanimous, "Yes!" hit the water-stained ceiling tiles.

"Miss Greenwood," Mr. Webb said with his I'm-warning-you eyes. "We'd appreciate taking a look at what you have prepared for us. But…"

"Yeah, we appreciate it! So, let's see it!" the buzz-cut said. Both of his fists punched the table as if a fork and a knife were clutched in each, and I was about to fulfill his hunger.

"But," continued the principal, "it will be me that will make the final decision."

# My Mistaken Identity

"Yes, sir," I said, "of course." I unrolled my sketch, or should I say Zelda's drawing of the gymnasium decked-out in Bitten. The diagram filled the length of the table. Eager palms pressed it to the chipped Formica surface to keep it from raveling. "Whoa!" the table exclaimed.

"You've got to be kidding me!" A voice screeched. "This is freakin' awesome!"

"Check-out the gargoyle fountains and chandeliers!" said the girl with dark purple lip gloss.

"I love the silver crescent moon balloons and dark tree silhouettes!" said the girl with spiked hair.

"Cool!" said another short skirt, "Look! Old-time streetlights and lanterns!"

"It's quite impressive, Tuesday," Ms. Andrews said, "I do like how you have the tables arranged in groups with the sheer cheesecloth curtains dividing them."

"And..." another teacher-sponsor said, "...the glittery spider web tablecloths are an interesting touch."

"Of course, you can make any changes," I said. "It's all just a suggestion."

"I'm sold!" the buzz-cut said.

"Me, too!" added a girl across from him.

"I'm in!" said another voice.

Mr. Webb walked around the table taking in the drawing with discriminating eyes. "Yes, most likely we will have to make some modifications. This certainly looks very costly. Our budget couldn't possibly cover the..."

That's where the even better news kicks in!" Brady Paul said standing up next to me. "Tuesday's recording company has requested to pick up the entire bill. Including a new stage, sound system and theatre lighting. And, they've asked to pay for both cover bands we hired for that evening – On the Brink and By the Seat of Your Pants."

My eyes could no longer hold back from sucking up the committee's praises. This is what having friends and being in high school was all about. And, having a for-real date to the prom with your steady. I smiled at his class ring hugging my right ring finger wrapped in the sizing-it-down red and black yarn – DuVal High Muskogee's fighting colors. I was going steady!

Unfreakin' believable.

## Chapter Twenty-Eight

### *For You*

My lips were made,

For you to kiss.

My hands,

For you to hold.

My eyes,

For you to read.

My feet,

For you to tickle.

I was made

For you…

To love.

~~~~~~~~~~~~~~~~~~~~~~~~~~~~~~~

"Please, Brady Paul." I held out a pair of ten-dollar button fly patchwork jeans. We were sifting at the Junkyard's Daughter vintage store referred to us by several prom committee members following the meeting. Killing time until the sun went down. Surf's up anybody?

Brady Paul lifted one of the pant's gargantuan bell bottoms and shook his head. "I don't think so, Tuesday."

"Just try them on." I squeezed the jeans in a prayerful clasp. "For me."

He shook his head again and added the abbreviated all-right-fine-whatever eye roll. I tossed them at him. "And, try this on with them." I pulled a honky-tonk white western shirt with multicolored patchwork yokes, pocket flaps and cuffs off a hanger and threw it to him. "You're going to rock that outfit!"

"Damn." He snatched the gingham curtain across the metal plumbing pole and disappeared like a child being scolded and sent to his room.

I had already traded in my clothes and purchased a pair of seventies-ish yellow and brown plaid hip-huggers and a 'You Be Trippin' tee that I now wore. Pure retro. The check-out girl recognized me but promised to not dish out the news. Especially after I autographed the wall behind her where so many other recording artists from the rock 'n' roll past and present had signed as well. My pleasure.

"Do you have it on yet?" I tried to peek.

His hand stretched the gingham curtain. "Hold on!"

"Sorry." I glanced around the store. It was way cool. From the chipped concrete floor splattered with psychedelic paint, to the industrial exposed piped ceiling. T-shirts from as far back as the 1950's hung like pieces of rare art everywhere your eyes roamed. The entire loft was devoted to retro hippie make-love-not-war times. Your nose was flooded with the whiff of incense. And, your ears filled with The Beatles singing Your Mother Should Know a soundtrack from their Magical Mystery Tour album.

Momma loves the Beatles. I wonder how she is. If only she would give Brady Paul a chance, I'm sure she'd love him too.

"How's your mother?" Brady Paul voice seeped through the cotton drape and hit my unprotected head.

"She's awesome. We talk almost every day!"

Liar.

"Glad to hear it."

# My Mistaken Identity

The curtain opened halfway. "You look amazing!"

He stared at his funkified look in the mirror. "You really think so?"

"Most definitely!"

"I feel ridiculous." His fisherman pride kicked in and forced him in the corner of the four by four foot dressing room.

"What about these?" I held out another pair of beige velour bellbottoms.

"What are you thinking?" Brady Paul sank further into his sanctuary. "No way!"

I struck a pout. It wasn't working.

"Tuesday, what about those?" He pointed at a pair of stone-washed black Levis.

I laughed and said, "What a tag hag you are, Brady Paul." I handed him the jeans.

"Uhh, Tuesday..."

"Yeah?" I stared at the curtain dividing us. From each other's arms.

"Thanks."

"For what?"

"The pictures...you...uhh...texted."

What do I say?

"Oh, yeah, those. Uhh...yeah...you're welcome."

Damn. I'd forgotten all about them. So embarrassing. Did I really send them? Oh my God! I so need to change the subject.

"Are you dressed yet?" I asked.

"Yeah." He opened the dressing room curtain. "I can deal with these."

"Turn around." I stood and stared. The Levi's fit. Nice. And, tight. And, low. Really, really balancing on his hips low. His bare chest was perfect, too. And then, there was what I thought was a tattoo. Way wrong. A birthmark surfacing just above the low-down back belt loop.

Sweet.

"I noticed that T-shirt when we first came in." He walked over and lifted the gray tee from the hook – 'Workin' for the Weekend'.

I nodded. "You're right. That is totally you."

"And this is you." He wrapped a long black crocheted scarf around my neck and pulled it like a lasso in his direction till we came together in the dressing room. He jerked the curtain shut. "A kiss for your thoughts, Tuesday."

"I love you."

Oh my God! Did I really say that?

"Tuesday!" said a gruff voice outside the dressing room.

No Way! So not fair! Does he have GPS on me?

"Unde Monty?" I unveiled our hiding place. "Umm, you remember Brady Paul, don't you?"

"Hello." Uncle Monty reached for my hand. "You shouldn't have lied to me."

I offered him up my I-don't-give-a-shit-shoulder shrug.

"It's time for you to leave, Tuesday. Our flight will be taking off in thirty minutes."

# My Mistaken Identity

How did the bloodhound sniff me out?

Over his shoulder I spotted several teens pointing at me.

"I'm not ready." I snagged my hand away from his tight grip and reached for Brady Paul's, who was also wearing now the what-the-hell-is-going-on expression.

More curious shoppers appeared. And the texting and cellphone pixing began.

Damn fame game!

"You don't have a choice. Now, come." Uncle Monty's voice was one of those under-the-breath stern requests. He hated scenes. His voice weakened. "Please, Tuesday honey."

"I don't want to." I snatched up my bottom lip.

Jeez, I sound like a spoiled brat about to throw a tantrum.

"Fine," I said, "but first I have to take Brady Paul home."

And ripcord from you!

"I have already taken care of that, Tuesday," Uncle Monty said. "The rental car company is taking him home. Okie-dokie?"

Just freakin' okie-dokie great.

"I had an awesome time, Tuesday." Brady Paul's lips met my eager ones.

"I'm sorry," I whispered against his.

"Is that really her?" asked a guy with a fuchsia streaked Mohawk.

"Yeah, that's what the chick at the counter said," said another guy.

Damn that check-out girl!

LL Eadie

# Chapter Twenty-Nine

## *Our Love*

Water it,

Fertilize it,

And plant it in full sun.

Our love will grow.

But…

There will be

Drought conditions,

And…

Contamination,

And…

Never forget,

Fertilizer is shit.

And…

Sunshine gives you cancer.

Tell me…

What's Our Love,

About?

~~~~~~~~~~~~~~~~~~~~~~~~~~~~~~~~

I stood and stared at the Rock-on-Videos reporter on TV revealing my recent sin to the airwaves of every household tuned in – Tuesday Greenwood in the Nude. The pictures. My pictures. Totally exposed. In the tub.

I hate Ashburn Fitzgerald!

I snagged my lip and my cell, hit favorites, and punched.

Answer! Please!

"The question is if it really is Tuesday then…" continued the reporter, "…who took these pictures of her?"

"Brady Paul, this is Tuesday. Please call me when you get this message!"

"And, is she really nude?" the Rock-on-Videos' reporter asked. "It sure looks like it."

My cell hit my ear once more.

Why don't you answer?

Text message. "Brady Paul, pleeease call me!"

"We've had a record setting emails and tweets on this," the reporter continued. "And here are some of your comments – I can't believe she would do this! What was she thinking? Hey, Tuesday, give me a call!"

I checked my cell. No messages. But the landline was now ringing. And ringing. And ringing.

How do these freakin' people get our unlisted number? We change it so often I don't even know what it is half the time!

I called his landline.

"Hello."

# My Mistaken Identity

Yes! Someone answered!

"Yes, hello, umm…" I said, "may I speak to Brady Paul?"

"Who is this?" asked the young girl's voice.

"Is this Alley?" I asked.

"Yes."

My door suddenly opened and there stood Uncle Monty. He mouthed the words – "hang up". I motioned for him to get the hell out of my room. Thank God, he did.

Damn, I need to confiscate that key from him.

"This is Tuesday," I said, "Tuesday Greenwood."

"How do I know it's really you?" she asked. "Mommy told me not to talk to any reporters while she was at the marina. They've been calling us a bunch!"

"I'm sorry, Alley," I said. "I know they're such a pain. But this really is me. Don't you remember how I texted you when I was at Brady Paul's school for the first time?"

"Yeah," she said. "Prove it! What did you say?"

Oh, God, what did I say?

"I think I said something like I wish I could meet you. And I wished you had been there to greet me. Didn't I?"

"Yeah, it's you," Alley said, "Wow! It is you!"

"Alley, listen to me," I said. "I need your help. Will you help me?"

"Of course!"

"I need to talk to your brother. Is he home?"

"Yeah, he's in his room. I think."

"I thought I told you, Alley, not to answer the phone while I was gone!"

Damn, it's her mother!

"I'm sorry, Mommy."

"Who are you talking to?"

"Please, Alley!" I said. "Go get your brother!"

"It's Tuesday," Alley said. "She wants to talk to Brady Paul."

"Hello!"

"Brady Paul!" I collapsed onto my bed with my cell committed to my right ear.

"No, Tuesday. This is not Brady Paul. This is his mother."

Oh my God!

"Mrs. Larson, may I speak with him?

"I don't think he wants or needs to talk to the likes of you."

Likes of me?

I shook my head. "Please, Mrs. Larson!"

"Brady Paul is grief stricken over those lewd pictures of you that have surfaced! We told him about you. Your own mother warned us. But he just wouldn't believe us!"

"Please, let me talk to him." I rolled onto my back.

"Your nude-y photos are plastered all over the place! And the high school no doubt is going to can your performance. And, I don't blame them if they do! It would serve you right! Besides, we promised your mother Brady Paul would never set eyes on you again. So, I'm asking, no, I'm telling you to stay the hell away from my son! Your mother told us all about you!"

Is this really happening? Maybe, it's a dream. No, a nightmare. It has to be. But…what if it's not?

"Please, Mrs. Larson." I hugged my pillow, my lip and stared at his class ring hugging my finger.

"There is nothing you can say to him…"

"Please."

"Mom!" Brady Paul's voice was muffled in the background. "Is that Tuesday? Alley told me you were talking to her."

"Yes, it is. And I'm letting her know exactly what I think about…"

"Give me the phone, Mom."

"Your daddy and I told you that girl was up to no good. But you wouldn't listen. You're just infatuated with who she is!"

"Tuesday…"

"Brady Paul…" I was beyond tears. Beyond calm. Beyond sense. Beyond myself.

"Mom leave the room. Please!" he said.

"Brady Paul give me a chance to explain. I'm telling you the pictures were just for fun. Zelda and I were just fooling around when we sent them to this stupid old boyfriend of mine. I didn't mean to hurt you. Please, believe me!"

"Mom, get out of here!"

"Brady Paul, I know they were sort of suggestive, but they didn't show anything! Not really. You know that! But I so understand how you must feel. It was way wrong. Forgive me!"

"I thought those pictures, Tuesday, were meant just for me."

"They were," I said. "You see Zelda sent them as a joke to Ashburn."

"Was it a joke to me, too?"

"No!"

"It's over, Tuesday. I don't know what I was thinking. It was stupid of me to really believe..."

"No!"

"Tuesday, I can't compete with whoever this guy is, or any other guy in your world."

"Believe me, Brady Paul, he means absolutely nothing to me!"

"Don't you see, we're too different, Tuesday. We'll never work out. I was just kidding myself to think that we would."

"Brady Paul..."

"I'm not through," he said, "and I understand if you want your boat back..."

"Hold on!" His mother yelled in the background. "What are you saying?"

"Mom! I asked you to give me some privacy!"

"No, Brady Paul!" I hit manic mode. "It's yours! Forever! I don't want it!"

# My Mistaken Identity

"I'm no good at this, Tuesday. And, neither is my family. We're tired of being a target for the press. Damn, they've made us out like white trailer trash! That's not who we are!"

"Of course, it isn't!"

Why aren't I reaching him? What should I say? What words would make a difference? WWZD?

"And, Tuesday, I've never asked you for anything. Nothing. And, I never will. I should have never allowed my parents to accept..."

"I know! I totally believe you! Don't even think about it! It so doesn't matter to me. I'm sorry about the pictures. But..."

"You're right it doesn't matter. Not anymore, cause I'm not interested in playing the Mr. Tuesday Greenwood role. Not ever. Besides..."

"What can I do to make it right?" I said. "Please, Brady Paul, tell me what it will take to make this up to you. Don't do this to me! I love you!"

The air-gulping tears made an appearance. Mine.

"No, you don't," he said.

"I do!"

"Tuesday, you have no idea what being in love really is."

 "That's not fair!"

Breath fading, heart hurting, crashing, soon.

"Like I was trying to say, Tuesday, there's someone else."

I tasted blood.

# Chapter Thirty

## *Reasons*

Give me a reason,

To not trust you.

Give me a reason,

To hate you.

Why am I so attracted...

To you?

I shouldn't,

Trust you.

I should,

Hate you!

For so many reasons!

~~~~~~~~~~~~~~~~~~~~~~~~~~~~~~~~~~

Zelda stuck her right hand into her mouth and began gnawing on her nubby nails as I lay in bed. "You stink."

I rolled onto my side in my bed away from Zelda. "Gee, thanks." I pinched my lip.

My focus was now tarnished, twisted, malignant, on the edge of another cliff.

Please, Brady Paul, forgive me. Or else...

Zelda spat one of her fingernails onto the marble floor. "Don't go and get all butt hurt. Do you think I care?" she said. "I don't give a shit what anybody does. Or thinks. Or says. Including you."

"Good!" I pulled the comforter over my head. It smelled way too familiar. I hadn't climbed out of bed in days. Or was it weeks. Not sure. Pure endless misery.

"Later!" Zelda said.

The door slammed. I sat up and panicked. "Wait!" I exclaimed. "Don't go! Please!"

"Beg," Zelda said, as her one exposed eye peeked around the door jam. "I so love it when you do that." She snarkled.

I smiled. Sort of. And shook my head and begged.

"All right." I grasped my hands as if in prayer. "Please, Zelda, my best bud and sissy in the whole-wide-freakin'-world, don't leave me."

"Brilliant! That's way better." She retraced her steps back into my room and shut the door behind her.

I took a deep breath, held it and nodded an exhale as my back reversed onto the headboard. I pulled my knees to my chest and began to rock. Back and forth and back and forth and...

"Hey, where's that dorky going steady ring you were sporting?" She picked up my hand.

I shook my head. Tears took over. "It's over! Didn't you hear? Everyone else has. The photos you texted were posted on the internet and surfaced on TV. And, now they're on the cover of every tabloid magazine."

"Yeah, yeah, yeah. I heard all about it. Bor-ing. But, hey, look at this way – you're more famous now than ever before. Seriously, you've never had so much press coverage. This scuffed-up image has totally rocked your web presence. You should thank me."

I shook my head and rolled to my side away from Zelda.

Does she really believe that?

Zelda sat down next to me. Then lay by my side and we spooned. "Your bubble has finally been popped. Just think, Tu-Tu, you've chewed your last piece of bubblegum. You should be celebrating!"

"His parents found out we were seeing each other."

"So? Why should he care? It's most definitely a fake-up, Tu-Tu, not a break-up."

I shook my head. "He has a girl friend."

"That sucks." Zelda's turn to shake her head. "Okay, what else is freakin' going on? Divulge the drama."

"The prom gig might be over, too."

Zelda didn't respond.

"It's all Stormy's fault. She even bragged responsibility for my pictures being released on her InUrFace blog. Ashburn must have shared them with her."

"Jaded by Stormy Gag-alicious Gallagher, huh?"

"Brady Paul is pissed. He said my mother must have been spot-on about me and my..." I blew my nose on the sheet. "...boy toys. And he said he's tired of being stalked and hassled by the paparazzi, and mad as hell at all the serious hits from the media. Their tabloid headlines making him and his family out as trash. And him as a gold suckin' leech. He says he doesn't want the title of Mr. Tuesday Greenwood!"

"I'm sorry, Tu-Tu." She wrapped her arms around me.

## My Mistaken Identity

"My life is so whacked!"

Zelda squeezed me tighter. "Hold on, don't slip that purity ring back on yet, Tuesday, and give in to your solo status." She released me and jumped to her feet. "Let's kick some Ashburn and Stormy butt!" She began to bounce. "And take care of those boyfriend hackers with a public poke! Let's find out where they hang-out their cushy asses on Saturday night. And, interrupt their fun. Together."

I leaped to my feet and shrieked, "9-1-1! Five, four, three, two, one! Dance!"

LL Eadie

# Chapter Thirty-One

## *Lucky*

I'm lucky,

You say.

Hey!

Be my guest.

Jump!

Into my skin.

And…digest,

My

Repressed, possessed, unconfessed

Suckie life!

~~~~~~~~~~~~~~~~~~~~~~~~~~~~~~

"What makes you think they'll be at this no-happening hot spot of a club?" Zelda followed me through the parking lot of the retro club – The Final Groove.

"Because Ashburn and Stormy's haunts were plastered all over club notes in the Grapevine," I said. "This is their hell hole of choice for the moment."

"Hey, isn't that…?"

"Yes, it is." I stopped. Zelda rear-ended me.

"You didn't tell me Ashburn was wheelchair material."

"He isn't." I watched in what-in-the-hell-is-he-doing as Ashburn parked up front and center in the $250.00 parking space. Of course, that was the fine.

"Awe, so glad we no longer have to say where is that camera when I need it?" Zelda snatched my Iphone from her pack and captured the fining moment.

"Perfect!" I exclaimed.

"That was way too freakin' easy," Zelda said as she slipped the evidence back in her bag. "Now let's deflate some tires."

After we flattened his tires, we headed to a thirty-five dollar per hour star-treatment-retreat upstairs lit only by the florescent glow of multi-colored lava lamps highlighting the vintage troll dolls lining the walls with their shocking colored mohair. The cushy room with a view of the adults-behaving-badly dance floor scene. The DJ, The Widow Maker, was stoking up the trendy crowd playing Struck by a Geyser by the fierce band Lost Cause.

"This place needs friction," Zelda complained as she plopped down on the sink-your-ass-in-and-can't-climb-out-of purple velvet covered waterbed with uncoordinated neon colored pillows. "Where's the stage diving and crowd surfing?" She picked up the furry orange one and tossed it at my face.

"Enough!" I pitched the lime green one at hers as I dropped into a leopard printed beanbag chair.

Zelda batted it into a life size florescent copy of an Andy Warhol print of Marilyn Monroe above my head. Other retro posters lined the walls: peace signs, zodiac symbols and a bra-burning for women's rights.

Zelda pulled off her kiddie-sized backpack and stretched out. She tugged at her wedgie in a pair of gutter-punk black jeans, which were most definitely booty-cutters. "Maybe they'll get down with a Jell-O slip 'n' slide tonight," she said and smirked.

I shook my head and laughed as a waitress dressed in Wonder Woman garb appeared around the tie-dyed curtain with complimentary glow-in-the-dark glasses of virgin-tinis and not-so-healthy hors d'oeuvres and cheese fondue. Delicioso.

"Leave the tray." Zelda snatched a fried stuffed mushroom and bit into it. It squirted juice down her chin and onto her Hello-Shitty T-shirt.

I shook my head, as the female superhero escaped our captivity. I pulled at my Power Rangers' XS tee. My chest circumference was stretching out the heads of the Power Rangers. Pure distortion.

"I spy," Zelda said staring through the one-way-mirrored window, "the totally top of your do-not-call list again."

My eyes meandered the crowd of torrid torsos of groomed guys and straight-up sexy girls till I finally spotted Ashburn next to an empty chair. The so-called I'm-not-gay seat with unknown guy friend seated in the next.

"I think I'll go mix things up." Zelda rolled out of the waterbed and headed for ground zero. "And check out the prey. Maybe I'll get lucky and take home some numbers."

"Maybe," I said, "I should make that trip, too."

"I don't think so, Tu-Tu!" Zelda disappeared behind the curtain. She stuck her head back around. "Take notes."

What is she up to? Did she come to play?

Marooned, I watched with blurred boundaries as Zelda moved in on my former bad habit – Ashburn Fitzgerald. He looked hot. Always did. Damn him.

Why does it still hurt?

Ashburn smiled his on-the-prowl grin as Zelda approached him and even got up and gave her a nice-to-meet-cha kiss on the cheek. Or, was it a so-good-to-see-ya-again smack? Strange.

They moved onto the dance floor as I stood at the picture window and soaked up the scene. They were rubbing and rocking to the music.

Zelda was way wrong. This place did have friction. Just the disturbing kind. Ashburn on Zelda. Or, was it Zelda on Ashburn?

I couldn't wait any longer and headed for the deep floor of accomplished dirty dancers and stopped in my Converse high tops at the sight of last year's Teen Choice Award recipient – Stormy Gag-alicious Gallagher with her electric blue contacts. The most recent queen of the social scene rocked a not-so-innocent mini skirt.

She stared-down Zelda and Ashburn with her scanty dressed crew of the bitching-hour. Then she made her move on Zelda. Her hip swung into Zelda's gyrating one. Zelda spun around and planted her lips right on Stormy's.

I can't believe Zelda just did that!

Why was I down here anyway? To dance with Ashburn?

No way!

I returned to my safety vault following the framed psychedelic posters of rock-n-roll yester-year – Pink Floyd, Jimi Hendrix, The Who, Led Zeppelin, and Bob Dylan.

"Excuse me." Wonder Woman reentered the enclave with a tray full of goodies. "Would you like anything else? Perhaps another 'tini of your choice? We have apple, chocolate cranberry, blueberry ..." She pointed them out.

I nodded.

"This one?" she asked lifting the chocolate one.

"Yeah, that's fine." I really didn't care.

## My Mistaken Identity

She handed it to me. "If you need anything just call," she pointed at the pink princess phone sitting on the round furry table. "Anything at all, Tuesday."

Shit.

I watched her tug on her Wonder Woman lifted-costume-cleavage as she hooked up with Superman in the hallway before my eyes dove back into the pool of fab bodies moving beneath me on the tri-level dance floor. The caged go-go girls in micro-mini skirts with shellacked boots, black lights, strobe lights and several rotating mirrored disco balls just added to the confusion.

Unable to identify my target I turned toward the tie-dyed exit. But before I did, I picked up the martini, drained it and set the glass on the tray.

Eww. That so wasn't a virgin.

I popped a mushroom in my mouth, chewed, swallowed, and, burped out loud. Really, really loud.

A momma and me de'ja' vu involuntarily nudged my mind – my mother totally splurging and taking me out to dinner for my fifth birthday, where I burped after downing a rare-to-my-little-girl-diet a complete glass of soda fountain cola.

"Tuesday," my mother had said, "don't you know how rude that is to belch? We learn our best manners from fairies. They would never do anything like that. They're fairy sweet. Only ugly trolls make disgusting body sounds."

I wanted to be her Sugar Plum fairy so badly that I never ever burped in public again. Until now.

Then another body function screamed for release – my bladder.

"I thought that was you, Tuesday Greenwood." Stormy said, as I entered the club's VIP ladies' lounge upstairs. She lit up a bidis – a flavored, leaf-wrapped cigarette from India.

She thinks she's so cool.

Isn't she the spokesperson for Smoke-out America Teens?

"Oh, yeah, it's me." I kept walking toward a corrugated metal stall trimmed in cheetah print faux fur.

"Do tell, Tuesday, where do you buy your clothes lately?" she asked and smirked.

"Like I would divulge that to you." I closed the door, pulled on my studded belt to release my jeans, and dropped onto the toilet seat. Without a seat cover. Eww.

"Did you guys see Tuesday?" Stormy said.

"Yeah, what is that she has on?" said one of Stormy's friends. "Totally skuzzy!"

"Maybe that explains her gutter-moves on Ashburn," another one said.

"Once a slut," Stormy said, "always a slut."

Don't lose it! Do something! Take advantage of this Kodak moment. Now! That's what Zelda would do.

I snagged my cell from my messenger bag, aimed it through the stall crack and click. Done. And so was Stormy's tobacco-free sponsors.

"My guess is, Stormy," Zelda said, as she suddenly joined the Tuesday-bashing party in the restroom, "you're just not into sharing, huh? Too bad. I so thought you were into boyfriend swapping. Guess I was way wrong, huh?"

"Shut up, bitch!" Stormy said.

"You make like a bitch," Zelda said, "and bark!"

"I said shut your mouth!"

# My Mistaken Identity

"You know what your problem is, Stormy?" Zelda said, "You have an oversized ego. And, ass!"

"What did you say?"

"I'm sorry, Stormy," Zelda said, "do you have one of those lazy thyroids?"

"I'm gonna kick your scrawny ass!" Stormy exclaimed.

"Come on!" Zelda exclaimed. "Let's take it to the club with a friendly competition for the sake of your fans. We so don't want them to miss out, do we? Or, Ashburn. Of course, I'll slay you in the end. You don't mind a little public poke, do you? In your cow patty brown eyes!"

"GET OUT OF MY FACE!" Stormy shouted.

"I am so not down with ripcording on a bad note," Zelda said. "Why don't we swap Ashburn stories? You first this time. Since last time, I sort of heard you got all hot and bothered and rushed out to hit it. I just wanted to get that off my chest. You understand, don't you, Stormy?"

"You're totally messed up!" Stormy exclaimed.

"Oh, I see how it is," Zelda said. "You want some more of me. I gave you a rush, huh? I'm pretty good, aren't I?"

"You are one crazy bitch!" Stormy said, as she and her suck-ups hit the club.

Without a kiss from Zelda.

LL Eadie

# Chapter Thirty-Two

## *At Day's End*

What do you think about,

At day's end?

Me?

Yourself?

Or,

Is there,

Someone else?

~~~~~~~~~~~~~~~~~~~~~~~~~~

"Hey, check it out!" Zelda exclaimed as she pointed to a TV anchored high in the corner of Henry's Diner after leaving The Final Groove. "It's time for some Good Bitch versus Bad Bitch sitcom reruns."

Jeez, The Jazmyn and Justyce Show. Hadn't I suffered enough this evening?

"Time to send out to cyberspace some good news to a current event magazine," Zelda said as she pulled her cell from her backpack. "The fine will not compare to the hot mess Ashburn will find himself buried in when the blue-designated-disabled-parkers' club get through with his lazy ass."

"I grinned and added, "I have a fun candid shot too of Stormy smoking." I held up my IPhone exposing the menthol suck.

Zelda high-fived me. "Doubt she'll be the smokeless spokesperson for that group much longer."

My smile widened. "Who should we send them to?" I shoved my plate of half eaten waffles toward the napkin holder beside me. "We most definitely want to spread the good news around."

"Let's send it directly to The Grapevine. Do you know they're email?" Zelda said as she tipped the syrup bottle into her mouth. I nodded as she swallowed and wiped her sticky mouth on the sleeve of her jean jacket. "Cool! They'll know just what to do with them. I can't wait to hear the raving reviews. Pure revenge." Mrs. Butterworth's found her way back to Zelda's lips.

"Young lady!" The 24/7 breakfast diners' waitress, with the fat stain on her blouse, stood with her hands encased on her XXL hips in a defiant pose at our table. "I'm not going to tell you again to get that bottle of syrup out of your mouth!"

The wasted looking couple in the next booth craned their necks to take notes, along with a Cro-Magnon criminal type at the six-swivel-stool bar.

"I'm sorry." Zelda dropped the sticky bottle from her lips and held it out. "I didn't mean to hog it. Did you want some? It is yummy, isn't it?"

The lame midnight diner's audience applauded with raucous laughter.

"That's it!" The waitress thrust her hand at the cloudy glass door three empty graffiti-decorated booths away. "Get out of here, you lunatic, before I call the law!"

The cook at the smoky grill stopped pouring waffle batter onto the griddle. He wiped his hands on his soiled apron and squinted through his fogged-up glasses with a way defeatist expression. Pure non-threatening specie.

"You want us to just dine and dash?" Zelda pushed her plate of waffle residue toward the waitress. "What about your tip?"

"Just pay the goddamn bill and get the hell out!" she shouted.

## My Mistaken Identity

I snorted a smirk as I laid a twenty-dollar bill on the chipped Formica table top and dug around in my purse for some change. Zelda snatched up the money and rushed to the door. "Hey, here's a tip – use soda water on that oinky grease spot."

The diner's pulse exploded with hysteria.

"You asked for it!" the waitress said. "Henry, call the police!"

I hopped into the driver's seat of my Benz and screeched my tires out of the parking lot. "You're freakin' crazy tonight, Zelda!"

Zelda started laughing and laughing. And laughing. And I had no choice but to…Too…How could I not?

"Detour!" Zelda pointed at the public park up ahead.

I pulled into the vacant lot and bailed out and ran straight for my all-time favorite playground equipment – the swing set. Zelda and I swung so high the chain jerked at the top. I closed my eyes and felt the mysterious tickle deep inside. The one that planted a smile on your face and forced you to giggle out loud.

That thought spurned-on a momma and me de'ja' vu moment. "The butterflies you feel when swinging with your eyes shut is just how fairies feel when they're flying," my mother had said. "Sometimes you might even see one flittering by when you peek." I opened my eyes to see if I could possibly catch a glimpse of a fairy. Just like old times. There's no such thing as fairies. And, trolls. And…is Zelda really Uncle Monty's daughter?

"Tuesday, come on." Zelda jumped out of the swing and headed for the car.

I leaped off too into the air just like a fairy.

"Talk about how I drive," Zelda said, "You need to revisit driver's ed. You're a freakin' road parrot!"

"I'm a what?"

"You're riding the shoulder of the road," Zelda said and snarkled.

It happened just then – a blue light in my rearview mirror.

"This sucks!" Zelda said.

"Do me a favor, Zelda, and don't say a word! Okay?" I pulled over to the curb.

Zelda stared at me with a smirk. "Why not? I can handle this T.G. shit-uation probably better than you."

"No, damn it, you can't! Now, pinky swear!" Our fingers locked in the promising embrace just before the officer tapped on my window. I rolled it down. "Yes, sir?"

"I need to see your driver's license and your car registration, ma'am." The deputy shined the flashlight into my car. He scoped out not only the front, but also the back seat as well.

"Yes, sir." I reached for my purse and handed him my wallet opened to Brady Paul's school picture. I pulled that picture out to expose my mother's. It wasn't one of her glamour shots that she liked, but it was the one I adored. It was her as a young girl around my age. "Here," I said pulling my license out from under that untouched photo.

The flashlight shined in my face. I squinted as I held out my license.

My hands were shaking. My heart was pounding. My stomach was sick.

Zelda reached into my glove compartment and handed me my registration. She smiled. I mouthed the words "thank you".

She whispered, "If all else fails rally the boobs." And, snarkled.

# My Mistaken Identity

"Could you not?" I said through clenched teeth.

"Are you the actress?" he asked.

"Yes, sir."

"I didn't recognize you," he said. "I guess young girls your age are always changing their hair. I have a lot to look forward to with my daughter."

"You have a daughter, sir?"

The officer cleared his throat. "Yes, but she's much younger than you."

"How old…"

He cut me off. "Well, Miss Greenwood, we have a complaint. I need to ask you if you were eating at Henry's Diner about thirty minutes ago."

"Where?" I said with as much innocence as I could suck to the surface. Thank God for my acting lessons.

"Henry's Diner," the deputy repeated. The flashlight continued its prowling.

"I've never heard of it," I lied.

"I believe you," the deputy said, "I doubt that's anywhere you would eat. But I have to ask where you were then around that time?"

I pulled up the sleeve of my 70's something jean jacket. "I was at the Full Body Detailing Tattoo Parlor. See, the artist there inked these amazing fairy wings on my wrist tonight." I peeled back the gauze for admiration and proof. The white wings were outlined intricately in black. Of course, I really received the tattoo way before the fun began at The Final Groove.

"Wings, huh?" The light hit it. "Nice."

"Yes, sir, thank you." I said, sealing it back up. "They remind me of my mother who tells the most amazing fairy tales."

He nodded. "Mmm-hmm."

I smiled. At the light.

"Are you under the influence?" he asked.

Yes, Zelda's.

I shook my head. "No, sir."

"Can you explain to me, Miss Greenwood, what you were doing when your car was riding on the shoulder of the road?" He clicked off his flashlight. Finally.

"I'm sorry, officer, I confess I was using my cell phone to call home and inform my Momma I was on my way," I said. And fibbed well.

"Do you know how many accidents everyday there are from people talking on their cell phones instead of keeping their minds on the road?" He leaned forward and rested his hands on my window sill.

"No, sir, but I'm sure way too many," I said. "It was foolish of me. Your car should most definitely be a no-phone zone."

"Yes, I agree. Now, Miss Greenwood." He patted the window frame and dipped even further to look me in the eye. He had a kind face. A father's face. If only. "I know you're a bright young lady with a promising future ahead of you and I would hate to see that come to a tragic end from a vehicular accident."

"Me, too."

Zelda nudged me in the ribs. I pushed her hand away.

"My daughter, Latisha, is a big fan of yours." He smiled. "In fact, she watches your show The Jackie and Jill…"

"The Jazmyn and Justyce Show?" I said and smiled. Another nudge from Zelda.

"Yes, that's the one!" He said and chuckled. "Latisha was so upset when they cancelled your season."

"Wow! What an awesome compliment," I said, "Hey, do you by chance have a sheet of paper I'll be glad to autograph it to her – Latisha – my biggest fan!"

"I thought I was," Zelda whispered and snarkled.

I reached out to shush her.

She giggled.

"Why sure!" the officer said as his entire face lit up more than his flashlight. "Why don't you sign this ticket that I'm not gonna issue you."

Thank God. Fame game.

LL Eadie

# Chapter Thirty-Three

## *Not Knowing*

Is it truly possible?

Not to know,

The difference?

Between...

Truth and lies?

Insomnia...Sleep?

Pleasure...Pain?

Resuscitate

or

Expiration?

Do you?

Are you really, really sure?

I'm not.

~~~~~~~~~~~~~~~~~~~~~~~~~~~~~~

"We need to talk," Uncle Monty said the following day, as I floated on a chaise. He stood in a pair of white linen perfectly pressed slacks by the stone steps leading into the pool. The early spring sun was blistering the top of his head where beads of sweat were forming. The palm trees offered little shade by the pool.

"We already did." I paddled away from him.

"No, you refused," he said. "Remember? So, let's talk this out. I'm not mad at you, Tuesday. I just want to help. So, like I said, we need to discuss what's been going on."

"No, we don't." I closed my eyes. Sleep was impossible. Pure deprivation. So unexplainable. One day I can't wake up and the next day my eyes refused to hit the rem button. I wondered if it was possible though to cat nap and then I would just roll off this raft into the water and...

"Yes, Tuesday honey, we do need to talk." He moved under the umbrella table and took a seat and a sip of his gin and tonic. The ice was melting at high def speed.

I'm not talking to you, Monty honey, about my pictures. Now if you want to discuss Ashburn and Stormy's I'll be more than ecstatic to share. Everyone else is enjoying them!

Or better yet – let's discuss Zelda!

Or...maybe not.

"First, let's discuss your mother. I'm having her reevaluated. It seems she's taken a turn for the worse."

I opened my eyes. The sun forced me to shade them even more than my UV eyewear provided. I waited for more news.

Did this have something to do with me? Did I cause this? Was Uncle Monty right? I shouldn't have called her?

"Could you like narrow that down for me," I said as I reached for my sore lip.

"It seems Constance, I mean your Momma, has not been taking her medicine. She's either been hiding the pills or throwing them away."

I attempted an I-don't-give-a-shit shrug. Botched effort. It just wasn't happening. Not now. My stomach growled. I was famished. Really, really hungry. Tired of my vending machine diet of late. I was way in need of some for-real food.

"You see, Tuesday honey, the medication was causing her to gain weight. And she was losing her hair. And, you know how she is."

"Yeah, pure vanity crisis, I'm sure."

I tried to float away. Momma and me de'ja' vu slapped me like a wave. "See, Tu-Tu, when dandelions dry out a parachute ball opens," my mother had said, as I held the white feathery flower in my hand. "Blow it, Sugar Plum, and watch the fairies float away."

"Once we get her stabilized," Uncle Monty said, "she'll be able to come home. Of course, even with treatment, mood changes can occur. She may have another severe episode and have to be hospitalized again. I'll be heading back up there for a couple of days for another evaluation. The threat of suicide is very real."

"I think I'm really, really set with all the decorations for the prom," I said. "The students loved everything I came up with. They're so stoked!"

"Tuesday, are you paying attention to me?"

"I was thinking about maybe doing another number. Something totally…"

"Tuesday!" Uncle Monty exclaimed.

He stood up and, walked over to the pool.

"Look at me!"

He squatted down, snagged my lounge, spun it around to face him and removed his designer shades.

"Are you on drugs?" he asked.

"What?"

"Let me see your eyes."

I raised my sunglasses to the top of my head like a headband and smirked at him.

"Okie dokie?" I shook my head while making a stupid face. "Do I look like I'm high?"

He sat back down. "You realize the prom deal is still up in the air. Don't you? You made a poor decision, Tuesday."

I flipped my sunglasses back on. "I don't want to talk about it."

"I think we should."

"I said I don't want to discuss it!"

Minutes, clouds and salty breezes past by.

"Are you still here?" I rolled off the raft and headed for the steps.

Z-moment ambush – "Monty craves full control over you as if you were his freakin' private property. That is just wrong."

"The principal, Mr. Webb, informed me of the school's position several days ago." Uncle Monty reached for my towel and headed toward me. "He said he's going ahead with the gym renovations."

I said and snarkled. "Of course."

"And for the moment," Uncle Monty said, "your scheduled practices with the students, which have been working so hard on your performance, with Baldwin, will continue. Just in case, it's a go. The prom is just a few weeks away."

"How convenient for them." I snorted a smirk as I stepped onto the sandstone pool deck.

## My Mistaken Identity

My horoscope for the day had read – A situation with your current position may make you realize you aren't doing what you really want. Look to someone who has always been there for you for guidance.

It damn sure isn't Uncle Monty. He doesn't know spit!

He stretched out the towel the length of his arm span. "But, it's in the hands of the school board, Tuesday honey, whether we pull this off. They're holding an emergency meeting soon to make a decision. I don't know what possessed you to take those pictures and send them…"

I walked away. Wet.

LL Eadie

# Chapter Thirty-Four

## *Is it True?*

I once heard,

That you could,

Smell fear.

Is it true?

What does it smell like?

Sweat?

Or

Shit?

Both caused by…

Created by…

Generated by…

Fear.

~~~~~~~~~~~~~~~~~~~~~~~~~~

"Zelda, are you here?" I knocked on her posh apartment's door above the garage that same week. I couldn't wait to share my latest scuffed-up existence with her – my shabby-sheek suite. It was her welcome-home-week surprise.

I had totally changed it up the two days that Uncle Monty was away. It was industrial. It was antique-y. It was mismatched. It was my taste. And I loved it! I had swapped everything I had for the thrift look at the same second-hand store Zelda took me to. I even donated my trendy clothes as well.

There was one dress I didn't toss and that was the black lacey one Zelda held up to her that first night we met. She had wanted to borrow it. Now it was hers.

I stuck the key into the door. "Zelda?" It didn't make sense I thought this was our week to hang. I hadn't seen or heard from her at all since last month. Not even a text. I walked in, shut the door and crammed the key back into my jean pocket. The place was totally trashed. Pure ripe. I wondered if Rosa had taken notice. Or, Uncle Monty. How long had it been like this?

I kicked her dirty clothes out of my way as I walked into one of the two bedrooms. "Zelda?" Everywhere I looked there was chaos. Clothes spilling out of drawers, to-go bags of forgotten food, mildewed bed and bath linens, mounds of cigarette butts...Serious ick.

Zelda was way too obscure. I scoured the place for a note perhaps. An explanation. Tonight, we had plans I thought. She had told me about this new club – The Squeeze-In the last time we hung. The band – Head in the Gutter that was playing there tonight.

It was our celebratory night-out springing from Ashburn and Stormy's demise. Neither had been seen in public. Pure low profile. Their character reputation management control was in high-def gear now. To repair, rebuild and redeem their regret. No doubt a public apology would be issued soon.

Hah! Good freakin' luck, you back stabbers!

But what was Zelda's deal?

I celled her. No answer.

Did she go without me?

Do I have the weeks confused?

Maybe it isn't her week to return.

# My Mistaken Identity

I flung the comforter to the footboard of her bed and there staring back at me with her head on a pillow was my limbless baby doll – Sissy. My breath reversed into my chest and I held it there while my feet attempted to back up too. However, they got tangled up in the handles of Zelda's backpack. I tumbled to the floor landing on my butt.

Underneath one hand were several candy wrappers and under the other one was a notebook. One of those composition books with the black and white marbleized covers. I opened it and began to read. It was Zelda's journal. A peek into her strange head.

First page – Tuesday is such a waste of time. Mine!

Huh?

Second page – How much longer can I take her? What a spoiled brat. I so need to end this relation-shit! No problem. She'll take care of it.

What?

Third page – Pure brutal hanging out with the pop princess! What a weak, insecure, withdrawn, over-protected, scared chicken shit chick!

I don't believe this!

I flipped to somewhere in the middle – She's licking out of my hand now. Pure mind control! Way vulnerable! So easily schmoozed!

No way!

Next page – Tuesday truly believes she's cool now! She's not!

Oh my God!

Skipped a few pages – Monty is a sicko!

Why does she hate him so?

And me?

Same page at the bottom – Constance is a constant pain in the ass!

You've never seen her other side.

Turned to next page – Tuesday still doesn't get it! What a freak!

Huh? Is she talking about her being Uncle Monty's daughter?

Two pages before that – She's throwing herself at BP! Just like she pushed herself on Ashburn! And, all the others!

I paused and pinched my lip. Harder. And, harder.

A few pages before the last one – Can you believe she still hasn't caught on??? Maybe she never will.

Another stumble.

The page before that – She's in denial. Can't wait for the big reveal!

Of what?

Last page – Hi, Tuesday! Fun read, huh?

Shit!

# Chapter Thirty-Five

## *Reality*

What is it,

Really...

Reality?

Be real,

Stay real,

For how long?

Is...

Back to...

Reality?

~~~~~~~~~~~~~~~~~~~~

I rushed to my suite to my computer. I checked my e-mail inbox – multiple messages from Zelda.

First message – Hi, T.G. – Ur album should be titled – 3rd Day of the WEAK!

Why is she doing this? Why does she want to hurt me? I trusted her. I loved her. She was my sissy.

Second message – Are you rocking back and forth yet?

Damn her!

Third message – Have you checked out your horoscope today, Tu-Tu?

-----PERSONAL DECEPTION IS APPARENT-----

Fourth message – What about ur fave tabloid mag The Grapevine? Seems like they have more than Ashburn and Stormy's pix. I heard they also have one hot pix of U and Ashburn. Oops! I mean – me and Ashburn. ;) And you on Stormy. I mean – me suckin' Stormy's tongue. 9-1-1! Later!

I hit the reply button – I HATE YOU!!!!!!!!!!!!!!!! BITCH!!!!!!!!!!!!!!!!!!

Brady Paul's e-mail address stared back at me from my BFF list. I had to try. I typed – Brady Paul, it wasn't me dancing with Ashburn! Or, kissing Stormy! It was Zelda! Believe me! Please! I LOVE YOU!!! TODAY!!! TOMORROW!!!FOR ALWAYS!!!

Why did I dye my hair? And cut it? Just like Zelda's? What an idiot I am!

Is anyone out there? I typed frantically onto Tu-Tu's InUrFace page. Do you ever feel like you are going crazy? Sometimes I feel a little bit ScHiZo. Do I have company? Please say yes! At least answer this for me – What's real? And what is delusional? Answer me! Damn it! I hate! Hate! HATE! MySeLf!!! Am I fixable? Is anyone out there? Please answer!

"Tuesday?"

"Oh my God!" I jumped up from the computer and knocked over my bottled water. "You scared the shit out of me!"

"I'm sorry." Uncle Monty picked up the capped bottle that rolled across the marble floor to the toe of his Italian leather loafer.

"What do you want?" I stared at him and his squinty right eye. I sat back down, reached over and unplugged cyberspace.

This is my room. I should at least have privacy. I should demand that key back!

"I'm actually the bearer of some rather interesting news." He walked over and pulled up a distressed wood chair next to the piano stool I was sitting on. "Is this new?" He looked down at the chair, next at mine and then around the room.

Two walls of my computer room were now covered with a grouping of old bookcases. Besides hardback books on the shelves there were also vintage ashtrays, wind-up alarm clocks, coffee stained mugs, chipped ceramic bowls, rusted tin lunch boxes, abandoned rag dolls, board games with missing pieces, just about anything dated, and most definitely nothing in mint condition. Across the room was an old park bench with a multicolored hand knitted afghan thrown around the shoulders of a headless mannequin sitting on it.

"What happened in here?" Uncle Monty's face turned to disgust. "Where are all your nice things?"

I stood up. "I got rid of them. It is my room, you know?"

"Of course, it is, Tuesday honey, but…"

"I like it. Okay?"

"If…" Uncle Monty stared at the enormous rabbit lamp sitting on an oversized plastic cube. The rabbit's ears were hidden beneath the black shade. "…if this is what you want…but…. I'm not too sure how your…"

"I don't care what she thinks!"

"Okay," Uncle Monty said. "I hope you had it all disinfected before…"

"Don't worry you're not going to be contaminated. Rosa helped."

Well, as I was saying about the good news…"

Why do I always have to listen? Maybe what he thinks is so good, is crap to me.

"Don't you want to hear?"

"All right, fine, whatever." I remained standing. "What's up with Momma?"

"No, my news has nothing to do with your mother, Tuesday, but she is doing much better," Uncle Monty said as he reached for my hand. "Actually, I spoke with Glissando Records today when I returned."

"So?" I yanked my hand away and walked toward my bedroom. The nightlight in my room advanced my steps. "Say it already."

Are they releasing me from my contract? That is good.

I think.

"Glissando is prepared to allow the first song on your album," Uncle Monty said as he shadowed me, "to go out as a free online stream a week before it's released. Just as you requested, Tuesday honey."

That is good news.

Why then don't I give a shit? I squeezed my lip.

"Great." I headed for my comfort zone – my new bed with the picket fence double gate headboard. The bay window behind it no longer was draped in luxurious curtains but oversized printed scarves tied together. I stretched out on the patchwork handmade quilt. It smelled unfamiliar. And so did the remnant pillows tossed on it.

"So," Uncle Monty said as he stopped and stared into my bedroom, "you refurnished your entire suite?"

"That's what I said." I smiled as I glanced around my cozy room. Zelda was way right. This felt for-real. Everywhere I looked there was inspiration. This was the new scuffed-up me.

# My Mistaken Identity

"It's certainly interesting," Uncle Monty said as he picked up a 33 album from the stack on top of an old record player. "Does this thing actually work?"

I nodded. "I guess Glissando hasn't heard about my little scandal yet, huh?"

Damn, it wasn't even me in those stupid pictures.

Uncle Monty sprayed halitosis relief into his mouth before continuing. "The pictures. Of course." He walked back and sat down on the edge of my bed, turned off my Felix the Cat lamp on the metal nightstand and patted my leg. I moved it away. "Glissando said, get this – great timing."

Huh? No way!

"I was surprised too." Uncle Monty chuckled. "They said they were happy with your illicit exposure. That it brought on a new vibe, original twist and fresh look for you. He stood up and walked to the footboard of my bed and faced me.

Eww. What is he looking at with that squinty pupil of his? Zelda's right – he is creepy.

I pulled the quilt up to my neck covering my black attire. My stirrup-ruffled legwarmers, spin-art fishnet tights, and Victorian-styled mini lace jumper.

"Glissando," Uncle Monty continued, "thinks the timing is perfect and will only help with the anticipation of the release of your album The Third Day of the Week to a new larger more mature audience with your new pop-soul sound. In fact, they said there's a young adult comic book series in the works for you!"

I shook my head in amazement.

None of this makes any sense.

"Oh, and if anyone asks you about the bathtub pictures," Uncle Monty said, "you're to answer that they were shots for the cover of your

CD, and someone secretly released them without Glissando's permission."

"Huh?"

"I know." Uncle Monty shook his head. "Baldwin talked them into this. He said they're just what you needed. So, believe it or not, one of the shots will be selected soon for the cover. They'll need the proofs, Tuesday honey, ASAP."

I shook my head in slow-motion.

"And," Uncle Monty said, "they didn't even mind your recent night club antics either."

What's up with ultra- conservative Glissando? They're totally twisted now.

"But what about the prom?" I said.

Why do I even care?

Please, Brady Paul, call me. You are everything to me.

"Oh, yes, the prom." Uncle Monty walked over to where my dresser once stood. He turned on the antique floor lamp and studied his majorly ick face in the cracked gold mirror leaning against the wall that stood taller than him. He especially took in that squinty right eye of his and his fine hairs stretched across his balding head. "Glissando wants you to speak to the school board that evening. They've hired someone to write a persuasive piece for you to present." He clicked off the lamp.

"That figures."

"So, everything might be okie-dokie after all. Let's celebrate!" Uncle Monty turned around. Cupped his hands together and smiled at me. "I ordered us a movie – Bye Bye Birdie. I'll make us some pop corn and..."

# My Mistaken Identity

"I don't think so." I rolled over onto my side. And stared at Brady Paul's class ring lying all alone on the antique fireplace mantle beside my bed, where only candles burned. My lip ached.

Why would I celebrate?

"Uncle Monty, I'm not up for that prom gig. It's way lame anyway."

"Now, now don't talk like that. You need a good night's rest and then we'll discuss it in the morning." Uncle Monty headed toward the door but stopped and turned around to face me. "I do have one question for you before you retire, Tuesday honey."

I closed my eyes.

Why doesn't he go the hell on?

"What, Monty honey?" I said and snarkled.

"I know you're tired. So, I'll overlook your sarcasm. I was wondering though…who took those pictures?"

Maybe I should tell him a piece of his own DNA clicked them. Would he be surprised? Or, has he already figured out I've met Zelda? He should know then that she took them. Then why is he bothering me about it?

"Was it that young man Brady Paul Larson?"

I opened my eyes, rolled over, propped myself up on my elbows and fessed-up. Sort of.

"Yeah, he did, Uncle Monty. Just before we did it."

LL Eadie

Chapter Thirty-Six

## *Too Difficult*

Why is it so difficult,

Not to think...

Of anything else,

But you?

As hard as I try,

Not to think...

Of us.

My mind takes me back,

To our place,

Our time,

Our dreams,

Our love.

Too difficult.

Not to

~~~~~~~~~~~~~~~~~~~~~~~~~

"So, you're a blonde again," said the Mr. Music Man himself – Baldwin Spikes as we headed toward the school gym's exit a week later.

It was the least I could do to separate myself from skanky two-faced Zelda.

"I like it. And I'm glad you changed your mind about coming, Tuesday," said Baldwin. "The kids were all so beyond themselves that you actually came."

I was actually hoping Brady Paul had changed his and would show-up. If only.

"That was the awesomest!" shouted one of the William P. DuVal High School's dance team members catching up with us.

I smiled. Sort of. My fingers squeezed tighter.

A crowd of stoked students – dancers, singers, band, and camera slash lighting techs emptied the newly renovated gymnasium. Compliments of Glissando Records and me, of course. Kudos hit me from every direction bouncing off me. I didn't care. Not anymore. Not without Brady Paul.

I wonder if one of these girls is his girlfriend.

"You kids," Baldwin turned and said as we headed for our airport limo, "totally ripped the stage today! Thanks for coming in while on spring break. Great performance!"

"Man, this is going to be one fierce prom!" said a guy somewhere behind me.

"I heard," said one of the dancers, "Rock-On-Videos was going to be at the prom and filming live."

"I can't wait to see our costumes!" a girl's voice said. "When will they be here, Mr. Spikes?"

"That all depends," Baldwin said, as we kept walking, "on the school board's decision."

Morbid moans and groans swarmed.

"Hopefully," Baldwin said, "Rock-On-Videos will be a go. And, you all will be sizing up your raging retro-garb soon. I know you're all going to be wowed by them! Tuesday helped design the outfits."

# My Mistaken Identity

I did?

"May I have your autograph, Tuesday?" asked a pretty one with mega-clear skin running up beside me.

Is she the one?

I sighed.

"I asked first," another girl said who pushed and shoved her way to my left.

What about her? Does she belong to Brady Paul?

Jeez, I don't want to know. I don't even want to live long enough to find out.

"Ladies," Baldwin said, intercepting their pleas, "Tuesday is going to personally sign and give her newest concept album – Tuesday's Evolution: The Third Day of the Week – to each and every one of you! "Aren't you, Tuesday?"

"Huh?" My mind was drifting in and out of a glaze-faze. There are degrees of insanity I'm sure. Although I've never visited a shrink. Maybe I should have invested in one's time. I thought about the edge way too much. Crept closer and closer to it. The edge of a cliff, a bridge, a blade... I was most definitely edge-fetished.

"You'll be signing everyone's copy, right?" Baldwin said again.

"Why not?" I answered. "Of course."

Jeez, I wish Zelda had not ended it with me.

But she was an imposter too. Just like Stormy and all the rest of my friendship fake-outs. Including Brady Paul!

But maybe I'll try to call Zelda again.

"Is it true," shouted a guy somewhere in the mix, "that you and Brady Paul split because of those pictures? Hey, Tuesday, you can send me some naughty Polaroid's anytime!"

Damn!

I could taste blood.

Oh-no-you-didn't displeasures echoed from the suddenly-morphed-into-Tuesday fans.

I turned around. "Who said that?"

"Come on, Tuesday." Baldwin took my hand. "Let's get in the car."

"There's always one in a crowd." Baldwin sat beside me. He combed the wrinkles from his slacks with his hands. He was totally into keeping-up his image. The one from ten years before. And, he nailed it every time.

"So, tell me," he said, "what's up with this Brady Paul dude and you? I thought I'd get to meet him. Is it a for-real high school love affair?" He chuckled that grown-up-you-just-think-you're-in-love laugh.

"I don't want to talk about it."

"Oh, I see." Baldwin laid his asking-for-forgiveness hand on my shoulder. "Sorry."

"Don't worry about it." I shrugged my I-don't-give-a-shit shoulders and stared out the window without really seeing, until our limo drove past the multitudes of protesting parents outside the gates of William P. DuVal High School. Signs blasting me filled the sky above their uptight shoulders

– DON'T NEED YOUR FILTHY $$$, STAY AWAY FROM OUR INNOCENT CHILDREN, TUESDAY GREENWOOD IS SEXUALIZING ADOLESCENCE!

Can they not? So cruel.

"Don't pay attention to them." Baldwin poured some bottled water into a chilled glass. "Like I said, there are always a few crazies in the crowd. The extremists. Don't let them stifle you, Tuesday. You're on your way. Universal! Poised for the next level! It's time for your updated style to be exposed!"

"Baldwin," I said.

"Yes, what is it? Name it, Tuesday, and it's yours!

"I need to make a stop before we head back."

Baldwin checked his watch. "We don't have a lot of time."

"I'll be quick." I opened the window separating us from the chauffer. "Please drive down to the Mayport Marina before the airport."

"My pleasure, ma'am," said our driver, as the window closed. Separating our lives from one another.

I dashed down the seagull-shit-stained docks as if I had missed my ride. My eyes scanned row after row of boats. I stood still.

I can't remember what his looked like. I should have brought that picture.

"Excuse me, Wes," I said to the dock master as he radioed to an approaching boat. "Do you know which boat belongs to Brady Paul's family?"

"Hi, missy," he said. "She's down in Miami at the moment and will be crusin' the Bahamas for a few days before returning. Not sure exactly. The couple that chartered her are avid fishermen. It's up to their wallets. You understand. And, yes, Brady Paul is on board."

"Do you know where she's docked in Miami?" I asked.

"The Miami Beach Marina, of course."

"Thanks, Wes!" I said.

"Hey, Tuesday," Wes said, "thanks for the reimbursement. But you still owe me."

Huh?

He smiled. "An autographed picture of the two of us."

My turn to grin. "We'll most definitely take care of that real soon."

I hope.

# Chapter Thirty-Seven

## *With Me*

Long after you had gone,

I took you with me.

Your face,

Your smile,

Your blush,

Your touch,

Your laugh,

With me.

~~~~~~~~~~~~~~~~~~~~~~~~

"What are you doing here, Tuesday?" Brady Paul stood in a pair of faded blue boxers on the spotless deck of the charter boat that very same evening. Of course, it was hours later after I had rushed back snatched the flyer with the photograph of the boat and changed clothes after our flight landed. I now had on my favorite pair of butt-defining jeans and see-through lace top.

I was planted underneath the moth-obsessed dock light. It was sort of late. Like ten-thirty-ish. It was still sort of warm too. Like seventy-ish. There were still signs of life in the marina, besides the lapping waves and salty breeze. There were the sounds of parties brewing, love-making sloshing sailboats and several trashed couples walking the plank to their yachts.

"I had to talk to you." I said. "May I come aboard?"

"Sure but let me help you." Brady Paul reached for my hand and I poured myself into his arms.

"I'm sorry, Brady Paul, I know you have passengers on board. And, your dad. And, it's late. And..."

He turned around. "Tuesday, no one's here. But us."

I followed him inside. In silence.

He shut the door, turned on a lamp, picked up a pair of jeans, a worn-out T-shirt, a bowl of half-eaten buttered popcorn, and a glass of milk.

I forced myself to look away. I so craved his attention. His kiss. His hug. His trust. His love.

"Your hair is blonde again." Brady Paul walked around the bar separating the galley from the stateroom. It was surprisingly a large area.

Momma really did kick-out. Damn.

"Do you like it?" I fingered the shaggy short ends.

"Yeah," he said and smiled. "Looks more like you."

"Don't you want to kiss me?" I walked toward him, touched his arm, his chest, his face, his lips...

"Tuesday." Brady Paul stepped back away from me.

Damn, the pull-back! That sucks.

"What's wrong?" I asked.

He shook his head and glanced down at the passengers' cat that was weaving his legs.

"Please, don't do this. Look at me," I said. "Don't you know how much I missed you?"

"I missed you, too. But…"

"Don't you believe me? I told you it wasn't me. It was Zelda!" I flung myself into his chest, laid the side of my face against his heart, my arms around his lean torso, and my legs took up where the cat left off.

My horoscope had read – You've been in a rut for too long. It's time to live, love and be happy. Rid yourself of what is working against you. And get on with your life.

"Oh, Tuesday." Brady Paul gave into his forbidden desires too and molded himself into me resting his chin on top of my head and his arms around my waist. "I don't know. I just don't know if this will ever work."

"It will! It will! If we want it to!"

Our lips spoke without saying a word and his aching heart spoke to me softly. My mouth reached for his. His latched onto mine. I reached up and felt his satiny hair. Pure optimism in every single kiss.

"Brady Paul, please promise me you won't leave me ever again."

"I promise," He whispered in my ear.

My neck exposed itself and invited his lips for a visit. A long overdue one. My body offered no resistance. When I opened my eyes, his were suggestive. A chill quaked my awakening body.

"I'm sorry I lied to you, Tuesday. That was cruel of me. There is no one else. Never was. Never will be. Just you. Only you."

My tears streamed across my cheeks and were met by his lips. He shared his breath with me as I moaned into his mouth.

BANG! BANG! BANG!

Shit! Who is that?

"Momma?" I exclaimed, as I stood in the center of the fishing boat's stateroom. "What are you doing here?"

"Sugar Plum!" My mother threw her arms around my too-shocked-to-budge body. I shook my head.

This so isn't happening.

Brady Paul lumbered over from the open door and snagged a blanket off the couch. He attempted to camouflage his boxers.

"What are you doing here?" I asked again.

"Oh, Tuesday, it's so wonderful to see you! And just look at your hair! It's blonde! I like it so much better! Of course, the cut and your clothes are still a bit edgy for my taste. But, believe it or not, they're growing on me." She held me out at arms length and smiled. Really, really smiled.

"I don't understand," I said. "Why are you here? And how did you find me?" I released her grip and peeked out a port hole. No answers available.

Is she for-real? Am I dreaming? Has she been cured? How did she get here?

"Don't worry, Tuesday," she said, "my ride will be right back. I sent him on an errand."

"Who?" I asked. Question ignored. Of course. Her annoying, confusing, overdone hug, eyes and smile moved on to yet another target.

"Why, you must be Brady Paul!"

Oh, no!

His eyes responded with a now-what expression in my direction.

"Momma, what's going on?"

"Are your parents on board?" she asked, as she now held Brady Paul in her arms' length let-me-take-a-good-look-at-you distance.

"No, ma'am. But it's nice to see you again." He brushed his hair out of his eyes with one hand while clutching the blanket around his waist, like a towel after stepping out of the shower, with the other.

"Oh, that is too bad," my mother said. "I so would like to get acquainted with them."

"My dad should be back pretty soon. He took our passengers to their rooms at the South Beach Marriott," Brady Paul said. "And then he was meetin' up for dinner with some of his old Navy buds."

"That's so American of him," my mother said. "To have been in our nation's service protecting our freedom."

Brady Paul nodded. "Yes, ma'am."

Crap! Why is she here? This is crazy!

"So, this is the charter boat." My mother released her latest confused victim and made herself cozy on the white leather couch.

"Yes, ma'am," Brady Paul said.

She puffed up the pillow to her right then patted the cushions on either side of her. "Please, sit down. Both of you." Another gyration to the cushions.

Momma and me de'ja' vu was released and invaded my head space. Momma patting the chair next to her at the kitchen table. "Sugar Plum, come sit down. We're going to have a fairy tea party with real china cups and saucers. And the fairies are serving us strawberry miniature cupcakes and tea."

"You are a handsome young man." My mother cocked her head in Brady Paul's face as he sat down to her right. "I had forgotten how precious you were."

I planted myself to her left. The leather felt cold against by back.

Why was I playing her game? By her rules that were most definitely being invented as the game rolled on.

WWZD?

"You make me wish I was eighteen again!" Her hand bounced off Brady Paul's blanket-covered thigh this time. "I can certainly see why you were so hot for him, Tuesday."

Please, Momma, no cougar tricks!

Brady Paul readjusted his pose. And, his blanket.

"Momma, why…"

"Hold on, Tuesday." My mother reached over and tapped my bare knee through my ripped skinny jeans. "I want to hear all about this boat. Tell me, Brady Paul. Everything!"

Brady Paul leaned forward and requested a permission glance from me. I nodded, did the eye-roll thingy and then introduced him to my I-don't give-shit shrug.

"We're booked throughout the summer," Brady Paul said. "Every week-end."

"How marvelous!" My mother clapped her hands in front of her overly percolated thrilled face while smashing her boobs together. Her saucy off-the-shoulders' top dropped almost to her elbows. "Isn't that wonderful, Tuesday?"

"Yes, Momma." I lifted up her left sleeve.

Could you not?

"I think," she said, "we should all get together for a boat ride!" More applause. More cleavage. "What a simply awesome way for our two families to get to know each other."

What is constantly-calculating-Constance up to?

"Momma, didn't you hear?" I stood up. "He said they were booked! All summer!

"But," my mother said, "only on the week-ends. Right, Brady Paul?" Another pat to his knee. Or was it his thigh?

"That's right, ma'am." Brady Paul smiled and winked.

At me, Momma! Not you!

"Now listen up, Tuesday," my mother said, "you see…"

Knock. Knock. Knock.

"Another uninvited guest?" I walked toward the vibrating door.

"Hold on, Tuesday," Brady Paul said. "I'll get that. It might be my dad." He jumped up, stumbled on the blanket and exposed his birthmark to my mother.

"Don't worry," my mother said and chuckled, "when you've seen one bare butt you've seen them all."

"Oh my God! Momma!"

Brady Paul laughed as he multi-tasked – pulling up his boxers, the blanket and opening the door.

"Uncle Monty?" I sat back down in a chair.

Of course. I should have known. It would be the blood hound.

"What's going on?" I asked. "Did you guys tailgate me all the way here? For almost two freakin' hours!"

"We're sorry to barge in on the two of you kids like this," Uncle Monty said. "Hello, Brady Paul. We met at the school."

"Yes, hello, sir."

Uncle Monty spritzed his insta-mouthwash before he reached down and caressed my hand. I moved it to my lap. Then to my lip.

My mother turned towards him. "Monty dear, did you get my cigarettes?"

"Of course." He pulled them out of his chest pocket of his silver silk sports coat.

"So," I said, "you drove all the way to Miami to buy a pack of Virginia Slims?"

"What did you say, Tu-Tu?" My mother said just before she opened the door and lit up on the deck. She left the door open and more uninvited guests made an appearance – the moths.

Uncle Monty attempted a chuckle. It was obvious he was doing his best to make light of this absurd situation. "We were on our way home and when we saw you, Tuesday, heading out from the house. We tried to call, but you didn't answer. And we had no idea where you were off to. We were concerned. So, we followed."

Must have tried Zelda's number. I so have to retain the rights to that cell.

"Naturally," I said with a roll-my-eyes-in-the-back-of-my-head look.

Brady Paul took advantage of my mother's absence and ducked behind the galley's chocolate granite counter and slipped on his jeans.

"So, don't you have some explaining to do too, Tuesday?" Uncle Monty said.

"No."

The cat meowed, the dark green water sloshed up against the boat's hull and Brady Paul looked panicked.

"Okay," I said, "I came to work things out with him. He's not who everyone thinks he is. He's not a gold digger or a wannabe Mr. Tuesday Greenwood. In fact, he broke it off with me after those pictures of me were released. I'm the one down on my knees, Uncle Monty. What's your excuse?"

## My Mistaken Identity

"Your mother wanted to surprise you, Tuesday honey," Uncle Monty said, "with her homecoming. But we also had some fabulous news to tell you."

"What?" I said. "That I'm all grown-up and am capable of making my own decisions. That I'm finally on my own? If so, you can leave now. Both of you."

"Oh, Tu-Tu," my mother said, sticking her head back inside, "don't be upset with us. You know we both love you. And we would follow you to the ends of the earth to make sure you were safe. Wouldn't we, Monty dear?"

"Of course, Constance."

"You just said that's not why you stalked me," I said.

"Well, you're right." my mother said. "There is another reason." She flicked her cigarette overboard and walked back inside. Over to Monty.

He wrapped his arm around her bare shoulders and said, "We're getting married!"

LL Eadie

# Chapter Thirty-Eight

## *Surprises*

You never can tell,

Or know,

Or be prepared.

For when one will,

Sneak up.

Or...

Speak up

Or...

Freak...

You out!

Damn surprises.

~~~~~~~~~~~~~~~~~~~~~~~~~~~~~~

"No way!" I stood up and stared in disbelief at M&M posed in the teak galley of the sports fisherman. I shook my head in slow-motion.

This so isn't happening.

"Look!" My mother held out the official I'm-engaged finger. Yes way. There it was proof positive. The diamond ring. "Isn't it gorgeous? We had just come from the jewelers and were heading home to share the news with you when we saw you leaving. We just couldn't wait to tell you!" My mother leaned back and pecked Uncle Monty's lips. He reciprocated. I recoiled.

"I've been in love with your mother for years. I'd asked her many times and she always rejected me."

Did you ever ask Rosa?

Your mother said now seemed like the perfect time," Uncle Monty said. "You're getting older, Tuesday honey, and it won't be long till…"

I filled in the blank. "…till I'm gone."

"That's right. So," Uncle Monty said, "will you stand up for us at the altar?"

I guess it's about time they got married. But what will Zelda think?

I shrugged and answered, "Sure, why not?" I sat back down.

"Congratulations," Brady Paul said coming around the bar from the galley. He shook Uncle Monty's hand. My mother kissed him too. Thank God on the cheek. "I wish I had some champagne on board for a toast."

"What are we toasting?" asked Brady Paul's father – Captain Larson. He filled the open door space.

Jeez. Now what?

"Dad," Brady Paul said, "this is the uh…" He pointed toward us. "The Greenwood's. Umm…that's Tuesday, her mother and her…uh…uncle. You remember…umm…" His shaky introduction expressed my concern and his.

"Captain Larson!" My mother was the first to make a move as usual. "Such a pleasure to make your acquaintance." She added, "In person." She smiled as she headed over to the too-shocked-to-speak Captain Larson.

"Mrs. Greenwood," Captain Larson said as he reached out for her hand. "Of course, I remember you. Is there a problem?"

# My Mistaken Identity

"No." My mother grasped her other hand around his like a clam shell. "We came, or should I say we followed Tuesday here tonight."

Captain Larson's head and eyes tagged mine first then Brady Paul's. We smiled. He frowned.

"Captain Larson," Uncle Monty stepped forward to add more believability to their absurd visit. Or invasion. "I'm Monty Simelski...and I'm not really her uncle. We're here only to check on Tuesday."

"I see," Captain Larson said releasing his hand from my mother's grip. "So, you're the famous Tuesday Greenwood." He smiled and reached out for my hand.

"Yes sir," I stood up. "I'm sorry for all this. It's all my fault." I shook my head and when I blinked tears dropped. He patted my hand as if he understood my embarrassment. "Brady Paul had no idea I was coming. It was rude of me."

Brady Paul came forward and wrapped his arm around my waist. "Dad, Tuesday and I are…"

Say it – in love.

"You twos aren't who we're supposed to be toasting are ya?" asked Captain Larson. He rubbed the back of his confused head.

"No! We are!" My mother revealed the rock once more and held onto to her prized catch – Uncle Monty.

Captain Larson turned back around and offered-up his congratulatory handshake toward Uncle Monty and my mother's. "Well, my goodness! Lemme see if I can't find a bottle of wine, beer or something." There was relief in his voice.

This evening was most definitely not going as I planned.

LL Eadie

# Chapter Thirty-Nine

## *Survival*

The sugar plum fairy...

Learned to fly.

Soar.

Sail.

Scout.

She learned to live.

Eat.

Sleep.

Dream.

She learned to survive.

Lie.

Liberate.

Fight.

Fly, Sugar Plum, fly.

Live, Sugar Plum, live.

Survive, Sugar Plum, survive.

~~~~~~~~~~~~~~~~~~~~~~~~~~~~~~~~~~

"It was so nice to meet y'all," said Brady Paul's father – Captain Larson.

My mother climbed into the backseat of Uncle Monty's black Escalade parked at the Miami Beach Marina. Midnight-ish. "Promise me, Captain, that you will save us a date for that boat ride."

Brady Paul squeezed my waist. The prom was only a week away and I had a date with Brady Paul again. Life was good.

"You can count on a call, ma'am." Captain Larson shook Uncle Monty's hand.

"Glad we were able to work this out. You can expect a payment from me for the boat every month."

"Don't worry," my mother said. "Send what you can, whenever you can."

"Thanks," Captain Larson said. "The kids really do like each other."

"We can see that." Uncle Monty glanced back over his shoulder at me.

I looked away into Brady Paul's eyes and wished I could stay with him forever.

"I know my wife will be pleased to hear it." Captain Larson reached in the car and shook my mother's hand too.

"You've raised such a nice young man." my mother said, and then she smiled puffing out her helium lips. "Monty and I look forward to seeing him real soon. Hopefully, at the prom. The school board meeting is tomorrow night."

"I have no doubt they'll vote to keep her act," Captain Larson said. "They'd be damn foolish not to."

"Okay, Tuesday, come on," Uncle Monty said holding the car door open wide. He was monitoring Brady Paul and me. "These sailors need to hit their bunks. They'll be shoving off in the morning bright and early."

I turned into Brady Paul with a hug and a kiss.

"I'll call you." Brady Paul spoke words of promise. "I love you, Tuesday."

He said it!

"I love you, too."

He took my hand and led me toward my ride home.

"Don't worry about your car, Sugar Plum," my mother said as she wrapped her arm around me in the backseat, "Monty will send someone down in the morning to pick it up."

I craned my neck and watched Captain Larson wrap his arm around his DNA, too.

"I really like him, Tuesday," my mother said, "and his father."

"Here, Constance," Uncle Monty said, "you need to take your medicine."

I turned back around and looked really hard at her as she swallowed the pill. She did seem sort of better. Was it possible the new treatment did the trick? Or was it Uncle Monty's proposal? I had not seen my mother this stoked since I was a pre-pubescent elementary age. She even recited fairy tales while we were homeward bound just before she hummed the Sugar Plum Fairy in my ear and we both dozed off. My head, on her shoulder. She almost had me believing once again in fairies, trolls and happily ever after.

Once home I peeled off my clothes and climbed into bed in my underwear. My mother planted a kiss on my forehead, tucked herself along with me into my cushy comforter, and wished me sweet dreams.

She didn't even mention my scuffed-up room. It was like she didn't see it. My eyes closed.

"I love you, Momma."

Did I really just say that?

She ran her limp fingers through my asymmetrical locks as we spooned. Her three-carat diamond ring grazed my forehead as my mother whispered, "I love you too, Tu-Tu."

Did she really say that?

Sleep was calling me fast.

"Good night, Sugar Plum."

"Good night, Momma."

His body spooned mine. His trembling hand outlined the length of my bare arm.

"Momma?" My eyes fluttered.

And, his nose led his lips to the scent of my perfume in the crook of my neck.

"Brady Paul," I whispered. I rolled over with haste to greet my surprise bedmate. My lips landed on his. Listerine fresh breath.

Mouthwash?

I jerked my head back. My eyes popped open. My nightlight revealed my nightmare. "Momma! It's the troll! Momma!"

"Shhh, Tuesday," Uncle Monty said.

I climbed across the bed pulling the quilt that was wrapped about my waist with me. "Where's momma?"

"I carried your momma back to her room. She's fine, Tuesday honey." Uncle Monty sat up. His shirt was unbuttoned. Totally. "I was just checking on you. You had a bad dream."

"Get out of here!" I slid further across the mattress away from him.

"Tuesday, come here." He crawled toward me. "You were having a nightmare. I heard…"

"How could you hear me?" I stood up still clutching the patchwork quilt to my shaken frame. "Your room is downstairs."

"I always come up and check on you. You know that."

I shook my head. "No, I didn't know that! I'm not a little girl anymore. You don't need to check on me any longer." I stuck out my hand. "Now, give me the damn key!"

"Tuesday honey, please." Uncle Monty reached out to hold my hand. "Don't do this."

"DON'T TOUCH ME     !" I backed into my metal nightstand. The nightlight flickered.

"You don't have to yell. You know I would never do anything to hurt you. I've always taken care of you. And I always will. You mean so much to me. I've watched you grow up into a beautiful young woman."

"So," I said, "what does that have to do with why you're in my room and trying to…"

"You're the one I truly love, Tuesday."

My head shook in disbelief.

He loves me? Of course, he does. But…not like…

"You just asked my mother to marry you!"

"Yes, well, to tell you the truth, Tuesday honey, your mother actually asked me, or as she put it, accepted a much earlier proposal of mine. I couldn't tell her no. Not after just getting out of the sanitarium." His gnarly feet touched the floor. "But I think you know I would rather have you as my wife."

"GET OUT OF HERE!" I shouted. "NOW! GET OUT OF MY ROOM!"

"Please, stop yelling, Tuesday honey!" Uncle Monty grasped my shoulders.

"LET GO OF ME! DON'T TOUCH ME! STOP IT! STOP IT! STOP IT!"

His gargantuan hand covered my mouth to drown-out my screams. I slapped, kicked and bit. I hit the mattress chest to chest with Uncle Monty.

No! This is so not happening! Please stop! Please stop! Please!

"Tuesday honey don't do this. I love you. I've waited so long for you. I've always loved you." His squinty right eye hypnotized me. And, his body anchored me. I couldn't move. Right. Or. Left. Front. Or. Back. Way penned. Pure tribulation.

"You don't want to upset your Momma now, do you?" he said. "She's so happy. And she just got all better."

There was another scent on Uncle Monty's breath. The one he tried to disguise daily with his fresh-breath habit. It was 80 proof.

"It would be a shame to put her back in the sanitarium now, wouldn't it?" His hand stroked the top of my head, brushing the hair out of my face. I spit in his. He licked his lips. "Besides," he said, as he covered my mouth once again, "she was a good girl tonight and took her medicine. She's sleeping soundly."

No wonder momma didn't notice the changes to my room. She's heavily drugged.

# My Mistaken Identity

"Now, you be a good girl too and behave yourself. Don't worry your pretty little self like this. You know you have nothing to fear from me."

Why didn't I see it coming?

Or, did I? Zelda must have. This must be what she meant about the big reveal. I'm such an idiot!

"That boy will never love you the way I do. Or will."

I hate, hate, hate, you!

He kissed my forehead. I closed my eyes. His hands took up where the sheet fell off.

Fly, Sugar Plum, fly...

Live, Sugar Plum, live...

Survive, Sugar Plum, survive.

LL Eadie

## Chapter Forty

### *Could You?*

Have you ever,

Felt the hate…

But chose to ignore it?

Could you?

Did you ever,

Cry sobs you'd never heard before?

Did it make you stop…

And think?

Could you?

Have you ever,

Wanted to slap yourself…

More than once?

Could you?

Or…

Did you?

~~~~~~~~~~~~~~~~~~~~~~~~~~~~~~

"GET OFF OF ME!" I screamed and aimed for every guy's Achilles' heel.

Uncle Monty rose up, rolled over and groaned.

I jumped out of bed away from the ugly troll. I reached for my pillow on the floor and held it tight. "GET! OUT! OF! MY! ROOM!"

Uncle Monty rolled like a tumble weed across my mattress. His feet hit the floor and his chest his lap. He sat in that collapsed gasping-for-air position for way too long.

I realized I needed to flee, escape, make a run for it, but, I was stalled.

"Tuesday," he said in a hushed voice, "you shouldn't have done that." He was pushing himself away from the bed. Up to his feet. Surprisingly, with the help of his strong, but scrawny arms.

I made like a cheetah and raced to my bathroom just inches from his wretched grasp. I locked the door. Not good enough.

"Tuesday, let me in, damn it!" He hit the door. "We need to talk."

NO! NO! NO! I WILL NOT! LET! HIM! IN!

I dragged my antique dressing table across the room. Vanilla scented talc powder coasted-off the marble top and blanketed the tile as I slipped and slid in it along with every charcoal colored lipstick, eye shadow and liner that rolled and smudged the floor. I shoved the vanity against the vibrating door. The one Uncle Monty was attempting to rip from its hinges.

"I made a mistake," he said. "Please forgive me. Please! I promised myself I would stay away from you. I couldn't. It was seeing you with that boy tonight. I just lost it! Don't you understand, Tuesday? I love you."

BANG! BOOM! SLAM! WHAM! BAM!

"OPEN THE GODDAMN DOOR!"

The Hollywood Gazette horoscope led me – You'll have mixed emotions regarding your personal situation. A change of scenery will do you good.

# My Mistaken Identity

Yes! I have to get away from here!

How did Zelda manage it? Moving in and out of my suite without my know-how, and theirs? She never explained how she did it. I checked out the balcony, the first place I remembered Zelda exiting. No way. This was not her entry of choice.

"TUESDAY!" Uncle Monty continued to shout and pound his fists. BAM!

How did she do it?

I rushed outside onto the meditation garden. This had to be it. I stared through the three-tiered Italian fountain at the cascading bougainvillea vine with its pink flowers and nasty thorns that was attached to the wall. Its lattice frame extended to the rooftop. Freedom was within my reach. I had no choice. I had to move on. Release myself from this sequestered hell. I climbed to the red clay tiled roof that overlooked the pool, wincing each time an inch-long thorn tore at my skin.

Don't look down. Keep your eyes straight forward. To the garage apartment.

I crawled on all fours across the roof. It was steep and my bare footing was unstable. I was still shaken. Inside and out. At one point I lay on the roof under the southern stars and listened to the ocean wash away the sandy beach. My thoughts were coming at me. In every direction. Inside. Outside. And, sideways.

Maybe I'll sneak in the kitchen and snatch a butcher knife. Or maybe I'll wake-up Momma and tell her. How could I? Or maybe I'll dial 911. What good that does…for The Grapevine. So not going there! I have to do it! I have to escape!

I began to crawl again scratching my palms and soles of my feet as I picked up my pace. I was wearing an oversized T-shirt I had snagged in my haste. A souvenir. Mayport Marina. I had to make it across the roof top of my 19,000 plus square foot asylum to the apartment. If Zelda could do it, then so could I. What if she was there? Would I forgive her?

I way needed her. Of course, amnesty would be granted with a pinky swear.

Finally, the light from her balcony was there. Beneath me. I inched my way down. Feet first. Clinching the clay tiles with bloody knuckles. The Spanish tiles moved. I dropped.

Thump...

Thump...

Thump...

Boom...

Ouch!

Shit!

# Chapter Forty-One

## *Fear*

It finds you,

Sneaks up on you,

And tracks you...

Down.

No warning,

It brings you,

To your knees,

Your tears.

Introduces you,

To your nightmares.

Up close!

Eyes-on-eyes,

Limbs-on-limbs,

Person-on-person.

~~~~~~~~~~~~~~~~~~~~~~~~~

"ZELDA!" I pounded on the glass doors. Shhh, I told myself and lowered my voice, "Zelda! It's me, Tuesday! Let me in! Please, Zelda!"

No answer. No signs of Zelda.

WWZD? Go for it!!! Freedom!

I reached down and picked up one of the broken tiles littering the balcony. Without another thought, I threw it at the door. SMASH! I reached through the serrated hole and unbolted it. I had done it! Entry! And soon…Escape!

"Owwee!" The bottoms of my feet were splintered by the shattered pieces of lead glass as I stepped inside into the darkness. I inched my way across the room till I found the switch plate next to a door. I flicked on a light.

Z-moment tip sheet – "Dead it!"

Damn!

I clicked it off, stood still and listened. Was the silent alarm set off? Had Uncle Monty been watching me? Perhaps he heard me? Did he see the light? Was he on his way to the apartment? Or, was he still taking his way-wrong-sexual-fantasy frustration out on my bathroom door?

I snatched a pair of Zelda's jeans off the floor and tugged them on. The apartment was still a wreck. Thank God, Rosa's extra car key still hung from the hook by the door. I snatched it, rushed down the steps to the garage below, climbed in, and took off from the asylum.

I followed the so-called guiding light of the full moon not knowing where the trail would end weaving in and out of traffic. I had no idea where my destination truly was. Pure screwed-up fate. Then I remembered an underground club Zelda and I were supposed to hang at The Squeeze-In. Her new favorite. It was close to The Tongue and Groove. Maybe she was there. But where was it? I wasn't sure I remembered how to get there.

Should I stop and ask?

Would Zelda help me if I did find it? Who else do I have to count on?

Nobody.

## My Mistaken Identity

Just Zelda.

I looked around seeking familiarity. None to be found. This was so the type of neighborhood where the doors of entry went into lockdown mode, and drive-bys were too God-awful common place. And frightened screams were I-don't-want-to-get-involved ignored.

I was channeling Zelda – "This is a dead zone, you fool!"

My fear was accelerated as soon as I noticed bright beam headlights in my rearview mirror. They were blinding me.

Oh my God! It's Uncle Monty! I know it is! He's found me! Again!

Please God protect me from him!

Head-jarring Z-moment – "Don't waste God's time praying for stupid things! Take action!"

I popped open the glove compartment in pursuit of who-knows-what. But, there it was – a cell phone!

Yes! Yes! Yes!

I called home.

Huh? You idiot!  No! No! No!

I tried Zelda's number.

Please answer! Please answer! Please answer!

No answer.

I called Brady Paul.

"Hello."

"Brady Paul! Oh my God!" My foot hammered the pedal to the floorboard. Rosa's car sputtered then lunged forward as my head whipped back.

Go! Go! Go!

But so did the one tailing me.

No! No! No!

"Who is this?" Brady Paul asked.

"Tuesday!"

"What's wrong?" he asked.

"I'm lost!" I passed the car in front of me. The driver laid on the horn.

Sorry! Sorry! Sorry!

"What?"

"I think somebody is following me." The city bus stopped in front of me to pick up passengers. I slammed on brakes. So did the vehicle behind me.

Shit! Shit! Shit!

"What's going on, Tuesday?"

I sped around the bus missing another car by inches. More angry horns.

Sorry! Sorry! Sorry!

"Tuesday!"

"Brady Paul, I think it's Uncle Monty! He's chasing me!"

# My Mistaken Identity

I turned the corner.

Faster! Faster! Faster!

Then another.

Faster! Faster! Faster!

"Tuesday!"

"He attacked me tonight! He was in my bed and..." The headlights were there again.

Shit! Shit! Shit!

"Tuesday, I don't understand what you're saying. You're breaking up."

"Brady Paul, I love you!" The traffic light up ahead turned red. No way could I stop. I took a chance.

"Tuesday, if you ... me... I don't ...good service...Bahamas. I'll be ... in a few .... Bye."

"OH MY GOD! BRADY PAUL!"

LL Eadie

# Chapter Forty-Two

## *There is Still Time*

When is the right time,

To call it quits?

Tell me...

I so need to know,

Is there still time?

Or, is check out...

At noon?

~~~~~~~~~~~~~~~~~~~~~~~~~~~~~~

"Welcome," said a woman dressed in white. Totally. "What's your name?"

"Who are you? Where am I?" I said. "Am I...dead?"

"No, sweetie, you're very much alive," said the same virginal image. "You're in Memorial Regional Hospital. You were in a car accident. Do you remember?"

"Sort of." I raised my right hand to touch the left side of my throbbing head. It wore a new piece of jewelry. A syringe needle accessorized with an IV bag on a pole.

"Paging Doctor Reynolds," an intercom said from the hallway, "you're needed in the ER."

"You've been coming in and out of consciousness for several hours," the nurse said, "Of course, the pain medicine makes you extremely drowsy. The doctor will be happy to hear you're awake. He'll be by to see you during his rounds."

God, I feel way trashed. What's that?

I reached down with my bandaged hand and felt a sanitary pad stuffed between my bare legs.

Damn! Why now? Why me? Where are my clothes? I'm freezing.

I shivered and pinched my lip. The nurse pulled the cotton blanket up to my neck. "Do you remember your name?"

"Zelda…" I stared at the bright white light above me. "Zelda Simelski."

Maybe, she's lying.

"Zelda with a 'Z' and Simelski with an 'S'?" she asked.

I nodded. "When do I see him?"

"Who?" the nurse said.

"God," I answered.

"Not on my shift you don't," she said and chuckled. "You're lucky, dear, you had on your seatbelt. Just a few stitches on your head, a couple of cracked ribs, broken hand…"

I closed my eyes and started drifting far away from here.

"Zelda? Are you still with me? Zelda?"

"What?" I looked up at the face. The one that kept insisting I was Zelda.

"Who should I call?" she asked. "You didn't have any identification on you."

"My daddy. Monty Simelski."

## My Mistaken Identity

I closed my eyes. I could hear Stormy. "Why not?" she asked. "Just because..." I answered. "It's not like I'm going to tell or anything. Just let me copy it," Stormy argued. "It's my homework! And I'm not sharing!" I exclaimed. I opened my eyes.

What's going on?

Is that a television?

"Yeah, it is. I got bored and turned it on," Zelda said, as she squeezed my nose. "You have one gargantuan honker of a zit right on the tip."

"STOP!" I said, as I tried to bat the pimple healer's hand away. But mine was still hooked up to a drip. "That hurts like hell!"

"Shhh..." Her finger pressed her lips. "Well, it's not because of me. You took a nasty blow to your nose too. And, one of your eyes is nicely blackened-up." She smirked. "Besides, I wouldn't be in this seriously sick-o place if you hadn't called me."

"Where am I?" I attempted to rise up from where I lay in sterile white linens. "Owwee."

"The hospital." Zelda said as she reached for the remote and turned off The Jazmyn and Justyce Show rerun.

"Why?" I asked.

"Your choice," Zelda said, "Not mine. My guess is you were looking for a way out. Planning to end it. To reduce the pain for all time. Pure RIP."

"I must have been in an accident."

"Yeah, spot on! You way kissed the side of that building!" She walked across the fourteen-by-fourteen Pine-Sol scented square room and snagged the black and white pinned striped curtain between my bed and the other vacant one.

"Maybe," I said, as I evaluated my head with the hand not in the cast, but hooked up to fluid lines, "...my airbag didn't go off."

"Do you like really think that old clunker actually had one?" Zelda walked back in my direction. Her shoes squeaked on the Linoleum tiled floor. "You are talking about Rosa's ride, right?"

"Yeah," I said. "You're probably right. No airbag."

"Is this like a bad time for you?" Zelda said. "Because I can leave and come back later. I'm not supposed to be hanging out in here anyway. There's some kind of no admittance shingle tacked to your door. I'm an intruder for sure. Again."

"No," I said, "please don't go."

"Beg! I so get off when you do that."

Damn her. Why did I seek her out? And, call her earlier? I so don't need her. I never did. She's such a bitch.

Why then can't I give her up?

"Please, Zelda." I attempted to clasp my hands as if in prayer. Botched effort. "My best friend, favorito fan and sissy in the whole-freakin'-wide-world don't leave me."

"So much better," she said and sneered. "So, you reverted back to your old ways, huh?" She lifted my hypodermic-needled-abused hand. "Pink polish. And, blonde hair."

I closed my eyes.

Damn.

"I am, who I am, Zelda." I looked up at her.

"And, tell me." Zelda crossed her arms at her chest. "Who is that?"

# My Mistaken Identity

My head hurt majorly. My eyes had trouble focusing. They begged to close.

"You told Nurse Nightingale you were me."

I shook my head. "No, I didn't."

"Oh, you most definitely did!" Zelda snagged my chart from the front of my bed. She peeked over her black horn-rimmed glasses. "See!" She shoved it at me. "Patient's name – Zelda Simelski."

"I don't remember," I said. I reached for my lip. Squeezing. Harder.

"Shed the innocence, Tu-Tu, please."

"Huh?" I looked up at her.

"Come on," she said, "tell me your woe-is-me story. I need a good laugh. And don't tweak it."

"I have no idea, Zelda, why I'm here, or how I got here."

"Sigh," she said. "Another case of convenient amnesia, huh?"

"Please Zelda," I said, "I'm having trouble focusing."

"I know what has happened is a rough patch for you. But, get a grip!"

"I don't remember anything!"

Now, I'm most definitely lying to myself. I so don't want to go there. Ever, again.

"Pure brain-cramp," Zelda said and laughed. "I so hope Uncle Okie-dokie is caught up on all his shots."

"What are you saying?" I exclaimed. "That is so not fair!"

"Life sucks. Do you remember that?"

"The last few hours, Zelda, are seriously gone from my memory."

"Like I said, how convenient."

"Why are you being so mean?" I rolled to my side. "Owwee."

"Why don't you call Monty honey and tell him how cruel I am. I dare you. You won't do it, will you?"

"No."

"Why not?"

"Because..." I touched my mouth gingerly. My lips felt way inflated "...I don't want to."

"And," Zelda said, "we both know why, don't we? You're scared shitless to discover the truth. You have always avoided it and I have always made you face it. Isn't that true? Admit it!

"Shut up! I don't ever want to talk to him!" Tears filled my eyes and spilled onto the chest of my back-ass-less gown. "Or, see his face! Ever again!"

"I warned you about him the first time I met you. The truth bites, doesn't it?"

"But, that was your daddy!"

Zelda nodded. "Yeah, it is. Uncle Monty. What a bummer." She disappeared.

"Excuse me, Miss Simelski," the nurse said as she entered the room, "but we called the number you requested and the gentleman that resides there said he didn't know any Zelda Simelski. He said he didn't have a daughter."

"Why am I not surprised?" Zelda mumbled, as she stood behind the curtain separating the twin beds. She snorted a smirk.

# My Mistaken Identity

"What did you say?" the nurse asked while opening the lid of my uneaten dinner.

"Nothing," I said as I shrugged my I-don't-give-a-shit shoulders.

"Sweetie," the nurse said, as she straightened my IV lines, "is there someone else we can call for you?" She pulled up the starched white sheet to my armpits.

"So you wanted Uncle Okie-dokie to come to your bedside?" Zelda whispered.

"Shut up, bitch!" I said.

"What?" exclaimed the nurse. Her head jutted back.

"I wasn't talking to you," I said, as I shook mine.

She looked around. Zelda stood still behind the black and white pin-striped cotton curtain. Only the toes of her shabby shoes were visible. To me.

"I know you need your rest," the nurse said as she cut the light off above my bed. "The police are here again. They want to speak to you, but the doctor wants them to wait. You have one serious contusion on your head, sweetie." She turned to leave. "A possible concussion."

"My name is Tuesday Greenwood," Zelda said.

"Excuse me." The nurse turned back around. "Are you really her?" She cut the light back on.

"I'm not her!" I said. "I never was! I don't know who I am."

"The gig is up, Tu-Tu."

"What?" the nurse said. "I'm calling the doctor!"

"I changed my mind, Zelda," I said as I watched the vision in white dash out the door as it slammed closed behind her. "I do want you to leave."

"Not yet," she said, as she exposed herself from behind the drape. "We need to talk."

"No! We! Don't!"

"Accept the obvious, Tuesday." Zelda sat on the edge of my bed. I moved my legs. "This is your kick-in-the-head moment." She punched my arm.

"Owwee."

"So sorry. Sort of." Zelda snarkled as she got up and walked around my bed and picked at my hospital baked chicken. "Don't go and get all butt-hurt."

"I don't know why I ever liked you!" I exclaimed. "You're not a friend! You never were!"

"I'm your only friend," she said and laughed as she took a bite of my dinner roll. "I believe I was there when no one else was. Isn't that true, Tuesday?"

"I don't care what you believe, Zelda! Just get out of my life!" I tried not to blink.

"Gladly, but first you will hear me out." She wiped the square of butter on the roll. "I get it all now, Tu-Tu. It wasn't Stormy or Ashburn that burnt you."

"You weren't there!" I couldn't hold the tears back. "You don't know what happened! You don't know spit!"

"Oh, yes I do. You pushed them at each other! You're the one that caused it! Shit, Stormy wasn't hitting on Ashburn. And he wasn't into Stormy. That is…until you suggested…"

"Shut up, Zelda!"

"Admit it, Tuesday! You enjoy playing the victim. Even Jazmyn was always being beat down by her evil twin Justyce. You're always the victim. It's the role you play the best. Even in life. Poor Tuesday. Everyone's so cruel to her. It's like they're all the evil fairy, isn't it?"

I shook my head in disbelief.

"And then there was your mother to blame for Brady Paul breaking up with you. Or, did you set that trap up for failure too? Didn't you tell Monty about him that night? About how you wanted to kiss Brady Paul and you told him not to tell Constance. But you knew he would, didn't you, Tu-Tu? Pure sabotage."

No! I don't screw myself over! I don't! I don't!

"You're crazy!"

"Do you really think so?" Zelda said and laughed. "What about those pictures you took of yourself? You sent them not only to Brady Paul but to Ashburn too!"

"LIAR!" I yelled. "You took them! You sent them! NOT ME!"

"What about the scene with Ashburn and Stormy at The Final Groove? I suppose that was me too, huh?"

"Of course, it was! Why are you doing this to me?"

"Think about it, Tu-Tu. Are your really sure?"

"And it was you, Tuesday, that sent The Grapevine those pictures, wasn't it? Even of Brady Paul's boat!"

"I did not!"

"You knew their number," Zelda said, "Remember that night at the diner when you emailed them those other pictures."

I shook my head. "You're the screwed-up one here, Zelda. I found my doll Sissy in your room! What's wrong with you? Are you some kind of sicko?"

"Hey!" Zelda said. "You didn't want her. Remember? She was just trash to you!"

"She was broken!"

"So, you just throw her away just like everyone else in your life you get tired of?"

"You're cruel, Zelda," I said. "By the way I found something else too. Your journal. And, I read it!"

"I left it there for you." Zelda raised and lowered my bed's side rails several times. Pure annoying. "I was hoping you would. Did you enjoy it?"

"Is it all true?" I asked. "Everything you wrote?"

"I'm so not down with lying." Zelda carried the lone straight back chair over to the door and blocked the entrance.

I shook my head. "You're such a damn liar! I hate you!"

"No, you don't." Zelda walked back to the bed and sat down again. "You can't exist without me."

"I so don't need you!" I said. "Not anymore! We're done! So leave!"

"You should get down on your scabbed-up knees and kiss my perfect ass." Zelda pushed the over-the-bed table with the dinner tray several feet away from her. "I helped your bubblegum-butt break away. Without me you never would be singing my songs or..."

"They're my songs! Damn it!"

She smirked. "I did everything you were afraid to do but wanted to. Remember?"

"You're whacked!"

# My Mistaken Identity

"Am I? Then, so are you. You see, Tu-Tu, I'm only a fragment of your life. A figment of your…"

"Miss Greenwood?" There was a series of let-me-in-NOW knocks on the door. "This is Dr. Shepherd. May I come in? Your door seems to be locked."

"As I was saying," Zelda said, "before I was so rudely interrupted, this is the kick-in-the-head moment, Tuesday. So, pay attention. I'm your…"

"Miss Greenwood!" the doctor said. "If you don't open this door I'm going to have to call security!"

"SHUT UP!" Zelda shouted.

"Call security," said the doctor.

"Open the damn door!" I said snagging off my sheet, forgetting about the intravenous drip, and attempting to stand.

"Not yet!" she said shoving me back into bed. "I haven't finished!"

"Zelda, I know what you think about me," I said. "You made it perfectly clear in your journal."

"Did I?" Zelda stood up and glared at me.

I looked down. Down at my bruises. Down at my cuts. Down at the scars that would heal. But, those I couldn't see I would feel forever.

"Miss Greenwood," the doctor said, "is there someone in the room with you?"

"You still don't get it, do you?" Zelda said.

"I do now," I said. "I fess-up, Zelda, I didn't see it coming. But, I know now the big reveal was…" I stared at my lap. "…Uncle Monty and, his sick-o feelings for me."

Zelda smirked.

I looked up at her. "Right?"

"Wrong." Zelda said and snarkled.

It was a stabbing laugh. The kind that makes you sit up straighter and check out your surroundings. Like something seriously gag-worthy is stuck between your front teeth, hanging off the sole of your shoe, or peek-a-booing out of your nose without your knowing how.

She sat down again next to me.

"Miss Greenwood, please answer me!"

"All right. Tell me," I said. I dug my nubby nails into my palm of my unplastered hand.

"Your feelings are always way transparent, Tuesday," she said. "You can't fool me. You never could. I see your pain."

"Duh, that's a no-brainer," I said, "I was in a car wreck last night."

"I so didn't show up here today to monitor your progress."

"Well, why did you come, Zelda?"

"To tell you…

"Miss Greenwood, if you don't open this door," Dr. Shepherd said, "we're going to have to force it open."

I shook my head at Zelda. "What? Tell me!"

"Aren't you tired of living a double life?" Zelda asked.

"What are you carrying on about?" I asked. "Me versus Jazmyn? M&M's? What?"

"I'm your alternative, all right?"

# My Mistaken Identity

"What?"

"It's me, Tuesday, inside your head."

"What?"

"I'm only in your mind."

"What?"

"I'm your mistaken identity."

I tasted blood.

LL Eadie

# Chapter Forty-Three

## *The One and Only*

Am I...

The rose...

Without the thorns?

Am I...

The ivy...

Without the poison?

Am I...

The one and only?

The bee...

Without a stinger?

The snake...

Without the fangs?

Am I...

Your one and only?

~~~~~~~~~~~~~~~~~~~~~~~~

"I promise," Dr. Shepherd said, as he stood by my hospital bed, "you are not crazy, Miss Greenwood."

"Thank God," I said. "And, please, doctor, call me Tuesday."

"I would like that, Tuesday," he said, "very much."

The midday sun peeked through the blinds as the nurse checked my vital signs: temperature, blood pressure, pulse, breathing, and pain.

Please, dead the pain.

"How old are you, Tuesday?" Dr. Shepherd asked, as he peeked over his reading glasses.

"Sixteen."

He checked a box on the paper that clung to his clipboard. "It's not unheard of for young ladies of your age to experience hallucinations during a full-blown manic state. Puberty in girls can frequently set it off. It begins in early adulthood. Much more common in young women. Sixteen to eighteen often times seems to be the average age for bipolar disorder."

Great. Just great.

"Is it usually around your monthly cycle, Tuesday," he asked, "that Zelda appears to you?"

Out of the past Z-moment – "So ya see, Tuesday, I'll be hanging out in this town for my monthly visitation rights. Thank God, for just a week at a time. Not my idea, I promise."

"You're right, Dr. Shepherd," I said. "Yes, that's when she comes."

The doctor checked another box and continued with his are-you-a-schizo quiz, "And, during your time of the month, Tuesday, are you experiencing extreme head and stomach aches?"

"Most definitely," I said. My stomach was already challenging my stitched head for the pain badge.

"I'm sorry," the doctor said, "is that a yes?"

I nodded.

"What about junk food cravings?"

# My Mistaken Identity

I thought about my vending machine diet of late and had to answer again. "Yes."

"Have you experienced sleep difficulties? Too much or too little?

"Frequently," I said.

"Another early sign," the doctor explained, "is being susceptible to suicidal thoughts. Have you ever confronted that issue, Tuesday?"

Damn, do I get an "A" on my quiz if I have?

I nodded my head in silence.

"What about dare-devil behavior?"

I answered that one with a shrug of my I-don't-give-a-shit shoulders.

"Have you acted out on false hopes or fantasies only to realize they're not real?"

Huh? What is he talking about?

"For instance you might believe you're stronger than what you are and try to lift something too heavy, or that you're invincible, or perhaps you believe a certain someone is really interested in you only to find out they are not."


No! He's wrong! Brady Paul does love me.

But am I really in love with him, or just the idea of it?

How can I be sure of anything that's happened?

Was Brady Paul right – I don't know what love really is?

I don't deserve to be loved!

"Tuesday?" Dr. Shepherd said. "Are you listening to me?

"Yes."

"I was saying that alcohol can make your condition worse," Dr. Shepherd said.

"It needs to be avoided."

I nodded.

Way true.

"Bipolar," he continued, "is hereditary, you know."

"How fortunate," I said, "for me."

"Actually, maybe you are," the doctor said. "Many gifted, endlessly creative people have been diagnosed – Axl Rose, Kurt Cobain, Ozzy Osbourne, Beethoven, even Florence Nightingale to name drop just a few."

I looked up at the nurse on the other side of my bed. She smiled and nodded.

"Do you have any questions thus far?" Dr. Shepherd asked.

"Yeah, I do," I said. "Does my mother know?"

The nurse nodded and smiled.

"Yes, Tuesday," the doctor said, "she's been made aware of your prognosis and is more than willing to help you."

She can hardly help herself.

He pulled a pamphlet loose from his clipboard. "I brought you some reading material to look over." He handed it to me. On the cover was a picture of an I-don't-have-a-problem pretty teen-aged girl with an ocean scene in the background. Pure tranquil. Pure misleading.

# My Mistaken Identity

"Sometimes teens with bipolar," the doctor said, "are missed diagnosed with ADHD or post traumatic stress disorder and other depressive ailments. You can read all about it in there."

I nodded. Again. And, again.

"And," Dr. Shepherd said, "parents often pass it off as a teenage growing-pains' phase. Or, make-up excuses for their kids that they're overly sensitive and imaginative."

"Been there before," I said and smirked.

"I'd like for you to keep a journal to keep track of your sleep habits and moods, for me, okay?"

"No problem," I said.

"It's not curable," the doctor said patting my shoulder, "but it is controllable, Tuesday."

Is that even possible? My mother never seemed to be able to get a handle on her inner mommy-monster. At least not until recently.

"How?" I asked.

"Through not only medication but a nutritious diet, aerobic exercise, getting enough sleep, and reducing the stress in your life. You should enjoy your environment, Tuesday." He laid his hand on my shoulder. "Especially, your home life. Also, part of the recovery process is getting past the guilt and pain in your…"

"Tuesday!" The intruder dressed in zebra striped pants raced into my up-classed private room two hours after Zelda had ripcorded my life for eternity. She threw her arms around me and cried tears of elation and regret on my choked-up chest. "Please excuse me, Dr. Shepherd!" my mother said. "But, I just couldn't wait any longer!"

"That's quite understandable," the doctor said, "We'll continue later, Tuesday." Another pat to my shoulder. "We'll be on our way…" He and the nurse walked toward the door. "…so you two can talk in private."

"Thank you," my mother said. She sat on the side of my bed. "I've completed the paperwork, doctor, if there's anything else, just let me know. I appreciate everything you all have done. And, thanks for the around-the-clock security."

"You're most welcome," Dr. Shepherd said, as he closed the door. This one on its hinges.

"I was so worried!" she exclaimed. "Thank, God, you're alive!"

I smiled through my tears.

"I'm so sorry, Tuesday, about what happened." my mother said, as she shook her head. "I had no idea."

Huh? I don't get it. Is she sorry about the accident? Or is she sorry...

"I kicked Monty out on his ass!"

Oh my God! She knows!

"He told me about his feelings. That is, after we got the shocking call from the hospital that woke us."

So it wasn't Monty following me?

Was it the paparazzi?

Or was it really nobody at all? Just different cars. In different places.

Oh my God, I am so whacked.

"Monty told me...everything."

My turn to shake my head. "Momma..."

"I wish," my mother said, "you had come to me."

"I just..." I turned away embarrassed. "...couldn't." I said, "I was scared..." I braved a glance at her face. "...you wouldn't believe me," I said.

"I wish you hadn't felt like that, Tuesday. You know it wasn't your fault. Even though he tried to say..."

"He did what?" I said.

Damn, my head hurts. I ache all over.

"Now, now, Sugar Plum, you're only going to cause yourself more discomfort." My mother rubbed my forehead softly. This time without a graze. Without the ring. "The doctor warned me," she said, "not to upset you. Are you okay? Maybe we shouldn't discuss this right now. You've been through..."

"Momma, what exactly did Uncle Monty say?"

"Well," she stared up at the IV bag. Almost empty. "He tried at first to say that you had come on to him."

"No way! That asshole! I hate him!"

"It's okay, Tuesday." She rubbed my arm. "I knew that was a lie. I saw you with that young man and there's no way in hell..."

I'm not so sure anymore.

My mother shook her head. Her choke point was emerging. "Monty finally confessed...he had fallen in love...with you." She started to cry. A different cry. A cry of a serrated, separated, shambled heart.

"I'm really sorry, Momma." I reached for her hand. She snagged mine and raised it to her lips and kissed it. Then, she palmed her face with it.

"As much as I thought I loved Monty," she said, "he could never take the place of my Sugar Plum!"

"I love you, Momma." My tears were a fusion of pain and relief.

"Well, you don't have to be frightened anymore," my mother said. "I told him to have all of his belongings out of my house before I got home. He was very remorseful and promised to never contact you ever again. But, I wasn't willing to forgive. Not now. I doubt ever. Still not sure if I'll press charges."

"No, please, Momma, let's not go there. Promise me you won't do that."

Let's just forget. But never forgive.

She nodded her head in agreement. I hoped. "Your career could do without that type of press."

"You're absolutely right, Momma. Please don't press charges. I don't want to have to…"

"It's okay, Sugar Plum." She stroked my head. "I guess I haven't exactly been the mommy-of-the-year. For a long time. Too long. I'm sorry."

"You've been sick, Momma."

And, so have I.

"I know. And, I promise you, Tuesday, I'm going to help you by doing everything right this time. No more episodes."

"That's great, Momma."

And, I will too. For now, on I'll blow my hereditary mind-altering-situation blahs off with medicine, diet and exercise. No more emergency dance parties. No more Zelda. I'm totally at risk for paranoia.

"The doctor said you'll get your stitches out soon," my mother said. "And as long as you don't have anymore headaches you should still be able to perform. You just might not be able to shake-it." She giggled. "Like you usually do."

# My Mistaken Identity

I smiled. "Momma, what day is it?" I glanced around the bleached art-free walls as if there was a calendar hanging there. "Have I totally skipped a day? Or, is the meeting tonight?"

"Oh my God!" my mother exclaimed, as she stood up. "The meeting is tonight! I have to call Baldwin! I'm sure he'll stand in for you. Damn! I left my purse and cell in the car. I'll be right back."

"Momma, before you go," I said reaching out for her hand. "There's something I need to say."

"What? You still want to sing at the prom, don't you? They'd be so disappointed, Tuesday. Those kids have worked themselves silly. But, of course, I'm sure they'd understand if…"

"Yes, Momma, if they still want me, I'll be there for them. But…"

"But what?" My mother sat back down. "What is it, Tuesday? Please, tell me."

"Momma, I love you."

"I love you too." She kissed my cheek. "And for now, on it's going to be just like old times. Just you and me."

I closed my eyes and shook my head. It was time. Time to pull the plug. Cut the cord. Unpack Momma.

"That's what I need to tell you."

I opened my eyes.

"I'm moving out."

LL Eadie

# Chapter Forty-Four

## *Mistaken Identity*

Are you there?

I can't find you.

I thought I saw you once,

But...

I was mistaken.

It wasn't you.

She only looked like you.

Or, was it me...

My mistaken identity?

~~~~~~~~~~~~~~~~~~~~~~~~~~~~~~~~

"Miss Tuesday Greenwood has always been professional every time she attended our school meetings," said Mr. Webb, the principal of William P. DuVal High School, as he spoke at the emergency school board meeting. "I have no problem with her singing at the prom. She and Mr. Baldwin Spikes, who spoke earlier in her place, have provided me with advance copies of lyrics, costume descriptions, diagrams of the stage setting, decorations...just about anything you can think of and I've always had the final word on all decisions."

He cleared his voice and continued, "In fact, Miss Greenwood has gone out of her way to make the students feel a part of her performance. And, she and her recording company, Glissando Records, have spent well over $50,000 on remodeling and updating our gymnasium."

"I LOVE YOU, TUESDAY!" shouted a young voice in the background.

"I LOVE YOU, TOO!" came another shout-out.

Brady Paul smiled at me as we listened on speaker phone from my hospital room already full of get-well-soon flower arrangements and cards.

"WE LOVE YOU, TUESDAY! GET BETTER!" a duet sounded.

Cheers, claps and chants from my fans. "TUESDAY! TUESDAY! TUESDAY!"

The superintendent attempted to intercept. "If you don't stop shouting we are going to have to ask you to leave!"

"They seriously love ya," Brady Paul said and smiled.

How am I going to tell him?

Shit! Maybe momma was right about me and guys after all.

"Just listen to that crowd, Tuesday!"

"It doesn't seem like that long ago," I said, "that they didn't connect with me. However, so many things have changed since then."

"Yes," he said, "they have. But some things haven't."

I frowned. "Like what?"

Does he know?

He touched the vase holding the single rose on the table. "Like me not being able to buy you the kind of..." He looked pass his single white rose in the milk glass vase to the crystal vase holding two dozen.

# My Mistaken Identity

I sat mute. He's so cute and nice. He would never hurt me. Brady Paul is the perfect boyfriend. Why don't I love him? What's happened?

"Hey!" His voice changed to his usual happy self. "It was sure nice of your uncle to charter a jet to pick me up in the Bahamas. Like I could afford that." He chuckled.

Is he really laughing?

"He even put me up tonight in the Seminole Hard Rock Hotel. And, flew my mother over to take my place on the boat as first mate."

Uncle Monty's scared shitless. That's why. Hoping for forgiveness.

But Uncle Monty didn't need to break a sweat. There was no way I would release to the world his sick-o feelings for me. But maybe I needed to fess-up to Brady Paul. Now.

"TUESDAY! TUESDAY! TUESDAY!" continued the chanting students through the telephone line.

"I'm so relieved you're going to be okay." Brady Paul began to lean forward.

Please don't.

He kissed me.

I pulled away.

"Did I hurt you?" he asked.

I can't lead him on.

This isn't fair to him.

He's so sweet.

What's wrong with me?

I shook my head while pamper-patting my bruised lips. "I have some news to tell you," I said.

"What's that?" he asked.

"I've decided to relocate," I said. "I was thinking about moving to the other Hollywood. As in California."

"California?" He stood up. "How long have you been thinking about that?"

Since I realized who I was. And who I wasn't.

"I need a fresh start and that's really where I need to be with my career, and it will help me personally to…"

"To find yourself?" Brady Paul said with a smirk.

The superintendent began to speak again. "The school board has voted, and the results are in. Its unanimous Miss Tuesday Greenwood will sing…"

"TUESDAY! TUESDAY! TUESDAY! TUESDAY! TUESDAY! TUESDAY!"

"Congratulations," Brady Paul said as he turned to walk away.

I reached out and caught his arm. "I'm sorry. Please don't leave like this. My life is so complicated. I'm so…"

"Tuesday, I wish you only the best, but I can't lie and say I'm feeling happy right now."

"I understand. I don't blame you. Listen when I get my act together, I'll call you and maybe you can come out and we'll see where we go from there. What do you think?"

He nodded. "Sure." Then smiled. "Sounds like a plan to me. Believe me, Tuesday, when I say I'm not sore at ya. I understand you've been through a lot and you probably do need to get away and figure this all out. And…get better."

I reached up with both hands and palmed his face. "Kiss me."

This time I did not reverse.

Maybe I do love him.

Damn, I am so whacked.

"Tuesday?" My mother's voice resonated through the speaker phone. "Are you still there?"

"Yes, Momma." My eyes were fixated on Brady Paul.

He mouthed the words "I love you."

"Did you hear?" she said.

I tingled.

"Yes, Momma, I heard."

"I wish you could see the students and all their posters of you they held up during the meeting! It was so exciting, Tuesday!"

"Hey, Tuesday, this is Baldwin. You scored huge tonight! The pulse in here was ricocheting! You are majorly off-the-popularity charts on this campus! If you needed a ratings' booster, which by the way you don't, you got one anyway!"

"Thanks, Baldwin, for filling-in for me tonight."

"No problem. Your mother is one awesome risk taker." He laughed. "She tells me you're coming home tomorrow. I'll be by to check on you then. Now, pop-soul diva, you get some rest. You hear?"

"Okay, Baldwin," I said. "I will."

"Tuesday," my mother said, "Umm...I won't be coming back this evening either...uhh...Baldwin is taking me out to dinner. Isn't that sweet of him?"

I nodded, smirked, and then shook my it-figures' head. My mother – Constance the Cougar.

"We're celebrating not only your success but mine too! My fairy tales are going to be published for children!" my mother exclaimed. "Can you believe that?"

Yes, Momma, I can.

"Congratulations," I said.

"I'm so excited!" my mother said. "But are you sure it's okay? I can certainly…"

"No, Momma, it's fine. Really. Go."

"I'll call you later on," she said, "and be back in the morning. I'll bring you some of your new tough-girl rocker clothes to wear home. I'm sure there will be dozens of reporters and…"

"Okay, Momma," I said. "Have fun." And, I meant it. "Bye, bye, Momma."

"Does your mother know?" Brady Paul asked after I had hung up. "You know about the other Hollywood?"

"Yes. She's not exactly thrilled about me moving to California. She says she understands and maybe she'll move out there too. I made it clear to her not with me though. She'll get over it."

He smiled. "Yeah, she will. But it's going to take me some time. I'm going to miss you, Tuesday. I guess we won't be going to the prom together either, huh?"

"Oh, I hope so!" I reached for his hand. "Will you still take me?"

"Of course. Damn, I didn't rent that penguin suit for just anyone!" He laughed.

I smiled and then yawned.

# My Mistaken Identity

"I need to go and let you get some sleep," Brady Paul said. "If it's okay with you I'll be back in the morning too." He lifted my hand to his lips.

"Please do." I clung to his hand, stretching his fingers before I let go. "Bye. Bye, Brady Paul."

"Bye. Bye, Tuesday."

The door shut, but my mind didn't. It was too confused to sleep even though my eyes would have preferred it.

They focused instead on Brady Paul's single rose. There, lying next to it was the newspaper. It was folded back to the page with The Last Word Horoscopes by Eugenia Word. My mother's favorite. I picked it up. And read mine – Your erratic behavior must be treated.

I shook my head and snorted a smirk.

Okay, so I'm not way insane. Just a little tinge of bipolar. Way easy. Just a brain disorder. Nothing serious. Just change your eating habits. Jog some. Perhaps take-up pole dancing. Swallow some pills. Get plenty of rest. And, most definitely move out!

Maybe my life was finally way worthy and controllable. I hoped.

I had that sudden urge to pee. I struggled with the IV pole and rolled it toward the bathroom. I stood outside it. The door squeaked as I pushed it open. "Shhh," whispered an intruder as her index finger raised to her puckered lips. It moved like a second hand on a clock ticking off the last thirty seconds to twelve. A disheveled looking girl stood in the dry shower with the plastic curtain wrapped around her. Half of her face grinned. The other half I couldn't see. It was hidden behind choppy hair that covered one eye. This time the intruder was different in another way too. This time I knew the stranger. It was Zelda.

I shut the door.